RUNNING
between dandelions

For Mommy,

As an adult, I understand what it means to sacrifice for loved ones. You fought to protect, provide for, and point me to the pinnacle of success. I admit, for years, I believed those fights left you depleted of confidence and hope. I didn't know your story, therefore, didn't understand your choices. As a result, unspoken anger led me to misjudge your passion as weakness.

Marilyn Joy Pitts Horton
(July 18, 1953-April 20, 2016)

The pain of loss is not lost on me. I've been flat on my back in the boxing ring after fighting with everything I had to live. I followed your example and wore shoes of steel to stay grounded, but being beat down, hurt, exhausted, and angry requires a safe place to heal. I should have leaned on you more instead of guarding my heart. I should have asked you to unlock your heart for me rather than making assumptions.

If I had been more sensitive, our collective strength and locked arms would have been a fortress.

This book came from a place I can't explain. When I was writing, I put on one of your shirts to feel close to you. To my surprise, the character Annabelle came alive. Her deep voice, singing "Amazing Grace," became a thread linking all of the women to each other. Their belief in something bigger than themselves gave them a common sense of fortitude.

Anabelle is a strong woman, but her deep wounds isolate her. She needs a healing circle and one of your long bear hugs to feel the presence of God. I found in your journal where you wrote, "I'm looking in the mirror to learn and grow from my mistakes." For Annabelle, learning to love through her pain, not despite it, was a long process. The characters in this story, and the readers, will find restoration when they face themselves in the mirror.

Daddy taught me to appreciate the dandelion moments in life. You taught me that love has power to heal and restore. I've broken through the unspoken anger that prevented me from honoring how incredibly strong, exceptionally giving, and remarkably resilient you were as a woman. Marilyn, you were one of a kind and we miss you immensely!

To keep living with purpose, I intend to tell powerful stories that inspire and encourage people to remember their strength. You once wrote to me, "I am committed to finding time and space to seek peace within, which is what powerful people do." That, Mommy, is a gift of your wisdom that I'll always cherish.

Running between dandelions,

Pen

Contents

IMPORTANT HISTORY

The obituary of Eldridge Charles Turner, Sr.
Annabelle's Husband.
Joyce's Father.
Nitty's Grandpa.

Eldridge Charles Turner, Sr. was born in Washington Courthouse, Ohio, in 1929 as the only son of his parents, Solomon and Lotus Turner. As Portia's baby brother, he was fiercely loved and protected by his family.

Eldridge shined in high school as an elite three letter athlete, winning championships in football, baseball, and track, earning the nickname "Hot Feet" for his speed and agility. Eldridge had a knack for evading his defenders on the football field, tripping them up and leaving them in his dust. No athlete has been able to break his coveted record of no sacks in a football game; although many have tried and failed since 1947.

Eldridge fell in love with Annabelle Dubose in high school. They were married in 1951, at the tender age of 23, after graduating from college. Eager to take the world by storm, Eldridge Sr. and Annabelle followed God's call on their lives by moving into ministry.

Eldridge's children were his pride and joy. Their first child, Joyce, was born in 1952. Eldridge Jr. came in 1954, and Enid was born in 1956. He always reminded people of the meaning of their names when he'd say, "I rejoice in the noble, brave, favored souls of my babies." Because of his work in the ministry and in the community, Eldridge Sr. looked out for children and cared for those who called him Dad. Many remain who will honor his legacy in life and ministry.

For his academic prowess, Hot Feet won a full academic scholarship to Wilberforce University, where he studied philosophy and education. Carrying the name Hot Feet, was prophetic for Eldridge, who accepted his call to the ministry, his first year of college. A natural born leader, Eldridge was nominated to serve his class as president. He didn't write a speech or plan campaign activities; he didn't think he'd win.

On the night of the campaign debate, he jokingly started his speech with the words, "They call me Hot Feet because I can run fast, and I know what it takes to evade and trip up the enemy." At the end of his speech, Eldridge and most of the people in the room were in tears because of the move of God. Needless to say, he won the election.

After graduating from Wilberforce, Eldridge earned his master's in divinity at Payne Theological Seminary. He was called to pastor the historic Third Baptist on The Hill in Xenia, Ohio, shortly after graduation. He served God and His people for over 15 years before he retired, having implemented a financial literacy program, mentoring, and a community kitchen for the less fortunate.

God took Eldridge to his heavenly reward on April 1, 1969. He passed away peacefully after a long battle with cancer, leaving behind a legacy of love and a yearning for hot feet to chase after God.

His mother preceded him in death.

FUNERAL PROGRAM

Opening Prayer, Deacon Leroy Battle

Choir Procession

Solo, Lady Annabelle Turner

    "Battle Hymn of Te Republic"

Prayer, Eldridge Turner, Jr.

Solo, Lady Annabelle Turner

    "Amazing Grace"

Eulogy – Deacon Timothy Freeman

Benediction

AMAZING GRACE.

Feel. Ask. Give.

PART 1 – BEFORE I WAS

Chapter 1

A baby at the door.

Her wig was nappy, crooked, and full of lint. When I opened the front door on my way to choir rehearsal, I saw her, a teenage girl huddled on my porch. She was curled up in the corner under a comforter, trying to shield herself from the cold December temperature. She must have been sitting on the porch for a while, but I don't know how long.

I won't ever forget that snowy day, Christmas Eve, 1971. It was fifth Saturday; the traditional choir only sings every fifth Sunday, so I was already in prayer for my solo the next day. I was leading *"Great Is Thy Faithfulness."*

When she heard the door crack open, the girl jumped up so fast that it startled me. Before I could ask her what she was doing on my porch, she said softly, "Hi, Ma'am. Is Eldrige Jr. home?" That's when I heard the coo of the baby inside of her coat and noticed that she was cradling something to her chest.

"Excuse me?" I stood in the doorway, blocking her view inside. "Who are you, and why are you at my house at 8:00 in the morning looking for my son?"

"He's related to this baby. We have nowhere to go." She sighed, "Eldridge Jr. said we can stay here."

There I was worrying that I might fall off key during my solo, and my son had fallen out of God's grace! I was stunned, as if somebody had hit me in the head with a skillet.

The girl cleared her throat and kept talking. "I start my new job on Monday."

I blinked my eyes trying to erase what I was seeing and hearing. One minute I was on my way to choir rehearsal to sing praises to my God, and the next, a girl holding a little baby wrapped in a stinky, dirty, blanket, was interrupting my plan.

"Eldridge Jr!" I screamed up the steps. "Make your way down here." I placed my hand on my forehead and massaged my brow while thinking, "Ugh! This is not the time for me to get a headache." I often get headaches, but the idea of my son getting someone pregnant made my body feel tense. I thought, "Did this little heifer just say that my son is her child's father?"

I heard my son's bedroom door scrape across the hardwood floor. Eldridge Jr. trampled down the steps wiping sleep out of his eyes, "Yes, Ma'am?"

I stepped aside to let him see the girl.

"Hannah?" He gasped.

"How do you know her name, Eldridge Jr?"

Waving at my son through the storm door, the girl said, "Hey." The girl stood on my porch with half a smile and a whole baby, and my insides were churning. I twisted my body to look at my son. "Who is she and why would you tell her that she could stay here? You don't pay bills in this house!"

"It's not what you think, Mother," he whimpered. I stared at Eldridge Jr., standing behind me looking sad. "I'm not the father of Hannah's baby."

Eldridge Jr. looked at the girl, and back at me. Then he stood between Hannah on the other side of the door, and me like he was her bodyguard. "But I do have a duty to watch out for her."

To the girl he tried to whisper, "You didn't give me time to work this out, Hannah." He gently nudged me to the side and looked around outside before opening the storm door. "How long have you been out here?" He shivered and said, "Come in, I can't believe you slept out there all night."

I looked at my son in his dingy white t-shirt and holey shorts and thought, "I'ma kill this boy." I glanced at the girl's bags on the porch and wondered, "*Why is she carrying rubbish?*"

Furious, but relieved he let them inside, I took a deep breath and asked my son, "How did she know where you live?" I was in shock! Eldridge Jr's lack of eye contact gave me my answer. "You know I don't condone this irresponsible behavior! You ain't got the two cents God gave you, boy."

I massaged the headache that was stretching across my forehead and watched Eldridge Jr. usher the kids inside. As he pulled the door closed, he was attentive to her wrapping her in the blanket. I noticed how she stood in front of him and how tall he was next her. She bent to adjust the blanket, and I caught a glimpse of too much of her behind. I covered my eyes and said, "Girl, you're out here exposing parts of your body that should be kept covered. You're out here ashy and cold." I pointed to Eldridge Jr. and said, "Look at her!"

My son took a deep breath but didn't speak. "Did you sleep with her?" He looked me in my eyes but did not respond and in that moment my heart dropped to my stomach. My knees buckled, my mouth got dry, and I wanted to pull off my hat and slap my son. "Now it makes sense why you don't want to serve on the Junior Deacon Board." Eldridge Jr. dropped his head.

"No, Mother." I saw the sincerity in his eyes. Something told me he was being honest.

"We did sleep in the same bed. Not. . . like . . . that."

"I don't understand," I said, trying to piece the puzzle together. "You ain't nowhere near ready to raise a baby. Can't even wash your own ass without asking where the soap is."

Eldridge Jr. interrupted my thoughts, "Once she tells you her situation, you'll understand. Please, Mother, just give us some time." He pushed the girl away from the door and rubbed his hands together to warm them. "We'll tell you everything."

I tapped my fingers on my forehead and asked, "How could you have slept with her and this not be your baby? Are you trying to imply that this was an immaculate conception?" I snorted. ". . . like Mary the mother of sweet baby Jesus? How ludicrous do you think that sounds?"

A corner of the blanket slipped through the girl's fingers and fell to the floor. I saw that she was wearing a thin summer dress and that made me shiver. Eldridge Jr. said, "Mother, you have to know that nothing happened." Hearing that, the girl, who had been timid, relaxed.

If I had a big switch, they both would have an ass whippin' coming! "We had a conversation about this six months ago, Eldridge Jr. You told me those condoms weren't yours." I turned my head to the girl, ready to unleash my wrath, but baby started to cry and I snapped out of my emotions. She pulled the blanket tight across her chest and shivered.

"It's okay, Elijah," she spoke softly to the baby and he calmed down at the sound of her voice. A vision of her laying down with my son and making that baby made the headache dance like a strobe light. "Where's your family, girl?" I asked, hoping she had somewhere else to go but my house.

"I'm on my own, Ma'am," she sniffled. "I do have family that's close, but right now. . ." She didn't finish her sentence. She looked at my son, then back at me. "I'm sorry for the inconvenience, Mother Turner."

I flopped on my praying chair, flustered, and found a peppermint in my pocket. I rubbed my forehead and massaged my temples talking to God. "This makes no sense," I said sucking. "So now I gotta be four grandparents rolled into one? Give me strength."

Chapter 2

Lies and Apologies.

I stood up from my chair and declared, "I need to get to choir rehearsal. We'll deal with this when I get back." I looked back and forth at both of them, "Since you already slept together, don't think you can mix pink and blue up in this house. God lives here and there better not be no purpling around here." I clapped my hands together and said, "There will be no more coitus until you're married."

I popped Eldridge Jr. on his shoulder, "Do you hear me, boy?"

"Mother Turner," the girl spoke softly, "We hear you." She rocked the baby over her shoulder and looked at the floor. "You really don't have to worry about us, as you say, purpling."

"Look at me," I demanded, taking my index finger and directing it to her left eye, "There are rules in this house." I tried unsuccessfully to massage the painful headache that was throbbing in my forehead. I put my hand on my hip and asked the girl, "How old are you?"

Eyes bowed, she said, "I'll make eighteen January 25, Ma'am."

"This girl is barely eighteen!" I whipped my head and yelled up the steps, "Joyce come down here! I need you to get down here to supervise your brother."

Just as I'd trained her, Joyce immediately trotted down the stairs. The sound of her feet against the wooden steps heightened the throbbing of my headache. Joyce gave her brother and Hannah a look of familiarity, but she tiptoed to the couch and sat with her hands under her thighs.

I looked at Hannah, and reached my arms out to her. "Let me see that baby." I turned my head and curled my nose at the God awful smell of either baby urine, or rotten dinosaur eggs, I couldn't tell. I let the blanket fall to the floor. I couldn't risk being contaminated by the odor.

I took the baby into my arms leaving just enough space between me and his little body. Pulling back the hood to reveal the baby's face, I was greeted by his big brown eyes, and he was so cute. I gasped at the resemblance to my son. "Mmm hmm," I hummed. "He's your child, Eldridge Jr." I handed the baby back to Hannah. "He's got the gray diamond in his curls."

Hannah let out a slow sigh, like someone had let the air out of a balloon, sputtering out of breath. I asked her, 'What is going on between you two?"

My son looked at me with his big brown eyes and I wanted to melt. "Mother," he sighed. "You don't need to worry." He put his hand on my shoulder, "But I need you to trust me."

I shook his hand off. "Trust you? Ha! I'm standing here looking at a 17-year-old homeless girl holding your baby. You've deemed yourself untrustworthy." I asked, "How old is this child?"

Hannah whispered, "He's three months old, ma'am."

"Three months old! You're out here gallivanting in freezing cold weather wearing a short dress with no sleeves? What kind of parent are you?"

Hannah looked flabbergasted. "I had no choice." She spoke delicately through tears, "I did not do this to myself."

I softened my tone hearing that. "I'm a Deaconess of the church and a former First Lady. What will it look like if people find out you fornicated with my son and I let you shack in my house?

"Mother," Eldridge Jr. interrupted. "You're an example of Christ. If you let her stay, you will be bearing the fruit of kindness, goodness and love."

"Boy, shut up!" I had to laugh. "Don't be trying to influence me with one of Pastor Davis' sermons." I chuckled. "You're right, but I don't want any appearance of evil. You just better pray for the fruit of self-control." Enid sauntered down the steps. I saw her lock eyes with Hannah in the same familiar glance as Joyce. "Enid, you know what's going on?"

"Mother," my 15-year-old daughter said. "There's a reasonable explanation." Eldridge Jr. shushed his sister before she could continue.

I glanced around the room, but they all avoided eye contact with me. I directed my attention to Eldridge Jr., and got in his face and stomped my foot at the same time. I know he could taste my peppermint candy. "Somebody better tell me what's going on, right now!"

Joyce spoke quietly. "We will, Mother," she said confidently, "but not right now."

"Joyce, don't pluck my nerves. You need to tell me what I need to know."

"I can't do that right now. Especially not with you in the state of mind."

"What do you mean by that, girl." I moved toward her, but Eldridge Jr. stepped between us. Frustrated, I straightened my coat and said, "I will call the authorities when I get back."

I tapped my foot and pressed my hand to my hip. "Oh my head aches," I moaned. I massaged my head.

I pointed at the girl and her baby. "There's a nice boarding house up the road." I pushed Eldridge Jr. on the shoulder and said, "You won't have time to play sports."

"No, he won't!" Hannah straightened her spine, "He doesn't have to give up his dreams for me. I'm moving to Cincinnati in a few weeks." Hannah took a deep breath and sat on the floor with the baby on her lap. "I'll make sure to give my son the best life I can." She rubbed the baby's cheek and sad, "I was already in a shelter. I left because somebody was stealing my baby's clothes."

I opened the door and the wind blew me back. "Go back there. They can take better care of you than I can." Joyce, Eldridge Jr, and Enid stood in front of Hannah as she started to fold the blanket around her.

She looked at Eldridge Jr. and said somberly, "I don't know why you thought this was a good idea." She moved toward the door. "My daddy taught me not to depend on nobody but God and myself. I'll embrace this challenge. It's painful, but I'll be stronger."

In unison, the children screamed, "No!" Eldridge Jr. put his hands on her shoulders and walked her back to where she was sitting on the floor.

Enid said, "Mother, please."

Eldrige Jr. added, "She'll be gone by the end of February. She has a job and everything."

"I'm starting a new job next week at Ambrosia Café." Hannah whispered. "Mr. Bennett and my daddy were good friends."

"Bennett gave you a job?" He's an old friend of me and my husband."

"I can take Elijah, too. His wife will help me because I don't have anybody to watch him."

"Me and my husband been going there for years. It's right down the street from my church, Third Baptist On The Hill. Do you know we're recognized around the world for our historical prominence and amazing choir."

"Yes, Ma'am." She nodded, "I'm familiar with your church. It's where my mother and father met."

"Oh really?" I lifted my brow. "Who are your parents? I've never seen you and I know everybody." I looked Hannah up and down, searching my brain for any recollection I could find of seeing her at church. The wig was throwing me off.

"I stayed in the background, Mother Turner. My mom didn't go a lot. Daddy, well that's a different story."

Changing the subject, Enid said, "Can I hold the baby?" Enid sat and rocked the baby without a care in the world. He looked so peaceful in her arms, but all I could do was turn my nose up at his stench.

"If you know my church, you know our Pastor, Dr. Evan D. Tide, Sr. will be devastated to learn that Eldridge Jr. broke his covenant." I spoke as Eldridge Jr. was grinding his teeth, "You made a vow in front of everybody that you'd save yourself, but you didn't. Is that why you took off your promise ring?" I popped Eldridge Jr. on the shoulder. "You're so simple, you'd rob a bank with your own deposit slip."

Watching him try to be a man in that moment made me think about my father-in-law, Solomon Turner. "What do you think your Poppa would have said about all of this?"

Chapter 3

Broken.

Let me take you back so you can understand how we got here.

My children were 11, 13, and 15 when we were knocked to the ground with a wrecking ball. My husband of 15 years, my pastor, and my high school sweetheart, walked out of our home. He divorced me to marry another woman without explanation.

When I arrived home from work, Eldridge Jr. was in Joyce's arms, crying. Enid was curled up in her father's favorite chair, rocking back and forth. "What's going on?" I asked, dropping my pocketbook.

Eldridge Jr. sighed, "I found this taped to the refrigerator." He gave me a cereal box and I saw Sr.'s scrawly handwriting in black letters. The first line made me drop the box, spilling little circles of oats all over the floor:

Annabelle,

I'm leaving you.

I'm not leaving because of anything you did. A lady needs a father for her daughter and God called me to go.

I don't know where we'll end up, but I left some money with my sister, Portia, to help you take care of the kids. Don't spend it all on church hats, dresses, or shoes. That money is for our children and their future. Encourage them to go college and pursue their dreams. Our children need their mother, but let them explore the world on their own terms.

I lifted my son from the couch and rocked him in my bosom. I reached for Enid and she cried on my shoulder. Joyce didn't move and I didn't reach for her, I don't know why. Holding my babies, I felt sad, and angry. I thought, *"He didn't have the courage to face me? I gave him the best years of my life, and he left me like I was a one-night stand."*

Determined not to break down, I swallowed my tears so the children didn't see me cry. I went to my room and played sad records with my mind racing. *"I was a good wife. I gave him sex whenever he wanted it and he got it from somebody else? I cooked, cleaned, and served that man. I know I did what I was supposed to do."*

I found out later that Sr. had left me for a younger, much bustier, and lighter-skinned woman. I washed my hands of both of them, not caring about what happened to him, her, or their bastard child. Ironically, two years later, Sr. died of cancer. I don't know if it was God's will, or his punishment for breaking our covenant. Either way, it was a terrible situation. I made the best of it, and took over planning for his funeral.

A few days after Sr. left us, I had meltdown. I dragged his ugly brown chair into the backyard. That heavy, brown thing was a nuisance, and I hated it. He'd sit there to study, pray, and read, but it reminded of him. I pushed and tugged to get it through the house and out the back door. Once I got it into the yard, I took an axe from the shed and chopped it up.

By the time I finished, I had perspired through my clothes and sweat out my press and curl. I screamed and cried swinging that axe. "I can't believe you did this to me." Swing, "You promised me forever!" Swing. "You are a liar!" Swing! "You broke me!" Swing! I swung so hard that I tossed the axe across the yard. That gave me Holy Ghost laughter, and I laughed until I cried.

My arms and legs were sore, but it felt good to get it out. When I was gratified, I tossed the springs and fabric in the metal trash can, and stacked the wood for the fireplace.

My father-in-law and Portia, Sr.'s sister came over the next day. Poppa sat with the kids and they sat on all sides of him, leaning, hugging, crying. His presence seemed to calm everybody's nerves, even mine. Portia helped me cook a few meals to leave in the freezer. I didn't feel like talking, nor did I care that she was trying to placate me.

Just before dark, Portia rounded up the kids for goodbye hugs. "We gotta get on back to Washington Courthouse." Poppa told them, "Call us anytime." They lived together and she was so happy to take care of her father. I always wondered why she chose caregiving over having a family of own. I couldn't have done it.

Portia hugged me and spoke, "Annabelle, lean on your faith. God will bring something good out of this. I promise." I rolled my eyes behind her back when she hugged me.

When I hugged Poppa, I had to swallow my tears. He was the closest thing I had to a father. Mine died when I was young and Poppa went out of his way for me. Having a father to lean on in that moment was consoling.

"Poppa," I said, letting go of my embrace. "You are like a father to me. I'm honored that you trusted me to own the home where you and Mother Lotus raised your family." I looked around. "Where she nurtured and prayed for her family, I emulated her. Sadly I won't be able to celebrate 35 years of marriage, but God is in control."

***

After they left and the children had scattered to their rooms, I started reminiscing. My mind drifted back to the day my son was born. "Let's name him Johnston Solomon Turner," I beamed at Sr. in the hospital. "I love the name Solomon, after your daddy."

Sr. looked at our son and shook his head in disagreement. "I will teach him to be a king, but I don't want to give him that name."

"Why not?" I shifted in bed. The pain was gruesome. "You don't like it?"

"No, I do," he adjusted my blanket. "I want him to have my name, Annabelle."

He lifted the baby from my chest and said with a smile, "Hello Benjamin Eldridge Turner." He lifted him toward heaven and said, "You have your daddy's smile and hair. One day, son," he chuckled, "People will be in awe of this gray patch that looks like a diamond. It's a family trait." He handed the baby back to me and said, "We'll always be able to bet on this child. He'll be our pride and joy."

"*B.E.T., the initials of my husband who left me, and the son who disappointed me,*" I thought.

***

Poppa came to see the children every weekend. A few weeks after the wrecking ball knocked us down, he and Eldridge Jr. sat outside chatting on one of his visits. I heard them talking through the window about where Poppa grew up in the deep south of Georgia. Poppa was whittling some wood, scraping, and blowing dust while he reminisced.

"Where I came from was a town so small everybody knew what everybody was thinking."

Eldridge Jr. laughed. "Really?"

"Yeah. When one of my friends disappeared, some of us made a plan to get out of town as fast as we could. Just one look, you could tell who was in."

"What happened to your friend, Poppa?"

"We don't know." I heard scraping as they sat silently for a few seconds. I clanged some pans to make it seem like I was working in the kitchen. When Poppa spoke again, his voice was soft, "He stood up to a man who pushed a little girl to the ground because she bumped into him."

"Poppa!"

"That night I left everything and everyone without a word. I jumped a train and rode it until it stopped here, in Ohio." Poppa was silent for a few seconds. "That's why I want you to be something, son."

When Poppa passed away a few months later, Eldridge Jr. was devasted. He tried to implement everything his grandfather and father had taught him at the same time. He tried to protect and provide, but I told him, "You ain't a man yet, Mother's got you."

That sad version of my son looked nothing like the man-child who stood in front of me, looking vulnerable. I snapped myself out of my memories and thought about what was happening in that moment.

Chapter 4

Wide open.

As I prepared to leave for rehearsal, I gave instructions, "Joyce, get Hannah cleaned up. Wash her clothes and give her something to wear. Enid, clean up the kitchen, and Eldridge Jr. throw those rags in the garbage." I flung open the door and proclaimed, "Everything better be in order when I get home." Behind my back, I said, "And make sure my Christmas pot roast doesn't burn in the oven."

"Yes, Ma'am," was the last thing I heard before I closed the door.

Eldridge Jr. opened the door. "Mother, do you really have to go out in this weather? The roads are slippery."

"I'll be fine," I responded. "I need to get out of this house for a while. I need to be near to God. This has brought on a headache that only God can remove." I turned on my heels and walked to my car.

On my way to rehearsal, I drove slower than usual. I didn't feel the need to be the first one at church. *"My world was just turned upside down by a little nappy-headed girl bringing me a grandchild,"* I felt sad thinking about that baby. *"What kind of life is he going to live with them two silly parents? They don't know nothing."*

By the time I got to the church, snow was everywhere. The parking lot was blanketed in white, and no one was there. I sat in my parked car for a while, staring at the Christmas lights around the church. While others were celebrating Christmas, I was sad. "On Jesus' birthday," I lamented, "I got a gift I didn't want, didn't ask for, and certainly didn't need." I drove back home, inching along the road, crying all the way.

When I walked in the house, Joyce was in the kitchen cleaning. I caught a whiff of lemon in the air. I closed the door and stood still for a few seconds. I don't know where she got it from, but she always put lemons in the water when she cleaned. I could smell it wafting from the kitchen into my sitting room.

"Mother," Joyce called out, interrupting my peace. I opened my eyes in time to see her coming out of the kitchen, wiping her hands on her apron. "Ms. Merlene, your choir secretary, called after you left. She wanted to let you know rehearsal was canceled. I couldn't catch you before you left."

"Where are your sister and brother?"

"Upstairs in their rooms."

"And the girl . . . Hannah?"

"She's in the bathroom. When I finish cleaning the kitchen, I'll make them a pallet in the sitting room."

"For a 19-year-old, she holds this family together like an old married woman," I thought. I wanted to say something nice, so I said, "You do a good job of taking care of the house." That was all I had.

Joyce exhaled and said, "Thank you, Mother. I'm glad you're pleased." Ignoring her attempt to crawl into my heart, I grunted. "I have a headache. I'm going to bed."

I tiptoed upstairs. I opened the door to Eldridge Jr.'s room and saw him lying down. "Get them dirty feet off my wall, boy!"

He jumped up, "Mother . . ."

"I don't want to hear it, Eldridge, Jr." I tapped my fingers on his wall. "The first thing you need to do on Monday, is look for a job, or talk to that military recruiter."

I slammed his bedroom door shut and walked to my room. I pushed back my purple velvet comforter and slid into the sheets, coat and all. "Lord, how will I explain to the church that I have a bastard grandchild? What would Sr. say if he were still alive?" I pulled the blanket over my face. "Is this Your will for my life?"

I laid in the bed, unable to still my racing thoughts. "*I ain't no fool,*" I thought. "*Eldridge Jr.'s nose is wide open by that girl. I wonder how long they've been messing around. Longer than six months, that's when I found those condoms in his drawer.*"

I had a terrible headache one day, and I left my cleaning job early. I planned to take a quick nap before going to work at the church. As I do on occasion, I walked around the house, praying and checking everybody's room. Joyce and Enid always kept their rooms tidy, but Eldridge Jr. often left dishes in his. I opened his door and saw a cup on his dresser. As I picked it up, I saw a box of condoms peeking out of an open drawer.

"What in heaven?" I said, pulling out the drawer. I fingered the initials B.E.T. in blue thread on his handkerchief and remembered how happy Joyce had been when she gave it to him for his birthday, "Aunt Portia taught me how to hand stich," she had said, grinning.

Poppa gave him a treasure box. "You're almost a man now," he had said, spitting out his chewing tobacco. "I carved that box so you can put a ring or a watch in there when you get one."

"If he had put his condoms in there, I wouldn't have found them, Poppa," I grunted. Fingering Eldridge Jr.'s treasure box, I recalled the rites of passage ceremony when he and 11 other young men stood in front of the congregation. Pastor Tide purchased rings for the young men, and he presented them with a prayer of covering. Each of the young boys had gone through junior deacon training and some other manhood exercises I wasn't privy to.

Wearing black suits, white shirts, and black ties, they looked so handsome. Eldridge Jr. spoke about how he planned to make his family proud. I was so grateful that I began to hum, *Amazing Grace*, and of course, everyone followed my lead.

The sanctuary was full of happy people. Joyce was crying tears of joy, "I'm so proud of you, brother," she shouted. Enid slid out of the pew behind me and twirled down the aisle. Portia, sitting in the choir stand, waved her hands in praise. That is one of my proudest moments, but standing in my son's room, I felt something different. Anger was rising from my toes.

"*He is a fraud*," I thought, tucking the promise ring into Eldridge Jr.'s hankie and then into my pocket. The headache made me want to scream. "If he's using condoms he has no need for this ring." I set Eldridge Jr.'s treasure box in plain sight on his dresser.

I squeezed the box of condoms between my fingers and went to the kitchen. "I'm going to confront him, when he gets home from school."

I made a feast fit for a king's court: southern fried chicken, macaroni and cheese, collard greens, homemade biscuits and apple pie. When Eldridge Jr and Enid got home from school, he came into the kitchen and said, "It smells so good in here, Mother."

"I made all of your favorites," I said, forcing a smile.

"Hi, Mother," Enid gave me a side hug. "Did you have a good day?"

"I did." I squeezed her arm. "Go to your room and change from your school clothes. Let me talk to your brother in private for a few minutes."

Enid looked at the food, and then at Eldridge Jr. "I thought Joyce said she was cooking. She told me she left a piece of ham and some pineapple upside-down cake for us." She opened the oven and looked around, bemused. "What time does Sissy get home, LJ?"

"Joyce has her late class tonight. She'll be home around 8:00, when you're getting ready for bed."

Enid opened the fridge, and saw the foil wrapped plates. With her head still in the fridge, she said, "I found it!"

I was so busy fuming about the condoms, I didn't notice that Joyce had cooked. Enid closed the fridge and looked at the chicken again. "Is it okay if I eat what Joyce made, Mother? I don't eat chicken anymore."

"Okay," I said, flipping the dish towel over my shoulder.

In an effort to get his sister out of the room, Eldridge Jr. pushed his sister. "Enid, go upstairs and do what Mother asked you to do." She turned without another word and obeyed her brother. I waited until her door closed before I asked, "When did she stop eating chicken?"

Eldridge Jr. looked perplexed. "Three years ago, at Aunt Portia's house. Remember, she saw Poppa cleaning a chicken, and it made her sick?"

"I don't recall that." I changed the subject. "Why don't you go sit in the dining room. I'll bring your dinner to you."

I added another dollop of mac and cheese to Eldridge Jr.'s plate and took the box of condoms out of the cabinet where I had stowed them. I dropped the box in the center of Eldridge Jr.'s food and carried it into the dining room, holding the plate in the palm of my hand, like I was his server.

"Here you are, sir," I said, setting the plate in front of him. I waited to see his reaction, but Eldridge Jr said nothing. He bowed his head and prayed over his food. When he lifted his head he squared his shoulders and said, "These condoms are not mine."

"If you don't want me to know your business, find better hiding places for your instruments of iniquity."

He cleared his throat, took a deep breath, and said, "Those condoms are not mine. I'm holding them for a friend."

"What friend?" I pounded the table. "What's his name?"

Eldridge Jr. took a bite of chicken, chewed slowly, and swallowed. "His name is John. You don't know him."

I hunched over a chair and pressed him. "Are you lying to me?"

"No. A couple of girls got into a tussle over John at school, and he felt bad about it. I told him about my promise to God, and he said he wants to try it for at least a month. I wouldn't lie on God. Although, I have been tempted by some girls on several occasions, I haven't had sex."

"Thank you, God!"

Satisfied, I pushed the plate closer to Eldridge Jr. and instructed him, "Eat your food, son."

He pushed macaroni and cheese around the plate but didn't eat. "I'm not hungry right now, may I be excused?"

I nodded. Eldridge Jr. stood up from the table and walked into the kitchen to put his plate in the oven. He grabbed my hand and held it for a few seconds. "Trust me, Mother."

"I do, son." I squeezed his hand. "I was worried that you were experimenting with things you don't understand." I fixed my eyes on the window. "Maybe I went too far this time."

Eldridge Jr. released my hand. He straightened his spine and took a deep breath. I looked at my son and relaxed my face muscles, "I'll try to get your ring resized by your birthday in November."

"That would be nice, Mother." He pivoted on his heels, paused, and turned back. "Mother, I haven't done anything to disrespect you. None of us have. I have not lied to you. None of us have. Me, Enid, and Joyce know how much your reputation means to you." He turned and walked somberly out of the kitchen.

I hesitated for a few minutes, before going into the sitting room. I sat in my favorite chair. I had spent many days and nights in my chair praying for my family like Nehemiah sat on his wall. I built my faith, brick by brick, praying fervently and crying out to God.

I crossed my legs and closed my eyes. "Enid," I called out. "You can come eat."

Hearing her rhythmic pace descending the steps, I knew she was leaping on her toes. When she walked past me, I felt the air of a pirouette, and she said, "I love you, Mother."

"Love you, baby," I hummed. Enid lives out loud with a sparkle in her eyes that comforts me. Without trying, she makes me laugh and helps me see when compassion is required. Her sensitivity and humor bring life to the house. While Joyce only speaks when spoken to, Enid communicates the messages of her sister's heart. When Eldridge Jr. fights to be a fierce protector, Enid shows him when to pick up his sword, and when to stand still. A perfect mix of hope and confidence, Enid is a gift.

I think Enid is the only one of my children who actually sees that I am exhausted in every way possible. While Joyce and Eldridge Jr. maintain a safe distance from me, Enid runs into my arms. She prays for me and even washes my feet occasionally. She seems to hear my unspoken struggles. I can't think straight. My body aches, and my head constantly hurts behind my eyebrows. I feel hungry for something I can't verbalize right now, but I can't hide it from Enid.

I nodded off into a sweet sleep for the last time before a baby on my porch turned my world upside down.

Chapter 5

Instructions from God.

My mother was tough on me. I don't talk about her much because she stopped talking to me. When I was a kid she gave me the essentials, but she was never a shoulder for me to cry on or a lap for me to rest in. When I got married, she washed her hands of me, I guess she thought I didn't need her anymore. Mother has been dead for some years now, but I still wish I had more time with her.

Eldridge Sr. loved my mother, and he tried to get us to reconcile, but she wasn't interested. Told Eldridge Sr., "That girl is mean. I dealt with her attitude long enough. She's your problem now."

That hurt, but what could I do? I poured my heart into my marriage and hoped that my relationship with my children would be better. When he left me alone to raise our kids, I was devastated. I didn't want anyone's pity, and I didn't talk about my feelings. It did hurt me that some of our church members turned their noses up to me because I was divorced. I didn't do nothin' wrong, but nobody wanted to hear that.

I was embarrassed and ashamed, yet I stood in front of my church and repented. I wanted them to know that it wasn't my choice to break my covenant. After that, I spent a year going through Deacon training so I could get ordained. I was determined to prove my loyalty to God and to my church, no matter the cost.

As I laid in my bed feeling sorry for myself, I felt the same pain I felt the day Eldridge Sr. left me. His letter was a 12,000 pound wrecking ball, that tore my life up. Again, I am being hit by a wrecking ball, and there is no one to help me rebuild after the devastation.

My kids and I don't have the best relationship. I'm hard on them, but I want to be closer. Take Joyce, she took it so hard that her father left. I saw her pain, but I couldn't find words to comfort her. I left her to heal alone while I comforted Enid and Eldridge Jr. When it came to Joyce, being around her made me think of Eldridge Sr. I was nursing my pain instead of her.

Joyce was so strong-willed after her dad died. She said she was okay, but acted despondent. I refused to let her become a soft woman, easily manipulated by men. I did my best to break codependency off of her; I pressed her as hard as I could to do whatever I thought was best.

"Lord," I prayed. "Help me be a better mother." I wiped tears from my eyes. "Now I have a grandchild, too."

I adjusted my blanket and sat still for a few minutes before praying again. "I know what love feels like when it cracks you wide open and leaves you feeling helpless. Sr. did that to me, and at first, his love covered me. When he left, I never thought I'd recover because I was exposed." I caught a tear that tried to escape my eye. "I surrender to Your will." I rolled over on my side and listened to the joy of life from the children downstairs until I fell asleep.

While I was in slumber, God poured out sixteen inches of snow. When I looked outside, I was blinded by the purity of the white blanket that covered the ground. The irony of the brightness outside, and the darkness I felt inside, were conflicting with each other.

Around 1:00, I got up, changed into my lounge clothes, and tiptoed down the steps. Hannah and the baby were asleep at the foot of my praying chair. When she heard me, Hannah sat up and said, "Is everything okay, Mother Turner?"

"It's fine, child," I whispered. "Go back to sleep." She laid back down, nestling with the baby and cradling her bags. I took note of how she guarded both.

I flicked the light on in the kitchen and pulled out the fixings to make my Grandma's apple pie. I needed something familiar to settle my heart; Grandma's pie always did that for me. I peeled and boiled apples and then added the special ingredients. While it baked, I prayed at the dining room table.

I flipped through Joyce's books and even though everything looked like gibberish, I knew Joyce was mastering her studies. I took the holy oil from my robe pocket and anointed her pens. "Joyce is brilliant. She graduated from high school and got into college at 16."

I prayed until the cinnamon fragrance crawled into my nose and I exhaled.

Chapter 6

Everything has changed.

Sunday morning, when I got up, the clock on my nightstand read 10:30. "I must have been tired," I yawned.

I heard Hannah singing in the bathroom, and it sounded good. I closed my eyes to listen, but there was a knock on my door. "Mother," it was Eldridge Jr.'s. "Are you okay in there? You didn't come out all day yesterday."

"I'm fine, baby."

"Okay. I was worried." His feet shuffled across the floor back to his room, and I continued listening to Hannah sing. When the creak of her feet on the steps let me know that the bathroom was free, I slipped into the bathroom and escaped into my own hot bath.

Hannah's wig, clean and looking brand new, was hanging behind the door. *"Glad she got that old thing fixed up,"* I thought. I placed my prayer request under a claw foot of the tub with some others and slipped into the steaming water.

"God, you always answer my prayers in this here tub. Don't let this be the time you turn your ear from me." Reheating the water every few minutes, I cast my cares at God's feet. "Am I resistant toward her because she scares me a little? You know I want to have total authority, yet this is something I can't control, Lord."

After a while, I heard God say, "Be not forgetful to entertain strangers, for thereby some have entertained angels unawares." Hebrews 13:2 was confirmation that God did want me to allow Hannah and her baby to stay with us.

By the time I dried my wrinkly off, I had prayed and cried so much that I felt like I had been cleansed in the Nile. The dirt ring around the tub was evidence that I'd been revitalized in God's presence.

I went back to my room, changed into my lounge clothes, and wrote in my journal before falling asleep. Around 6:00 p.m., Joyce came to get me for dinner, but I declined the invitation. "I'm not hungry right now," I lied. The smell of her handmade biscuits and cabbage rolls made my stomach flip, but I had to hold on to my fast a little while longer.

Joyce, sounding concerned, said, "I'll leave a plate for you in the oven." She descended the steps; I rolled over and went back to sleep until around 8:00 when I got the unction to go downstairs. I opened my door and yelled, "Family meeting. Meet me at the table."

I made my way down the steps and stood on the landing to watch my children. Eldridge Jr., wiping sleep from his eyes, took one step at a time and glared over the banister at nothing in particular. Enid skipped down the stairs, while Joyce, with her hair in rollers and a scarf tied around her head, marched like a soldier. I patted them all on the shoulder as they passed me.

I was the last one to make it to the dining room. I sat at the head of the table, looking everyone in the eye. Watching everyone fidget in their seats, I broke the ice. "Listen. I know we got off to a bad start, but God spoke to me, and I have to be obedient." I looked at Hannah, nursing her son. "You can stay with us for the sake of that little soul." The blue comforter covered her body, and it smelled lemony fresh. I turned my attention to Joyce, "I don't know what you did to make that blanket so clean, but good job."

"Thank you, Ma'am." Hannah spoke softly. I observed how different she looked. Her freshly braided cornrows were shiny. *"With a nice press and curl, she'd look nicer. At least she doesn't look like a streetwalker anymore."*

As I watched her rock the baby, I said, "When you get up in the mornings, fold up your pallet and put it under the couch. I hold prayer meetings, Bible studies, and voice lessons in that sitting room. Keep it clean." Hannah nodded

"She can have my bed," Joyce spoke up. "I'll sleep on the floor.

I rotated my head toward her, "Why?"

"She didn't tell you that she had complications during her delivery. Joyce locked her eyes with mine, "I want to help."

I turned to my son and said, "If anything, Eldridge Jr. needs to give up his room."

"She can stay in my room," Enid offered. "I'll go to Joyce's room."

Joyce agreed, "That's a good idea, Sissy."

Enid flipped her hair back and laughed, "What would you do without me?"

I looked at Eldridge Jr. and clarified, "I don't care what ya'll do, no closed doors."

Hannah spoke up again, "I promise to do everything you ask, Mother Turner."

I asked. "Where is your father?"

Hannah wiped her eyes. "My daddy died two years ago from cancer."

I looked at my children, "They understand your pain. So sorry to hear that. Since your mother didn't look out for you, make sure to tend to him immediately."

As if she was reading my mind, Hannah said, "My mother doesn't want me. When my son was born, she came to the hospital, looked at him, and left. I haven't seen her since."

"Well," I breathed. "I have a heart for missions and hospitality. You can stay here until you move to Cincinnati." Satisfied with the family meeting, I dismissed everyone from the table.

Alone, I looked up to heaven and said, "I'm only doing this for you, Lord."

Chapter 7

Clarity.

We made it through the New Year's celebrations, and the month of January, with no problems. I hardly saw Hannah around the house. At dinner, the week before Valentine's Day, she asked me at the dinner table, "Do you mind taking me and Elijah to the doctor next Thursday at 3:00 in the afternoon? It's in Washington Courthouse?"

I nodded. "Maybe we can stop to see my sister-in-law, Portia, after your appointment. I haven't seen her in a while."

Hannah lowered her eyes. All I heard was the clinking of forks against plates.

***

I took off work, on the day of Hannah's medical appointment. That rest did my body good. Cleaning houses, teaching, and working at the church was exhausting. I slept for most of the day and enjoyed my break. At 2:00, I was ready to get on the road. I stood at the door jingling my keys, and Hannah was moving so slowly in the bathroom. I yelled upstairs, "Get that molasses out of your ass, girl. We need to go so you can be on time."

When she came downstairs, she carried the baby in her arms and clutched a new bag. "Where you going with all that stuff?" I asked as she passed me.

"This is everything I came with."

I must admit, the girl looked beautiful, and I was shocked. "You don't look anything like you did a few months ago. You're a completely different person!" I nodded at her, "That yellow dress complements your skin tone."

"Thank you, Mother Turner. Joyce made this outfit and my bag."

"Oh? Joyce made that?" I watched as Hannah struggled to put the baby in a sling across her chest. I didn't reach to help her, so when she asked, "Can you hold Elijah for a minute?" I wasn't moved by her heavy sigh or the expression of agony on her face. "I just need to zip up my jacket and adjust my socks," she explained.

"Chile, you'll be carrying him for the rest of his life. Get used to it." I put on my hat and gloves. "He's your responsibility." I opened the door, and a gust of wind knocked me back. "It's cold, wrap that baby up."

Hannah adjusted herself, put the baby in the sling, and bundled up. I watched her carry him and all of her belongings outside to my car. I opened the door for her, and when she got in, I cautioned, "Watch your leg," before closing the door behind her.

The 35-minute ride to Washington Courthouse was silent. I didn't have anything to say, and Hannah didn't either. While she and the baby dozed, I talked to God. There was no marked moment of Him responding, but when we got to the city, the sun lit up the sky. I woke Hannah up to give me directions to the doctor's office.

When we walked into the office, the receptionist, a young girl in her late twenties, greeted us. "Hey, Hannah Eve!" She lit up when Hannah walked to the counter. "Let me see that baby."

Hearing the name Eve, I was caught off guard. "That's my middle name," I said under my breath.

"My daddy named me Hannah Eve," Hannah informed me with a side glance. "It means grace to live."

The receptionist looked at me from the side of her glasses. "You doing alright, Hannah?" Clarice stood up to peek under the blanket and beamed. "Elijah is getting so big! What are you feeding him?"

"I'm still nursing."

"Good for you!" Clarice sat down. "I gotta say, I see you glowing, girl. Because we need to be walking around looking pretty at all times."

Hannah tossed her head, and joined the receptionist in a cackle. She took a strut across the floor and said, "I just walk around looking pretty." Hannah did a twirl to show off her dress. "It's been a long process, but I've been getting myself back together."

"Walk around looking pretty?" I repeated. "That's comical." I snickered.

The receptionist looked at me and frowned, "Did you say something?" I felt the heat coming from her eyes.

I squelched my laugh. "I mean . . . walk around looking pretty is an interesting thing to say."

"Ma'am," Clarice pointed to a row of brown wicker chairs, "Have a seat. We'll call you if we need you." I clutched my pocketbook and walked to a chair close to the door. When I was seated, Clarice continued, "What else have you been doing other than walking around looking pretty?"

"Just studying and working."

"I like that flower on your dress."

"This was made from an old tie. It's one of my new favorite things."

The flower on her dress was pretty. *"I didn't notice the flower,"* I thought. *"She must have put it on in the car."*

Clarice kept chatting. "That's so creative, your friend is doing a good job of styling you. And your hair is growing! Have you been using the cream Momma gave you to get it to grow back?"

"Every day." Hannah reached into her bag and pulled out the wig. "That reminds me, thank her for letting me use the wig since it fell out when Elijah was born." She handed the wig to Clarice. "I deep-cleaned it and conditioned it for her."

Clarice fingered the wig, "It looks brand new." She slipped it under the desk and said, "I'll let her know. She misses you coming to the shop to get your hair done."

"I'm going to miss her too, but I'm ready to get out of here and start over in Cincinnati."

"You're going to be a great doctor." Clarice pushed her chair back and stood up. "I'll let Nancy know you're here.

"Thanks, Clarice." The receptionist disappeared to the back, and Hannah sat across from me.

"How did you find out about this doctor?" I asked her.

"My Daddy has been bringing me here since I was a baby." I watched the baby bounce on Hannah's lap. "I went to Xenia after I had Elijah. My mom was gone, and my daddy was dead. They all helped me get set up at the shelter."

I didn't want to be fake, so I said, "Your Daddy must have been a good man. If he were alive, do you think you would have gotten yourself pregnant?"

"Ahem." The nurse disrupted my question. "Come on, Hannah." When Hannah got up, the nurse gave me a hard look, that gave me goosebumps. "*What did I do?*"

I caught a glimpse of their tender embrace before the nurse closed the door with a snap.

As I waited, I flipped through magazines, wrote in my journal, and twiddled my thumbs. Time crawled along like a snail avoiding salt. It felt so long, I thought horses and chariots were going to take me to glory. Light turned to dark, and I switched chairs because I got tired of being poked in the back by wicker.

After about an hour, which felt like two days, the nurse opened the door, "Ms. Turner?" I looked up, not realizing I had dozed into a nap.

"You want me?" I pointed to my chest with a snort.

"The doctor wants to speak with you privately." I picked up my pocketbook and shuffled myself to the back, following the nurse. I passed Clarice, typing on the typewriter, keeping her eyes on her work. I peeked into exam rooms admiring the decor.

When we arrived at the office, where the doctor was waiting, the nurse opened the door and stretched her hand inside. I walked in and she closed the door behind me with a soft click. Hannah was there, visibly upset. Tears rolled down her face, and she wiped them with a handkerchief I recognized. I saw B.E.T. in blue letters.

Before I could address why she had my son's handkerchief, the doctor stood to greet me. "Hi, Ms. Turner, She extended her hand for me to shake. "I'm Dr. Warner. Thank you for bringing Hannah to her appointment today."

"No problem. But I don't understand why you need to talk to me." I glanced at Hannah. "I'm not this child's mother."

The doctor swallowed, and said, "Have a seat. Let's chat, Ms. Turner." I sat, crossed my legs at my ankles, and shifted to the side like a lady should. Out of the corner of my eye, I saw Hannah, still crying, yet poised.

"She showed up at my house one day. God told me to care for her because her child belongs to my son."

I inspected the doctor and her office. "*She's pretty, well-dressed, and looks like she's in her early thirties. I wonder where she goes to church.*" To her I asked, "What's all this about, Dr. Warner? Enough of the small talk."

"I've been seeing Hannah since she was three days old. I know her family, her family history, and I know she has a heart of gold. Have you seen that side of her?" She tilted her head and waited for my response.

I coughed, "Well, I can't say we've had much conversation since she came to my home."

"I think you truly are a woman after God's own heart." She cleared her throat. "We all have rough edges that He needs to smooth out for us."

"Well thank you Dr. Warner." I beamed with pride. "My pastor would be pleased at your compliment."

Dr. Warner leaned back in her chair and wiped her brow, "There's something that you need to know and you're not going to like it. Hannah and your children are siblings."

"What! I'm sorry." I swallowed. "What?" I gripped my pocketbook, feeling humiliation sit on my chest. My blood vessels started to dance. "Is this some kind of joke?"

Hannah let out a loud sob that startled me. "Is your mother . . ." I tried to ask if her mother was the woman Eldridge Sr. left me for, but the words wouldn't cross my tongue.

Sensing my confusion, Dr. Warner instructed Hannah, "Go find Ms. Nancy and Clarice."

Hannah clutched the baby close and stood. She didn't make eye contact with either of us. As soon as she opened the door, Nancy fell in. "Come on, honey, let me get you some water." Nancy tried to play it off, but I was insulted that she was eavesdropping.

Dr. Warner waited until Hannah closed the door before speaking again. "Forgive Nancy," Dr. Warner said standing. She moved from behind her desk and sat in the chair Hannah had occupied next to me. "We've all known Hannah since she was a baby. She's been given nothing but rotten lemons from her mother, but she finds a way to see the good in everything. I don't know many people with that kind of optimism and faith." Dr. Warner pushed her hair behind her ear. "Nancy was the doula who delivered Hannah."

The headache monster dug its long fingernails into my skull. I massaged my forehead with my fingers upside down, trying to keep the room from spinning. I straightened my back and screamed out, "This can't be happening!"

"I know you're upset Ms. Turner," she said, leaning into me. "I need to tell you something else."

I crossed my arms. "I don't know if I can bear much more." I shook my head, making the decision not to listen, "Mmn, mmn, I don't want to hear anything else right now." I started slapping my cheek to wake myself up from this crazy nightmare. "That girl is the illegitimate child of my husband? The bastard child he left me for?" The wrecking ball swung back on my head.

"Ms. Turner," Dr. Warner sighed with frustration. "Your deceased husband was Hannah's father. She and your Eldridge Jr. are two months apart."

Dr. Warner stretched forward and slid Hannah's folder to herself. I saw several sealed envelopes as she flipped through. She picked out an envelope and handed it to me.

"What is this?"

"Every year for Hannah's checkup, Mr. Turner brought me a letter.

"What is happening?" My heart thumped in my chest.

Dr. Warner continued her explanation. "Hannah's mother took advantage of him. All we know is that someone paid her to discredit him." She sighed and said, "Destina broke

Hannah's arm when she was three months old. Mr. Turner knew how reckless and irrational she was, so he chose to end your marriage to preserve Hannah's life."

"Ummmm," I hummed. "I'm so confused. How? Why? When?"

"Mr. Turner coordinated Hannah's appointments as visits for the children. We kept the office open as long as he wanted to be here. He'd bring a treat, and Portia would bring your kids. He made a mistake that he desperately wanted to rectify."

I searched my brain to make sense of what this woman was saying to me. "He left me to start a new life. This can't be true. How can a man of God get a hussy pregnant, leave his family, make a whole new family, and keep his old family together?" The reality of what she was saying continued to unfold before me. "Hannah is my husband's daughter!" I tapped my foot against the hardwood floor. "I didn't deserve any of this!"

The wrecking ball that slammed into me when Eldridge Sr. left us took another swing at me. "She has his pointy nose and his brown eyes. The gray streak in the baby's hair is from Sr.!"

I slumped into my chair, "I was so focused on the fact that she had a baby, I never paid attention to how much she looked like my children." I huffed, "Why didn't anyone tell me?"

Dr. Warner leaned into me. "While they didn't want to deceive you, they were instructed by him not to speak about it to anyone. They knew the rumors. . ." She glanced at the clock and said, "This is going to take a while longer to explain. Would you like a cup of coffee?" I nodded. She stood to open the door. "Nancy, could you or Clarice put on a fresh pot of coffee for us?"

"Clarice is gone for the day, I can do it." I heard the baby cooing, and Hannah sounded so happy talking to him.

Dr. Warner leaned back to ask, "How do you like your coffee, Ms. Turner?"

"Cream and two sugars, please."

"Nancy, two coffees. Add cream with two sugars."

"Yes, Ma'am. Dr. Warner, you mind if I take Hannah and the baby to the deli for a quick meal before …"

Dr. Warner interjected, "That's a good idea. Take a few dollars from the petty cash and bring me the receipt."

Dr. Warner closed the door and took her seat next to me. "Are you ready to read your letter, Ms. Turner?"

I forgot about the envelope in my hand. I slid my pocketbook beside me in the chair, I never put it on the floor …bad luck. Sliding my finger across the back of the envelope, I held my breath until I pulled out the letter. In the top corner of the page, it said, "1 of 5."

Sr.'s cologne greeted me before his scrawly handwriting did. Without realizing it, I held it up to my nose, closed my eyes, and took a big whiff. Holding back tears, I sat silently in that moment, reminiscing about good times with the love of my life.

I heard the knock on the door and opened my eyes when Dr. Warner said, "Come in, Nancy."

"Be careful, it's hot." Nancy slid the coffee onto the desk. Dr. Warner nodded in gratitude. Nancy left, closing the door behind her. I took a sip of my coffee before reading. It was just right.

Then, I settled into the chair, planted my feet, and started to read the cryptic, yet heartfelt letter from my husband:

Dear Annabelle,

For months I have wanted to come by the house to have this conversation with you, but I couldn't bring myself to see your face again. You are the love of my life, I hope you'll always believe that.

I made a mistake and drifted into another woman's arms. I was trying to console her and as a result, turned off all common sense. I never should have let Deacon Hent make tea for me, I never trusted him. I let my guard down and got myself in a jam.

People say that Destina put a root on me. She and Deacon Hent put something in my tea, but to be honest, I was feeling lost, confused, unheard, and overlooked long before I met her. She was the camel that broke everything around me. I don't know if it matters, but I saw your face that first time she and I were together. When I woke up, I saw her, standing over me, smiling and looking satisfied like a lioness killing her prey.

After she told me she was expecting, I wanted to protect the baby from the schemes and tricks of her mother. She didn't have tenderness in her heart. I knew I had to be a father for the child. I had many good years with Hannah and she is a good child, Annabelle.

"My children needed their father, too." I said out loud. Dr. Warner looked at me with sympathy. I kept reading silently.

When Dr. Warner told me that I have cancer, I was sad that I wouldn't be able to see the children grow up. I gave everything to Eldridge Jr. that I could think of. I know he will pass on those lessons to the next generation of men in the family.

I'm so sorry I hurt you. Destina wanted to move away, but I couldn't leave you our children. I kept tabs on you through Portia, and I'm proud of everything you have accomplished.

I believe I followed my own will, but God's permissive will kept me covered. Your prayers for me are not in vain.

I took a gulp of coffee, but I forgot it was hot, and it burned my tongue. I massaged it on the roof of my mouth for a few seconds, before I started reading again.

I wrote letters to you as often as I could and Dr. Warner has kept them safe for me for such a time as this. I pray that these letters will help you find the healing your heart deserves.

You are a wonderful woman, my Bell-Bell. Let your kindness ring and open up your heart to love again.

You loved the hell out of me, figuratively and literally.

I am forever grateful,
Eldridge Sr.

I sat dumbfounded, gripping the letter and holding it to my heart. As much as I wanted to be angry, I felt relieved, and rebuked at the same time. I dropped my head and said to Dr. Warner, "I asked the questions and answered them myself. I have behaved terribly."

That's when I lost it, right in the doctor's office. Years of unspoken pain formed into tears that I had never allowed myself to cry. I wailed, "I'm so sorry, Lord!"

Dr. Warner was trying to console me, but I didn't hear anything she said. I felt her rubbing my back, until it felt numb. I slid to my knees, and wiped my face on the inside of my blouse. I began to sing a slow, soulful rendition of "*Amazing Grace*."

I tried standing to stop the uncharacteristic acting out, but the dizziness forced me back to my knees. I kept singing, moaning, praying out loud, until I felt a cold glass on my lips. Dr. Warner was telling me to drink, but water dribbled down my numb lips and chin.

"Let it out," Dr. Warner said. "God knows your heart, Ms. Turner." Her words were salve to my hurting heart, but I felt as guilty as the law would allow. "*It's going to take time to forgive myself for turning my back on God's child.*"

All I could do was plead my case with my song. "My heart was repentant," I said through tears. I felt the weight of regret sit on my head, it started to bounce, making my head feel heavy. "I was so rude and judgmental to that baby girl. I hope she'll forgive me. She was so scared to knock on my door that she curled up in a blanket and slept on the porch."

"Hannah told us some of the things you've said to her. It's really understandable with everything you've been through. Perhaps the healing can help all of you reconcile."

I relented. "I can tell that Nancy loves Hannah."

"Your ex-husband saw how Nancy cared for Destina when she was delivering Hannah and named her Hannah's Godmother. She takes that role seriously."

"I see."

"When Elijah was born, Hannah's mother moved out of the house. Nancy started working extra shifts to buy a house. Her goal is to open a home for pregnant teens. When Mr. Turner died, he left a generous donation in his will for the house. As a matter of fact, today is her last day."

"Oh, wow!"

"She bought a house in Cincinnati. She's secured donations for it. She's calling the house Hannah's Haven. She's taking Hannah, Elijah, and another young lady and they're leaving on the bus tonight."

Clarity. "That's why I brought everything."

There was a knock at the door, and Dr. Warner looked at her watch. "I think that's Doris. Excuse me one second." She trotted out of the office leaving the door open. "Coming!"

A young lady's voice said, "Hi Dr. Warner."

"Ohh, Doris," Dr. Warner sounded cheerful. "I'm so glad you didn't change your mind. You can sit in exam room 1 until Nancy gets back. I have someone in my office."

"Okay."

"Any pains or concerns?"

"No, Ma'am."

"*Is that Mable's granddaughter? That's why she hasn't been to church!*" I thought. "*She done gone and got knocked up.*" I had to check myself, "*She's pregnant.*"

"One of my friends will take over your medical care when you get to Cincinnati. You're going to love her."

"I hope so. I'll miss you, but I have to get out of this small town."

"I know, baby. I'll be in my office if you need me." A few seconds later, Dr. Warner returned.

"Doris is only 15," she whispered. "She has her own set of problems, but pregnancies like hers happen around here more than I care to repeat."

I tried to swallow the lump in my throat, "So you're saying she was. . .?"

"Yes." Dr. Warner looked to heaven. "I thank God for the vision that He gave Nancy. She helps these young women find some joy in this life."

"I feel so bad for assuming the worst about Hannah. I thought it was Eldridge Jr.'s baby."

"They do favor, don't they?" Dr. Warner smiled. "I loved watching him with the children. Joyce always tried to take the lead with discipline or caring for the children. One day he accidentally knocked over his cup of hot tea with lemon. She ran over trying to clean it up and he said, 'I'm the Daddy around here, you're a nine year old kid. I'll clean it up.'"

That revelation opened my eyes, "*The lemons!*"

She turned to cough and clear her throat. "Excuse me." She coughed again, "He always said that he never wanted to cause you any shame."

"The secrets this family kept from me," I crossed my arms. "I just don't get it."

"Her mother, like you, assumed that Hannah was promiscuous. Unfortunately, as I suspected, Hannah confirmed that the father of her child is her mother's boyfriend."

I clutched my pearls. "Huh?"

"Unfortunately, he has skipped town, but if he comes back, we'll alert the Sheriff." The door slammed. "Sounds like they're back."

"Hey baby!" I heard the delight in Nancy's voice greeting Doris. "We need to leave for the bus station soon. Dr. Warner, are you almost finished in there?"

She looked at me, "Do you want to see Hannah before she leaves?" I nodded. "Nancy, can you and Hannah come here for a second?"

I stood up, straightened my blouse and skirt and moved to the door. When Hannah came in I grabbed her by the shoulders and turned her to me. I choked back tears. And said, "Please accept my humble apologies. I wasn't good to you." I pulled her close, "Will you forgive me?"

"Mother Turner." Hannah's voice cracked as she laid her head on my shoulder. I felt Elijah's hand rubbing my face. "Daddy told me you had been hurt. He knew that you could learn to love me unconditionally." She handed me the baby, "Nancy is his surrogate Grandmother, but he needs you too, Grandma Annabelle."

"Oh?" I teared up holding the baby. "I'm honored."

Nancy looked like an angel in her nurse's uniform. "Nurse Nancy, can we have a second chance?" Her face softened at my question, and I extended my hand to her. "Hi, I'm Ms. Annabelle Turner. Nice to meet you."

"My pleasure," she spoke through gritted teeth.

"I apologize for not being an example of God's love toward your Goddaughter. I pray that you will allow you to show you my repentant heart."

Nancy smiled. "The prayers of the righteous availeth much. You can start by praying for the young girls who will live in Hannah's Haven."

"Well, that settles it." Dr. Warner clapped. "As we embark on a new journey of faith, God will order our steps. Ms. . . . I mean, Grandma Annabelle, do you mind leading us in prayer before the girls go to the bus station?" She turned her head and called for Doris.

As I had thought, Mabel's granddaughter waddled into the office with a very pregnant belly. When she saw me, she put her head down and lowered her eyes. "Doris," I reassured her, "there is no shame in the presence of God. Lift your head." She sighed with relief and I said, "I promise, there will be no judgement from me."

I closed my eyes and hummed, "*Amazing Grace*," this time not from grief, but from gratitude and love.

"Heavenly Father," I prayed, "Thank you for allowing me to see things through Your eyes. Thank you for replacing my stony heart with a heart of flesh. I am here with your daughters, who have shown love unconditionally." I gripped Nancy's left hand and Hannah's right hand; they squeezed me back and I kept praying. "Forgive me for turning my heart from you and for not showing the fruit of love to your children, or mine."

When I opened my eyes, we were all in tears.

For the first time, I looked at Hannah and saw how much she resembled her father.

PART TWO – SHE IS ME

Chapter 8

Hello, Joyce.

The night that Hannah left for Cincinnati, was my birthday. It was a bittersweet goodbye, but I was glad Hannah wasn't a secret anymore. I was going to miss her. Having my siblings close was special for me. I planned to visit Hannah for a week. I was moving to Toledo to start a new job and a new life, away from my mother.

LJ, Enid, and I couldn't be at the bus station with Hannah since she was leaving from Washington Courthouse. Mother didn't go to the bus station to see her off. She let Dr. Warner take Miss Nancy, Hannah's Godmother, Elijah, and our friend, Doris, to the station.

We had a party for Hannah, Doris, and Miss Nancy a week before they left. Dr. Warner opened her office for us to share the 1,000,000 reasons we had to celebrate them. Hannah had finished high school early, she was a good mother, and she worked hard, often putting in long hours at the café.

Listening to everyone talk about how proud they were of my sister, I cried so hard while holding her baby, my nephew. I wanted to be close to Elijah so I could be his favorite auntie, although his Auntie E did a good job of loving him, too. I wasn't necessarily crying because they were leaving, I think I was grieving my own pitiful life.

Hannah sat next to me and for at least thirty minutes, consoling me. "I'm not going far, Sissy," she said, rubbing my back. "You're coming to see me in Cincinnati in a few months. It won't be long."

"I know," I said through sniffles. "But with you leaving us, it's like a piece of my heart is being ripped out."

"Aww, Sissy," Enid had said, "In a few months we'll all be living our lives. I'll be at Howard, LJ will be in the Army, and you'll be in the big city, nursing and making people look good. It's an exciting time for all of us."

"I promise to write and call once a week." Hannah reassured us.

"You better, twin," LJ laughed. "Call us on Sundays, but send your letters to Aunt Portia's."

"Your secret is safe with me," Aunt Portia put her finger over her lips. We didn't want Mother to know that we were planning our escape. It was because of Hannah that we all got serious about leaving the nest. She inspired me to see life beyond the four walls of Mother's house.

"What makes it worse," I lamented. "I'm the oldest. I was supposed to be the example for you, not the other way around." Elijah started to cry. Hannah took him to the side to nurse him.

LJ put his arm around me, "Sissy, we know that Mother kept you close so that you could care for us. We all love you for the sacrifices you have made for us. Don't be so hard on yourself, you couldn't help that she kept a tight leash on you."

"So tight, I haven't even had time to find a boyfriend." I cleared my throat. "I promise you, when I leave this town, I ain't gone be weak like I've been under Mother's roof. You'll see." I sat up. "I am going to be a force to be reckoned with. Nobody will run over me anymore. Not a man, not a woman, not anything."

"Sissy," Hannah had said between bites of cake, "Next week act normal, but I want you to celebrate your birthday, you hear me?"

"Birthday celebrations remind Mother of Daddy." I teared up. "He loved to celebrate us in big ways. She only allows us to celebrate our special day with a piece of cake."

Dr. Warner tapped me on the shoulder and said, "Turning 21 is a major accomplishment, honey." She leaned in for a hug. "Spend time with your friends, take in the birthday festivities. Remember what your Daddy told you, "Live your life, Joyce." We repeated it in unison.

I planned to do just that, live my life. Being a college graduate with a budding business meant that I could make some of my own decisions without Mother shooting me down. I planned to leave Xenia, Ohio, by August and take a job in Toledo with one of the premier Negro seamstresses in the country, Alfreda Burns. She had agreed to take me on as her apprentice.

On my birthday, I wore a form fitting, handmade, red dress, a color Mother never allowed me to wear. I bent over the ironing board and pressed out my curly afro with the iron. It took a few hours, but the end result made me happy. My hair was so long and thick when it was straight, I had to be careful so I wouldn't sit on it.

Miss Sally closed the library early and let me sit outside with LJ, Enid, and some of our friends. We ate some of LJ's pound cake leftover from one of the church mothers. We drank sweet tea and danced in the courtyard. Before they left, my siblings gave me a beautiful purple silk scarf that I still cherish to this day.

"In a few months I will be starting a new life in Toledo." I lifted my glass of tea. "Here's to new beginnings."

"To new beginnings," everyone repeated.

Keeping Hannah a secret was hard for me. She didn't deserve the treatment she got from her mother. Although my relationship with Mother was strained, she didn't abuse me on a regular basis. She made certain our needs were met, and she always made sure we had a safe place to sleep.

Mother never told me that I was a mistake, she just never made me feel wanted. I was grateful that my mother, although distant, was in my life. Hannah's mother had abandoned her. She didn't let that stop her, Hannah was determined to beat the odds and prove her mother wrong.

Daddy was intentional about us knowing Hannah, and I'm glad he was. When she and LJ were five, Enid was three, I was nine, Daddy introduced us to her at Aunt Portia's house. That weekend, Aunt Portia came to take us to her house. She told us she had a surprise for us. When we got there, Dadday and a little girl who looked just like us were sitting on the porch.

"Daddy!" Enid jumped out of the car.

"Who is that?" I asked him.

"You look just like me!" LJ exclaimed.

"This is Hannah, and she is the sister I've been telling you about."

"What happened to your arm?" LJ inquired, pointing to a long, thin scar.

"She had a tumble. Her mother was a little bit too rough with her., but she's okay."

"I'm sorry that happened to you, Hannah." Enid said. "Can we go play?" LJ and Enid ran off to play with her while I pondered what it meant to keep my new sister a secret. Over the years, we kept in touch through Aunt Portia, even after Daddy died. His passing meant that he couldn't protect her anymore. She didn't want to burden Aunt Poria, she chose to be autonomous, going into a shelter, sacrificing comfortability for independence.

Chapter 9

Daddy's departure.

The note on the refrigerator was LJ's idea. He knew that Mother would turn her focus to him and not ask a lot of questions. She hated to see him upset. Mother catered to LJ, supported Enid, and ignored me.

I could tell that she was hurting, but Mother kept the tender emotions locked up. She only emoted when she was angry or frustrated, usually with me. A few weeks after Daddy left, she was already slamming the hammer down on me about any little thing I did wrong.

At night when we were all in our rooms, I would hear Daddy and Mother arguing through the thin walls. "Annabelle," he'd say in a hushed tone, "You don't have to be so hard on the children."

Mother, unmoved by his quiet tone, would raise her voice and say, "I have to stand before God and give an explanation for these children. I carried them, and I'm responsible to raise them up for Him."

"Why are you so hard on Joyce?" he had asked her once when they were getting ready for bed. "She's only nine, you expect her to do things that a married woman has to do."

"If I don't turn her toward God, she's going to go astray," she had grunted. "She looks like trouble. I need to nip that devil in the bud."

"You're wrong, Annabelle," he stood up for me. "Joyce has done nothing wrong. She is special. I can see the anointing on her to help people."

"Hmph. If you say so. Ain't no anointing on that girl. I don't know what you see. Eldridge Jr. is the anointed one. Enid too. Joyce will be in the background." Those words stung. I vowed to make her proud of me.

My mother had no idea who I was, who I wanted to be, or who I was capable of being. "She will know it when I'm gone," I thought while lying in my bed. Day by day, I was taking steps to get out of her shadow, trusting the God Daddy taught me to believe in, turning my back on the one Mother represented.

I was in my room studying when Mother returned from Washington Courthouse. I knew she was going to be on a rampage when she came home, but I didn't know what to expect. When I heard her calling us, "Joyce, Eldridge Jr., Enid, come on down here," my heart froze for a second.

We all opened our doors at the same time, giving each other a look of concern. "Do you think she's mad at us?" LJ whispered.

Enid looked scared, "I don't know, Brother."

I shrugged my shoulders and whispered back, "Come on, we gotta go." I could feel the cloud of a headache coming over the horizon looking for me. I waved my hand at my siblings, and of course as the oldest, I led the troops down the steps.

I couldn't think straight, nor could I see, my headache was lifting me off of the ground. We all knew that keeping Hannah a secret was a major infraction.

In the dining room, Mother was sitting at the head of the table with her Bible in her lap. No one at the table moved, not even Mother. We sat silently, for a few minutes at the dining room table, like we did whenever she wanted to berate us or tell us something we needed to correct.

After a few minutes, she licked her index finger and flipped through her Bible. I braced myself against my chair, preparing for a sharp tongue lashing. Mother had a way of using the Bible to berate us, and I didn't like it. Part of the reason I stopped going to church was because she used His word as a weapon.

Mother flipped to 1 John 1:9 and began to read aloud. Her voice was soft as she read and emphasized the words, "If we confess our sins." It surprised me that she sounded so humble. She licked her finger again and flipped to a chapter in the Old Testament. She chose a couple of more passages and held them with her fingers. Mother passed the Bible to LJ who was to her left at the head of the table. "Hold these pages, but read here."

LJ replaced mother's fingers with his own. As he stood and read the whole chapter, of Psalms 27, Mother sat back in her chair with her eyes closed. I closed my eyes, too, and listened to my brother's calming baritone voice as it floated through the air.

"Pass the Bible to Enid," Mother said.

LJ slid the Bible to his left. When she slipped her fingers to hold the spots LJ had saved, he sat down. "Flip back to Ephesians 6," Mother said, eyes still closed.

Mother said, "Read chapter six." Enid read as mother instructed, her melodic voice rang through my ears like a sweet bell until she finished. "Now pass the Bible to your sister," Mother said. With another swoop, the Word of God was slid across the table to me, to Mother's right. My reading was from I Corinthians.

Enid sat down, scraping the chair against the floor. Mother opened one eye, looked at me and said, "Read chapter thirteen."

I did as I was told, standing to read about love, something I yearned for, especially from my mother. The cloud had moved over my head, and I wanted to lie down. But as I always did, I pushed myself to be present in the room. When I had finished reading, I took a deep breath and sat down. I glanced at my siblings who looked back at me with the same confusion I felt in my heart.

Mother cleared her throat, sat up in her chair, and opened her eyes. "It will take some time for me to fully forgive you all for keeping such a big secret from me," Mother said. "I don't appreciate being kept in the dark about the fact you have a sister, and your father left me for her mother."

Mother reached for the Bible and put it in her lap. "I had to repent to God for my actions. Now I must apologize to all of you." She leaned up and looked at LJ. "Eldridge Jr., I'm sorry for jumping to conclusions so quickly and not listening to you. You have told me several times to trust you yet, I didn't. Forgive me, son."

She turned to Enid. "Baby, I'm sorry that you had to see me only as a gruff, angry mother. I appreciate the joy and imagination you bring to us. Thank you for seeing me as I should be. Forgive me."

"Oh, Mother," Enid said. "I love you."

She turned to me, "Joyce," she patted my hand, "You were conceived in love, on my wedding night." She looked at each of us to emphasize her point, and said again, "My *wedding* night."

I pondered, "I was conceived in love, but if the demonstration of what she calls love is love, I don't want anything to do with it." I shook my head trying to move the cloud of a headache. I affirmed to myself, "Love is bigger than my mother. God is love."

Mother said, "I know I'm hard on you Joyce. You remind me of some people I know from high school. They were girls who lacked confidence, were people pleasers, didn't amount to anything. I just want you to be better than them. In a way, I want you to be better than me, too. The Bible says in John 10:28 that nothing can pluck us from God's hand, and I was shaping you to be Unpluckable."

Mother was quiet for a few seconds, then I heard her utter the words I had been longing to hear, "Joyce, look at me," she patted my hand again. "I love you." What she said next moved me to tears. "I'm sorry."

I tried to hold back my tears. I wanted to be strong, but hearing those words, years after losing my father, I let myself go. I bowed my head and sobbed silently. I felt Enid rubbing my back. "It's going to be okay, Sissy." She consoled me, "Let it out."

Mother started to sing Amazing Grace and LJ harmonized with her. I then thought back to a time when Daddy had to defend me against Mother in the same chair that I sat in. I clearly remembered him watching us eat dinner as he sat at the head of the table.

"How was your day, Annabelle?" He asked plopping some mashed potatoes on his plate, butter flowing around it like a stream.

Mother didn't engage in much conversation that night. "It was a regular day. I taught my students and dealt with selfish entitled children who don't like to listen and don't want to learn." She scarfed down her food almost without swallowing.

We all finished our food in silence with only the clinking of forks against plates. Mother finished her food, and she stood over the table to give me directives. "I'm going to women's Bible study, and I want my kitchen clean when I get home." She pushed her chair in. "Sweep and mop the floor." Before she left the dining room she said, "And don't forget to wipe down my stove."

Daddy always looked out for me. He stood up and walked into the kitchen, following Mother as she put on her coat. "Annabelle," I heard him say, "why don't you stay home tonight? We can spend time as a family and go get some ice cream or something."

"I don't want to miss Bible study tonight, Sr. We are talking about walking with God, trusting Him when times are lean and worshiping Him when times are good."

"I know, Baby," Daddy sighed. "I wrote the Bible study months ago."

"Well, you're no longer my pastor." I heard the door creak open, "You can take the children to get ice cream. I don't want any." I heard the door slam.

Daddy came back into the dining room and slumped in his chair. We had seen Daddy cry before, he never held his emotions back from us; but that night, his vulnerability spread across us like a wildfire.

"I have loved your mother for more than half of my life. I don't know how my leaving is going to affect her, but you have my word, children," he held a gaze with all of us. "You will always, always have me in your life."

"Daddy," Enid said, "Hannah needs you right now."

LJ punched the table, "I can't believe her mother broke her arm. "If I could, I would . . ."

"Jr., I will handle this," Daddy dropped his head. "I made a covenant with your mother, and she just . . .," Daddy cried. "I committed infidelity, but I can't believe they set me up. I can't take it back, but I can redeem myself by protecting Hannah."

"Daddy," I said standing to clear the table. We can see how unhappy you are with Mother. It's even worse now, since you retired from pastoring without giving her any explanation. You don't chase her around the house for kisses anymore. I never see you hug, or even whisper in corners to each other."

Daddy wiped away tears and said, "I don't know why, but your mother has changed so much that I don't recognize her anymore. Her light is fading."

Sitting at that same table, I digested Mother's apology and I started to understand some of her story.

Chapter 10

On my own.

I didn't plan to run away from home in the middle of the night, but unexpected circumstances forced my hand. I had to get away from Mother, or I was going to do or say something I couldn't come back from.

You might not believe me, but the next day, after Mother prayed heaven down, asked for forgiveness and had us pour out our hearts to each other, she reverted right back to her old evil self. I don't know if her prayer wasn't genuine, or if God's power wasn't strong enough to keep her on the straight and narrow.

Enid and a couple of her friends were sitting around, while I made some adjustments to their Sadie Hawkins' dresses. The atmosphere was light, everyone was laughing and joking until we heard Mother's key in the door. As she entered the house, the girls scrambled to sit on the couch with their legs crossed. Everyone sat frozen. Bertha had on a black polyester dress, and she sat down so fast that she slipped right back onto the floor. We all burst out in uproarious laughter.

I was on my knees hemming the bottom of Enid's dress when mother walked in. I made sure the house wasn't dirty, but I did have a pile of scrap fabric and a couple of pairs of scissors near me. When Mother walked in, we were chuckling, and I accidentally poked Enid with a straight pin. "Oh, you got me, Sissy." She hopped on one foot.

"Sorry, Sissy," I looked up at her. "Bertha is so funny." We laughed again. I continued removing straight pins from the hem.

"It's okay," Enid looked down at me, "It didn't really hurt. I was just teasing you."

Mother stomped her foot and said, "What didn't hurt?" The thud of her dropping her bag startled me, I shuddered. She smiled at everyone in the room, but gave me an evil look. "What's all this mess you in my sitting room, girl?"

I looked up at Mother and glanced around the room but kept my lips sealed. Mother asked again, "What is all this mess you got in my sitting room?" She snapped her finger and said, "Clean it up." I had placed all of the scraps into a piece of fabric. I picked up the four corners and held them together, cleaning up the mess with one scoop. I slid them into my apron pocket along with two pairs of scissors. That one action returned her sitting room to its pristine condition. Mother's face relaxed briefly, but she raised her voice and said, "You know I don't allow anyone to sit in my sitting room! You just desecrated my safe space. I pray in here."

Hearing the commotion, LJ came running down the steps. "Is everything okay, Mother?" LJ said over the banister. Mother's face softened toward him. "Oh, my sweet boy!" She smiled. "Come here and give your beloved Mother a big hug." She opened her arms and LJ walked down the steps into them. "Who are all these people in my house?" She said over his shoulder.

"Mother, you know these are Enid's friends. You gave her permission to have them over today to try on their dresses for Saturday. They are going to the Sadie Hawkins dance at school."

Mother nodded, "But I don't remember saying anything about Joyce doing this," she waved her hands in a circle. "Whatever this is."

I stood up, took a deep breath and faced my greatest fear, my mother. "This" I said, waving my hands in a circle, imitating her, "is me helping my sister and her friends feel good about themselves when they go to the Sadie Hawkins dance." Mother grunted.

"Enid and her friends saved their money to buy these dresses at the thrift store. I told them to bring their dresses to me so I could breathe new life into them, like God did for us, Mother. I did the same thing for Hannah before she left."

I had Hannah to thank for most of my business. She'd model my creations at the deli, where she worked, and the highfalutin people in town ate. People would ask her where she got her clothes from and she'd tell them, "Joyce Turner did this for me."

I loved recreating clothes and making people look good in them. Many of Mother's friends stopped eating there when Hannah came to live with us.

Sometimes I wished that Mother knew what I could do with my sewing machine. I wanted to make adjustments to some of her suits and hats, but she would never be caught wearing anything form-fitting, though she had a nice figure.

Mama and her church friends found a new place to have their after church brunches, because Mother wanted to keep the news about Hannah away from them. In every way that she could, she hid herself from the reality of our life and tried to protect the image of Daddy, that she remembered. Most people knew the truth, they just didn't talk to her about it.

Mother's absence at the deli was good for me. Hannah always talked about me because she only wore clothes I picked out for her. The church people never put it together that I was the Joyce they were talking about because there were so many Joyce's in our town. Anyone who was serious about finding me did so without announcing their intention. Our secrets were safe with each other, and I liked it that way.

Mother's foot tapping arrested my attention. I looked up to see her rolling her eyes at me. "Don't bring God into this foolishness, Joyce."

"Mother," I said looking into her eyes. "These are good girls. They plan to go to youth choir rehearsal and serve at the church picnic before the dance on Saturday." I held my sister's hand. "Enid has worked hard this year, she is the Valedictorian of her class. You already know that she got a full scholarship to Howard."

"You don't have the right to tell me anything about my child." I heard her neck crack as she whipped her head away from me. "I know what I need to know about her."

I pointed to Bertha, "Mother, do you remember that Bertha is the Salutatorian of their class?" I looked to Mother for a reaction but there was none, so I kept talking. "Bertha's polyester dress was plain, it had holes in it, and it was frayed at the ends. I hand stitched those flowers," Bertha, still seated, lifted up her dress to show Mother the flowers. "To bring her dress back to life, Bertha helped me cut off the frayed ends and rehem it. To get it to the condition it is in now, we soaked her dress in baking soda for a few days to make sure we could get the stench out."

I stepped over to Eunice and stood her up. "Eunice liked this dress." I twirled her around, "But it was one size too small for her. I found a piece of fabric to match the color and added it to this dress so she could wear the dress she wanted and feel beautiful in it." Mother crossed her arms and planted her feet. I emphasized my point about them being good girls by saying, "Eunice is singing the solo on Sunday at church."

Mother looked at Enid's friends and kept her lips sealed. She stared at Enid who straightened her dress, stood up tall, waiting for the inspection, and frowned. "Why are you making Enid's dress so tight?" She flipped the bodice and pulled on the waist.

"Mother, please stop pulling the dress. I put loose seams in it to hold it in place until I can get to my sewing machine." I tried to grab the fabric from her, "You're going to pull them out if you keep tugging at it like that." She didn't stop so I resorted to begging, "Mother, stop tugging, I've been working on Enid's dress for hours." I scrambled to pry the fabric from Mother's fingers, "What are you doing?" I huffed.

Mother's ironclad grip on the dress surprised me. I kept trying to move her hand, but she pushed her elbow into my chest. I let go and stepped back. Our tussle caused Mother to yank my sister off the block she was standing on. As she stumbled forward, LJ stepped up and caught her before she fell. Mother stood there triumphantly until she realized that she was gripping one half of Enid's dress in her hand.

"Why would you do that, Mother?" I asked. I looked around the room and everyone's faces displayed how mortified I was feeling for myself and for my sister.

Enid swiped a quilt from the couch and covered her lower body with it. "You picked out this dress I'm wearing, Mother." She said, "We bought it on Senior day at the thrift store two weeks ago. When I tried it on for you in the store, you made sure that the fabric fell right below my ankles." Enid sniffled, "Mother, we agreed that this dress met all of your requirements and you gave me your approval." She adjusted her quilt, and said softly, "Now, you've ruined it."

Mother turned and looked at Enid who cowered behind my brother. "I'll get you a new dress, girl. Stop all that crying."

Mother tossed the fabric to her side, "I remember how pretty you looked in the store, but I don't remember seeing your ankle bones." She put her finger to her temple and looked up in thought. "Nor do I remember the waist of this dress being tight on you like it was just now."

She whipped her head at me and rolled her eyes. I met her gaze with my own. Mother broke her gaze with me by turning up her nose and wrinkling her lips. "From what I can see," she looked back at Enid. "The changes Joyce made to this dress has invited the devil into my house." She put her hand on her hip to stand her ground, "and I don't like it, not one bit."

"Mother," I uttered, "I didn't make too many changes to Enid's dress. I cinched her waist just a tiny bit, but there was still room between her skin and the dress. It was still long, and it covered her ankles."

"I'm not talking about no hem, Joyce." She crossed the room and stood in front of me.

Mother looked at Enid's friends and shook her head at them. "You girls ought to be ashamed of yourselves letting Joyce make your dresses so doggone tight." She cleared her throat and sucked her teeth, "I ought to call all of your mothers right now." She flicked her finger at Bernice and hissed, "You, of all people, should know better, your grandmother is president of the choir."

Bernice dropped her head and took a deep breath. The girls sat motionless as Mother continued her tirade against me. "You ought to be ashamed of yourselves. On Sunday, make your way straight to the altar, get on your knees, and repent."

"Mother Turner" Bernice muttered, eyes still down, "My mother likes my dress. She even thanked Joyce for fixing it up for me." I appreciated that Bernice was trying to defend me. I could see them looking up at Mother from the corner of my eye, but I kept my eyes on Enid and LJ.

"Your mother is a little off her rocker, anyway," Mother declared. Bernice looked perplexed, but Mother kept talking, "You know what I ought to do?" She took a breath and said, "Never mind that, you all just go home. You can come back when you can follow the rules of my house." They looked at each other and Mother moved to open the door. "Go on, now."

After the last girl crossed the threshold of the house, she slammed the door behind them and directed her wrath towards me. "Joyce, I don't know who you think you are, but you will no longer be the devil's influence on my children or anyone else's children."

She looked at LJ who returned a sorrowful glance at me. "Enid, Baby, Mother needs you to take a couple of steps back." As soon as Enid lifted her foot to move, Mother reared her right hand back as far as it would go and swung it right across my cheek, sending me to the floor. Enid and LJ gasped, but they knew they could not move toward me to help.

Enid choked back her tears and LJ cried out, "Mother, please calm down. You're hurting Joyce!" I often wondered what Daddy would have thought about the woman Mother had become. I thought, "Could my Daddy have fallen in love with a woman who has this heart posture toward his child?"

The cloud in my head and the bells ringing in my ears after the slap made me nauseous. I gulped and swallowed the lump of emotions forming in my throat. "Joyce," I affirmed myself patting my heart, "remember this moment. The sting you feel in your right cheek is the alarm. It's time to wake up your sleeping soul, girl." I shook my head trying to move the clouds bringing with them a headache.

Through the clouds I heard Mother say, "Let that slap be a reminder to the devil that he has no place in this house." She pointed at LJ and Enid, "Go to your rooms, while I talk to your sister." The way she said, "sister" sounded like the hiss of a python. I heard their footsteps creep up the steps, slowly. I imagined they were walking in a sad parade, behind my casket.

As that irate woman stood over me with her hands on her hips, face grimaced, and teeth gritted, I didn't recognize my own mother. I searched her face, but I couldn't find anything good in her bloodshot red eyes. "I once saw a mirror reflection of myself in her," I thought. "But tonight, she has shown me who she really is." That was the moment I was able to surgically remove myself mentally from the woman who birthed me and become the woman I wanted to be. "I have to land on my feet," I declared to myself.

"Are you listening to me?" Mother bowed down and put her nose to my nose. I hadn't realized that I had tuned her out. "Get up!"

I prayed to God to give me strength. "I don't know if I will ever know my mother's love, Lord, but don't forget about me. Please provide a way of escape." I squeezed my eyes shut and let myself feel the sting of my cheek and the ringing in my ears. I wanted to get up, but all I could do was be still, like a possum would play dead. "Lord, what would make a mother hate her own child so much?"

That's when I heard the sound of LJ and Enid's harmonious hums of "Amazing Grace." The family song that Mother always hummed, when she was in a good mood, seemed to arrest her attention and she backed up off of me.

I took that as a sign from God that it was my opportunity to make my escape. "I knew that you didn't like me," I said, finding my footing by gripping the plastic on the couch. I moved slowly so as not to succumb to the dizzy feeling that danced around my head.

"You're my child. I don't have to like you, girl." She retorted, wiping sweat from her brow, "I'm responsible to love you, but I can love you from a distance." She was letting me know that she really was ready for me to go.

"Mother," I whispered. "I can read between the lines. You don't have to worry, I won't be a burden to you anymore." I moved toward the steps, "This will be the last time you will ever put your hands on me, without expressing love. You will no longer embarrass me, or have the ability to control me." I started walking up the steps, "I haven't done anything but serve you as God commanded me to." From the middle of the steps I said, "I have honored you, Mother."

"Joyce," LJ said from the top of the steps.

"Stay out of this, son," Mother called up to him.

"I've got this brother." I reassured him walking up the steps. "I'll be alright."

Without remorse, mother tilted her head at me and said, "God be with you." That was the confirmation I needed. For weeks, I had been slowly packing up things around the house that meant something to me.

"Mother," I said to her, "I never would have imagined that you would stoop this low." I ran up the steps and into Enid's room. She was sitting on her bed. LJ followed behind me whispering behind my back, "What are you going to do?" He closed Enid's bedroom door, stood in front of me and said, "Let me see your face." He put his thumb and index finger on my chin and moved my head into the light. "She slapped you so hard. Are you sure you're okay?"

I shook my head left and right. "This was the last straw for me, Brother."

He wiped his brow, "I hate to say this, but maybe it's time for you to go explore the world, Sissy."

"What do you mean?" I furrowed my brow.

LJ continued, "Go live your life. It's obvious that this situation with Mother is not going to change right now." I shook my head in disbelief. "Anything that brings you happiness is snatched from you by her. She doesn't seem to like anything that you represent. You cannot stay in this house anymore."

"Why doesn't she love me?" I started to cry.

"I can't answer that for you, Sissy. But I know that Mother has had to fight for us and about us. No weak woman worth her weight in salt, would remain in a town where her husband committed infidelity, left her to marry another woman, and took care of their illegitimate child. Walk in Mother's shoes before you decide what's in her heart or what she believes."

Enid covered her face with her hands and cried silently. I felt empathy for my sister as I watched tears roll out of her eyes and down her cheeks. After a few seconds, she gathered herself and said through her fingers, "Where will you go?"

I honestly hadn't thought about the next step in my plan. I closed my eyes and took a deep breath, centering myself in the moment. "I'm never, ever, having children." I let a few tears fall before wiping my face. "I'm so scared of being a bad mother."

"Don't make that decision right now, Sissy," Enid said. "When you fall in love, you might change your mind." She looked at LJ, "Just like we helped Hannah, we will help you." She put her pinky finger up indicating to LJ and me to intertwine with hers. "We'll hold you accountable."

We affirmed our declaration in unison. "Promises made. Promises kept."

"Okay LJ," I breathed. "You have ten months to make sure that Enid has everything she needs until she goes to Howard in August. I'll be going to Toledo to work with Ms. Alfreda in December. I'll send money to Aunt Portia's for you when I can."

"Oh Joyce!" Enid wailed into my shoulder, squelching the volume. "I'm going to miss you."

I squeezed her shoulder. "Enid, you are the heart of us. Don't change your direction for anyone, do you understand me?" She shook her head up and down. "You make sure that LJ takes care of himself and maybe has a little fun sometimes. When the young ladies at church smile at him, tell him to pay attention." We all chuckled.

"I'm not looking for a girlfriend right now.

"LJ," I laughed to lighten the mood. "I don't know if there is a contest between the church mothers for who has the best food to get their dibs on you for their daughters, granddaughters, or nieces, but they are working hard to get your attention."

Enid cracked up, "Mother is always bringing him pound cake, fried chicken, pork chops, ham, and homemade lemonade. Somebody is looking."

LJ blushed. "Stop it, now." He snorted and covered his face.

"In all seriousness," I said. "When you're safely away at college, LJ will enlist in the Army. Stick to the plan."

I heard Mother calling from downstairs, "So what are you gonna do, Joyce?" I ignored her taunting and focused on my siblings. We all sat on Enid's bed, holding each other in a tender embrace. LJ started to hum "Amazing Grace" just low enough for us three to hear. Enid joined him, and I added my harmony.

I felt God moving and the tears started to fall. "I didn't want it to happen this way."

LJ started to pray, "Lord, we release our sister into your hands. Protect her, order her footsteps, and give her peace."

The reality of my impending leap of faith overwhelmed me. I felt pressure in my chest and I choked on the words, "This is real. In this moment," I breathed. "I have to trust God like I've never trusted Him before." I rubbed my sister's shoulder in order to console myself. I pulled my siblings into a tighter embrace and held them like I wanted to be held.

Enid said, "God won't forsake you."

I regained my confidence at that moment. "I have to stand firm on my convictions and walk in what I believe." I stood up, hugged my brother, and got on my knees to look under Enid's bed. I grabbed my packed bag, my coin purse and headed to the door. "I'm ready to go."

"Wait!" LJ said, handing me the coffee can we had been using as a bank. "Take this. You're going to need money."

I shook my head, "No, you and Enid need it."

"Take it," LJ whispered, pushing it into my chest.

"Mmmn, mmn," I muttered.

"Joyce," Enid pleaded.

"Sissy, I have money in my coin purse, and I have some alterations lined up within the next few days. I'll be alright." I pushed the can back.

I looked around Enid's room and bid farewell to the chapter of my life that was written to describe me as unworthy. "I am ready for the freedom I have been yearning to feel."

I walked slowly down the steps with LJ and Enid on my heels. "Mother, what have you done? Joyce graduates in a few months." Enid sighed. "I wish you two could work this out."

She sat on the steps, tears watering her cheeks. LJ stayed behind her, his face sad and proud.

I walked past my mother, who stood with her hands on her hips glaring at me with her red eyes. I fought to hold back my tears, I did not want to let her see me cry. "Mother," I said, "I declare my independence from your opinion of me which keeps me bound." I opened the front door, raised my hand to heaven and said, "May God be with you, Mother. I'll always pray for you. I will always pray that God will restore us back to each other." I will pray that you will find it in your heart to receive me back into your good graces."

I opened the door and stepped into the dark. "God," I prayed. "Order my steps."

Mother said behind my back, "I'll be praying, too." I turned around to see her pressing her fingers into her brow and massaging her forehead. She closed the door and I stepped into the night, tears falling, ready for the unknown. I took the first step down the stairs of Mother's house and when I got to the last one, I started running.

I ran until my feet couldn't carry me anymore.

Chapter 11

A safe place to rest.

I don't know how long I ran, but it felt like 10 country miles. My bag and heart were heavy. Lugging around the weight I was carrying made me feel tired. I felt anxious, hiding in shadows as cars passed me. I made sure to hide my silhouette so that no one could say they saw Annabelle Turner's daughter out in the streets.

Once I reached Second Street, I leaned against Ambrosia Café, taking a few moments to gather myself and catch my breath. It was closed, but I knew that I could have gone in there and Mr. Bennett would have helped me like he had helped Hannah. I cried, regretting that I had left home without a plan. I wanted to step over the invisible line that separated me from where I was and where I needed to go.

I slumped against the building to try to warm up. If I didn't find shelter, I was going to freeze. A burst of energy hit me when I remembered how Mama used to warn us, "The only people who are out after dark are looking for alcohol, drugs, or sex."

"Annabelle, now you know that's not true." Daddy used to say, "Your mother is exaggerating. You can be out after dark, just be aware of your surroundings. If you're in the center of town, don't cross Second Street after dark."

No one was outside that night, but me. I wondered, "Where do people go when it's cold outside," I thought.

I walked, seeing my city for the first time through the eyes of my faith and freedom. "This city is beautiful," I thought, gazing into the holiday decorations. I could feel the air changing from cool to cold. The cold air on my face felt good because my cheek was still burning. I hadn't grabbed a coat, the thin sweater, long skirt and apron weren't enough to protect me from the elements. "Lord, I don't know what to do now," I questioned. "This bag is heavy and I made a hasty decision to leave home without a plan. "Why did I put these nursing books in here?"

I answered myself aloud, "Joyce, it's time to release the mental rocks of negativity." I switched the bag I was carrying from my left hand to my right hand, and kept walking, mindlessly. When I realized that I had walked to school and ended up at the library, I let my shoulders relax. "My feet led me here?" I had been walking blindly, along a two-lane highway along the grassy edge. Normally I don't even like the dark, but somehow, my intuition, which I guess was the Holy Spirit. led me to the safest and only place I felt like myself.

I was exhausted by the time I saw the clock tower that let me know it was 8:30 p.m. I was relieved to see my boss, Miss Sally, standing outside the library, locking up for the night. I slumped my shoulders and relaxed.

When Miss Sally saw me, she left her keys in the door and scurried over to me. "Joyce, are you okay?" She took the bag from me, "What are you doing out here at this time of night." She led me to a nearby bench. "You look upset. How long have you been walking around in this cold weather?"

"I don't know. I started running and then . . ." I stuttered, "and then I ended up here."

"What happened?"

"My mother…" I started to sob. "We had a bad argument that turned physical." Miss Sally gasped. "I chose to leave home." I sniffled, "She unleashed her fury and pent up anger towards any and everything that ever hurt her was dumped right onto me!"

"What made Annabelle so angry?"

"She got upset," I spoke through choppy breaths. "She wasn't happy with the alterations I made to my sister and her friends' dresses for the Sadie Hawkins dance."

"I know sometimes she can be a bit overzealous with her interpretation of Pastor Tide's sermons. I hope she didn't say or do anything too harsh."

"It was more than that, Miss Sally, when she came home she looked different."

"Oh Dear!" She clicked her tongue. "I think I know what set her off." Miss Sally took off her coat and wrapped it around me. She shivered and said, "You know the choir director, Helene?"

I nodded, "We sang together in the youth choir."

"Well, at choir rehearsal she was so excited to announce that she had gotten engaged to her long-time beau, Oscar, and that they were having a quick wedding and then moving to Colorado."

"Awww," I stretched out the word. "I'm so happy for her. But I'm confused, that set my mother off?"

"Your mother mumbled something under her breath about how she must be pregnant. "I didn't hear it, but Helene's mother did, and they started going back and forth exchanging strong words."

"Helene's mother didn't take the bait your mother was dangling. She led a powerful prayer for her daughter and future son in law. Rehearsal then turned into a prayer meeting that led into a discussion of love and matrimony. She didn't have time to rehearse her solo."

"Let's get you out of this cold." Miss Sally stood, "Let me lock up. You're coming home with me tonight. My sister and I would love to have you."

When Miss Sally was ready, we walked to her house, not too far from the school. I'd only been to Miss Sally's house, to drop off some alterations for her. I knew she lived in a quaint little home with her sister. I was nervous and excited. "Thank you, God, for hearing my request," I prayed as we walked.

We entered the house, Miss Sally called for her sister, "Cecilia, I'm home! We have a guest."

"Oh! I love guests. Are they staying for dinner?"

"Yes." She said, taking off her coat.

"Good. I made a tuna casserole, you know I cook enough for an Army." Miss Cecilia chuckled. "I'll join you in the kitchen in a minute, finishing up rolling my hair."

"I'm putting on a pot of tea for us."

"Perfect. "

"Bring your prayer jar when you come. I have a feeling we're going to need it." She smiled at me. I lowered my eyes and took a deep breath.

She pulled out a chair and motioned for me to sit. "Have a seat honey," she said to me. "Take off your shoes and make yourself at home." I followed Miss Sally's instructions. She floated into the sitting room and returned with a quilt and a blue and white patterned tea set. "Would you like a cup of hot chocolate or a cup of tea?" She said, handing me the quilt.

"I'll have a cup of tea, please. Mother usually only keeps coffee in the house." I wrapped myself in the quilt and crossed my arms. "I love how the temperature of hot tea forces you to slow down. If you drink too fast, you can burn yourself. If you sip slowly, you can savor the flavor."

"Good insight," she smiled. "A nice cup of tea and

that quilt will warm you right up."

I looked around the house, "Everything in here is so dainty," I thought. "I love it here."

A few minutes later, Miss Cecilia came into the kitchen. She smiled when she saw that the guest was me. "Joyce, it's so nice to see you." She bent to hug my shoulders. "I haven't seen you in so long. You're looking more and more like your mother as you age." She clapped, "You are just so beautiful."

The last person I wanted to be compared to was Mother. I wrinkled my lips and said, "Thank you Miss Cecelia. It's nice to see you too."

"I haven't seen you at church in a while."

"Work a lot on Sundays, now." I didn't have the heart to tell her that I didn't want to be under the extreme teachings that guided my mother's conscience. As long as I was serving her needs by cooking and cleaning, she didn't bother me. Plus, she held a family meeting every Sunday, recapping the sermon.

Mother found a way to be in the Lord's house more than at home. Part of me wonders if she was at church so much because she wanted to be in other people's business to ignore own issues. She'd always be writing something in her "prayer journal," but was it her who was keeping the rumor mill of the town spinning?

I could hear Mother on the phone, "Pray for sister so-and-so," she'd whisper, "You know she's going through a storm." I always wondered what kind of prayer warrior tells everybody's business?

When Mother wasn't home her absence made the house peaceful and gave me freedom to exist without her breathing down my neck all the time. I needed space and to be something outside of being her lackey, "Do this Joyce," she'd grunt at me. Or "You didn't do this right, Joyce." Even my siblings knew that she was riding me too hard. Sometimes they would do my chores so I could focus on my homework, or alter clothes for extra money.

Eyeing my bag under the table Ms. Ceceilia asked, "Are you traveling, Joyce?"

Miss Sally answered for me. "She and Annabelle need some space from each other."

"Oh. Okay."

Miss Sally joined us at the table with a tray of hot water, tea and sweeteners. She poured hot water into three mugs. I watched the steam rise from my mug as she dropped in a tea bag. "You want sugar?"

"No thank you." Miss Sally dropped two cubes of sugar into her cup, and Miss Cecelia added a few drops of honey. We all sipped our tea quietly.

"Sal," Miss Cecelia said, "get some plates, we need some casserole with this tea." She stood and grabbed the dish. "I know you must be hungry Joyce."

Little did she know how hungry I was. For food, love, and God. "Yes, Ma'am, I could eat."

The sisters worked together to serve the food. It smelled so good, and I enjoyed being on the other side of the serving spoon for once.

"Tonight, I stood up to Mother. She reared her hand to hell and slapped me with the force of every demon she could summon." I rubbed my cheek in a circular motion, remembering the pain and the headache for the first time since leaving home. "I was planning to leave town after my graduation, but I don't think I can stay here that long."

Miss Sally looked into my eyes and spoke with empathy. "I won't have you missing graduation, that is not an option." I could see a reflection of myself in her glasses. "You can stay until you graduate." Ms. Cecilia rubbed my shoulder.

I felt overwhelmed with emotion. "Thank you both." I spoke broken words through my tears. "Is it okay if I call my Aunt Portia? I want to let her know that I'm safe so she can tell LJ and Enid."

Miss Sally stood up to clear the plates, "Of course."

"I feel so lost right now." I sipped my tea, holding back tears. "I had to get out of the house before something bad happened. I never want to disrespect my mother."

"Why do you think you would?" Miss Cecelia looked at me with sympathy.

"I don't know, Miss Cecilia. She told me, 'I have to love you but I don't have to like you.' When Daddy left she grew distant. When he died, she grew cold."

Miss Sally shook her head, "I can't believe it's been four years since he passed."

"I remember you speaking at his funeral," Miss Cecelia recalled. "You were so poised. It's remarkable how Eldridge Sr. kept you all together." She sipped her tea, "Your father was a good man."

"Yes," I nodded. "I think Mother blames me for his infidelity, his untimely death, and the fact that he had my sister. I understand why he did what he did, but it doesn't mean that I wasn't hurt when he left."

"You all are wonderful children," Miss Sally affirmed to me.

"Tonight I realized that I helped everyone else find their footing, but I don't know who I am."

"You're only 21, Joyce," Miss Sally said. "Getting to know yourself is a lifelong journey. One thing you should know about yourself," she beamed, "is that you have far more strength to endure trials and tribulations than you give yourself credit for."

I sat silently, soaking it all in.

"We've known you all of your life," she said. "You come from a long line of strong people. You may not understand it now, but this season of your life is preparing you for something. You are gathering the tools of fortitude, faith and fastidiousness. When the time comes, you'll remember your strength."

"It's getting late, girls. We can solve the world's problems in the morning, but for now, let's get some rest." Miss Sally stood, grabbed my hand and led me into the sitting room. "We have plenty of blankets and quilts for you to make yourself at home." They waved and left me alone.

Chapter 12

Scraps of me.

Aunt Portia, my father's older sister, by four years, walked with me through life in a way that Mother didn't have the capacity to. Mother fortified my hard shell, while Aunt Portia opened up her life to me, flaws and all. Mother kept her heart guarded at all costs, while Aunt Portia was tender and sensitive. Calling her, I knew she'd not only let my siblings know I was okay, but she'd be able to mediate a conversation with Mother if I needed her to.

I don't know whom I would have become had it not been for Aunt Portia. She taught me how to sew, how to cook, and how to expect the good in life, even though I couldn't always see it. Aunt Portia was a safety net, but she never overstepped Mother's boundaries. "I'm your Aunt," she would say. "Always remember that your mother has the final say."

I always understood her role as my aunt, yet it didn't stop me from leaning on her for support. Mother kept her distance from sensitive topics, but Aunt Portia didn't hesitate to explain things we didn't understand.

When Daddy was our Pastor, Aunt Portia was active in church, singing in the choir, serving as a missionary, being on the kitchen committee, and working in a nursing home. Her purpose was to serve others, and Aunt Portia took care of herself, too. Her life was balanced with obedience to God, serving others, and allowing herself to be served.

I watched how Aunt Portia cared for Poppa and Daddy when they were ill. I don't remember Grandma Lotus, but I can imagine that Aunt Portia's kind heart was passed down from her mother.

At church, Aunt Portia kept a low profile. She sat with her friends in the choir stand. In contrast, Mother sat in the front row and would rise from her front row seat so everybody could see her.

When I experienced the change in my body at 12, Mother called it "Lady Time." She gave no explanation for the pain I was experiencing in my stomach, or the cloudy feeling I had in my head. "Some things you have to learn on your own," she'd said when I asked. "This is one of those things."

Daddy took me to Aunt Portia who she gave me the talk about womanhood. She was soft, yet edifying. "This is how your body prepares for a baby. It's nothing to be afraid of, all girls go through it."

Mother had shared no remedies with me. However, Aunt Portia made sure to teach me and my sisters what to do, which added to what Mother had shared. Aunt Portia took me to the store and bought all of the tools I needed: a heating pad, Epsom salts, and pads. She showed me what to do and told me, "Your body has to rest when your cycle comes. You can't do a lot of heavy lifting."

"If Mother will allow me," I sighed.

"She knows what a period feels like." She rubbed my head. "Have you ever seen her massage her forehead?"

I put my hand on my head, fingers on my brow imitating Mother. "She often does this." I closed my eyes and massaged my head.

"When she does that, she has a headache."

"Ohh," I said, with the revelation falling on me. "My head doesn't hurt that way. Sometimes I feel like I'm in a cloud. I can't hear, I can't think. I can't see." Aunt Portia gave me everything I needed to survive, literally.

Those moments with Aunt Portia fortified me. I shook my head to free the headache. As I dialed her number, I imagined that she was in her sitting room sewing, or in the kitchen nibbling.

"Mmm hello," Aunt Portia coughed when she answered the phone.

"Hey Auntie, it's me, Joyce."

"Hi Joyce. How are you, baby?" I heard her fork scraping across a plate.

"What are you eating, Auntie?"

"I'm enjoying a piece of sweet potato pie."

"That sounds so good." I took a deep breath and said, "I left Mother's house, Aunt Portia."

"What happened, Baby? Where are you? Do I need to come get you?"

"No. No. I'm with Miss Sally."

"Sally and Cecelia?" I could hear the relief in her voice. "Can I talk to Sally?"

"They went to bed, but I'll tell Miss Sally to call you tomorrow, Aunt Portia."

She exhaled. "Tell me what happened?"

"She said I brought the devil into her house." I shook my head, trying to move the cloud. "She said I made Enid's dress too short, then she slapped me."

"How short was the dress?"

I straightened my spine and said, "A smidgen above her ankle bone."

"What!?" Aunt Portia guffawed. "Her ankle bone? What in the world!"

I couldn't help but laugh, too. It was a silly argument. "She was so angry."

"When you were born, she couldn't stop doting over you." Aunt Portia got silent for a few seconds. "I've known Annabelle for a long time. She's always been reserved and guarded, I always compared her to a porcupine."

"A porcupine?"

Aunt Portia chuckled. "They can be gentle when they are not threatened. Your mother shoots her quills only when she feels threatened. Being an only child makes a person strong in ways we don't understand because we have siblings."

"What do you mean, Auntie?"

"As the oldest child we are given responsibilities to care for our siblings, often sacrificing our own needs in the process. For example, I have held your daddy's burdens and confidential matters in a vault since we were children. I protected, supported, and prayed for him."

"Like I do for my siblings."

"Yes, like that, Joyce." Aunt Portia spoke softly. "I have seen my brother in every season. When he was happy, heartbroken, sick, thriving, I knew. Being his vault, especially keeping Hannah from your mother overwhelmed me. Your Poppa and I begged him to tell Annabelle about her."

That surprised me. "You did?"

"Yeah, Hannah went through hell with her mother. We thought Annabelle would embrace her. Poppa and I had a fantasy, but your daddy knew Annabelle better."

"She didn't take it well when Hannah came to the house, Aunt Portia."

"I wanted to tell your mother so many times. I'd bring Hannah to church, but she stayed in the back. It hurt me that she couldn't be recognized as our family."

"Me too, but she's good now, Aunt Portia. Cincinnati has been good for her and Elijah."

Aunt Portia let out a hard breath. "Joyce, in this life, we only get one mother. Annabelle isn't perfect, but God picked her for you. When she's gone, you're going to miss her. You have to understand her story and her history in order to understand your own."

"Why doesn't she love me?"

"Don't say that. She loves you, Joyce, even though she doesn't acknowledge it publicly."

"I don't know if it is possible for me to let myself trust her, Auntie."

"Baby, the journey we walk in this life is a result of our choices. I miss my mother deeply. I give to you and your siblings what she gave me and your daddy—unconditional love. I think Annabelle became consumed with protecting you when there was no threat."

I could almost feel her caressing my shoulder through the phone. "Let your face relax, Joyce. I know you're frowning." I relaxed. "Now," she continued. "I can't tell you how to feel about your mother, that's something you're gonna have to figure out on your own."

"How do I do that?"

"It will take time, but you'll need to think through your emotions and try to speak them from a healed place."

"Why is it my responsibility to reconcile with her?"

Aunt Portia spoke softly, "That's not what I said, baby." I could hear her tapping her fork against the plate. "You have to figure out your feelings about your mother. Over the years I've watched her, and I can't figure out why she's indifferent toward you. She does love you, I believe that."

"Why is everything so complicated?"

"Life isn't a straight path, baby. Sometimes you have to run between the dandelions."

I crossed my leg and kicked it. "I don't know what that means, Auntie."

"It means that for every step you take towards something that you want for yourself, you will most likely run into an obstacle. Don't let those obstacles stop you from running, but if you do stop, look for God all around you. Dandelions lean, but they are hard to break. Sometimes something as simple as the yellow color of a dandelion can give you strength."

"I love you Aunt Portia." Aunt Portia, with her calm, neutral, introspective, demeanor always helped me see situations from a bird's eye view.

"I love you, more." She yawned and moaned, "I'll get you Saturday."

"Save me a piece of pie, Auntie." I felt a weight lifted off of my shoulders, after that phone call.

Even though I didn't receive the love I expected, or even hoped for from my mother, Aunt Portia affirmed that I am valuable and worthy of love. Until her death when she was in her late 90's, Aunt Portia kept her word to us and our dad. She never missed an important event. She encouraged us, and protected us from Mother's fury, whenever she could.

I opened my bag to change my clothes and found the crumpled ball of money that either LJ or Enid had slipped in there. "Thank you, God, for keeping me covered," I prayed. "Restore to them what they sacrificed for me."

I laid down on the pallet, took my coin purse out of my bag, and looked at my favorite picture of Daddy in his Army uniform. "You always told me that my steps are ordered, Daddy. I understand what that means now." I pulled out his obituary, unfolded it and began to read. "My hot feet led me here, Daddy."

I pulled out a piece of my favorite dress, one made from scraps of Daddy's old shirts. "I'm going to make you proud, Daddy." I blew out the candle and fell asleep with a smile on my face for the first time in years.

Chapter 13

Prayer answering God.

I woke up the next morning to the sisters laughing in the kitchen and the smell of eggs, turkey and biscuits. I folded up my pallet and joined them in the kitchen. Miss Cecelia was dancing at the stove while Miss Sally ironed her skirt. "Good morning, Sunshine!" She smiled. "Ready for some breakfast?"

I took my seat at the table, and Miss Cecelia put a plate in front of me. I could see the pepper in the eggs and smell the butter on the biscuits. "This looks so good, thank you again."

"No need to keep thanking us," she wiped her hands on her apron. "You're welcome here."

Did you sleep okay, Joyce?" Miss Sally said, pressing down the iron. "Mama's packed her quilts with a lot of love and extra batting." She and Miss Cecilia cracked up.

"Yes Ma'am." I left Mother's house with no plan, believing I was on my own, but I was surrounded by a love I didn't expect.

"We spend most of our time in the kitchen so the sitting room is really just the place where we pace and pray." She held up the iron and the whoosh of the steam covered her face. "If you want, I can bring the foldaway bed down from the attic, but I'd have to wipe it down for you to get the gook off. We haven't used it in so long, we haven't had a lot of overnight guests. There may be cobwebs on it, and if you're anything like me, you don't want to be anywhere near a spider."

"Oh, no," I said, putting my hand up. "Don't bother with that trouble. I slept peacefully. I know I felt grounded, it was peaceful and I needed that."

"Good," Miss Sally said, breaking a piece of biscuit and dipping it in a dollop of strawberry preserves. "I don't want you to feel uncomfortable."

"I'm still wondering if I should stay here until my graduation, or not. I don't want to be any trouble for you and Miss Cecelia."

"You've only been here for one night, and you're ready to leave us? What kind of hosts are we, sister?" Miss Cecelia joked looking at Miss Sally. "Maybe if we let her sleep on the cobwebby foldaway bed, she'll want to stay."

I appreciated Miss Cecelia for trying to keep the atmosphere light. I finished my breakfast. "I'm fine on the pallet, I promise." I patted the table, "I guess I better get ready for work. I don't want to be late today."

Miss Sally chuckled, "I left a towel and wash rag for you in the bathroom."

I stood up from the table and said with tears in my eyes, "Thank you. You are an answered prayer."

***

I didn't have to worry about seeing Mother around town. She only went four places: the grocery store, work, the thrift store and church. Being with Miss Sally and Miss Cecelia, I was close enough to my siblings that I could see them whenever I wanted to, and I could keep my promise to myself to graduate.

Enid and LJ would often come to my job, bringing me items that I needed, slipping them past Mother's watchful eye. They would fill me in on what was happening at home and with Hannah. I wrote letters and when Aunt Portia came to get me, I was glad I could talk to her.

I not enjoyed only the tranquility of being with the Dowd sisters, additionally I got to sit at their feet and soak up as much knowledge as I could about life. I imagined what I was gleaning from them is what Ruth in the Bible was able to glean from Naomi.

I spent the next seven weeks getting to know myself, while at Miss Sally and Ms. Cecilia's house. It was peaceful for me there, but I was always conscious of what I was doing. I didn't want to overstay my welcome. I did everything I could to show them I appreciated their hospitality. I offered to fix articles of clothing, tended to the plants, and I thanked them as often as I could.

I counted down the days, 58, even though I didn't have to. They didn't pressure me to leave or stay. I wanted to see Hannah and my nephew, so I often thought about when I'd mount the bus and go on another adventure.

When the sisters went to work, Miss Sallie at the library and Miss Cecelia at the elementary school, I left the house, too, even if I didn't have any place to be. If I was ever at the house when they weren't home, I would cook. They loved when I made pineapple upside down cake, pot roast, and mashed potatoes with garlic.

To make sure I protected the peace they provided for me, I cleaned for them. I always chopped up lemons and put them in my cleaning water. The lemon smell reminded me of Daddy and lifted my spirits when I felt sad. Miss Cecilia used to come in the house and gush with glee, "It smells so good in here!"

On Thursday nights we had a standing appointment at Roller World skating rink. Miss Sally and Miss Cecelia loved to skate, dance, and sing, which surprised me, since they were both so introverted. They came alive on their skates. I was intrigued by their ability to balance fun with holiness.

Living with Miss Sally and Miss Cecelia exposed me to things Mother never would've allowed me to participate in. Much of the wisdom they passed down to me came in the form of those activities.

The first time they took me roller skating, I tried to make excuses about why I couldn't go. The truth is, I was scared of falling and hurting myself. "I need to study for my nursing exam," I said. "I can't go skating tonight."

"Oh, girl, stop it!" Miss Cecelia said, waving me to the door. "We're taking you skating tonight, and you're going to love it!" She put on her coat. "You need to have a little fun in your life."

"Yes you do!" Miss Cecilia grinned, "Roller World on Thursdays is the place to be. We go there on a group date every week."

"I don't want to intrude." I stared at them in their two piece sweat suits looking like college students half their age. "I don't know how to skate."

"Oh honey," Miss Sally laughed. "We've been skating since we were kids. We can teach you."

"What kind of music do they play?" I asked, thinking about what Mother would think of me skating.

Miss Cecilia doubled over in laughter. "You are so funny, Joyce." She locked eyes with Miss Cecelia and said, "Jesus came to give us life and life more abundantly."

Miss Cecelia gave her a high five and said, "Life more abundantly, indeed." They both held their stomachs in amusement.

"I . . . I mean . . .," I stuttered. "You go to the same church as my mother, and I know she doesn't enjoy anything . . . fun."

"There is a lot about your mother that you don't understand right now." Miss Cecelia said, "At your age of being a daughter, you haven't gotten the chance to meet your mother as a woman yet." Miss Cecelia looked at me with sympathy. "When you have your children, a lot more things will make sense to you."

"I doubt that" I said, flipping a page in my book pretending to read.

"We know more about the Annabelle who used to be than you know about the Annabelle who is now." Miss Sally added, "I want to encourage you to extend grace to your mother. Didn't you learn in school that a woman carries the eggs of her grandchildren? So when you were in your mother's womb," she pointed at my stomach. "The eggs that will eventually become your children were forming in your womb."

"I've heard that before, but I never thought about it like that."

Miss Cecelia smiled, "To give your mother grace means that you honor the invisible thread that ties you to her, and the thread that ties her to your children. If there are knots in that thread, and you do everything in your power to untangle them, you can rest assured that God sees your effort."

"You know what, Joyce," Miss Sally added, "Once upon a time Annabelle was full of joy, optimism, and compassion. Would you believe that she even used to go skating with us?"

"Whaat!?" I slammed the book. "No she didn't."

"Your mother did have life before you," Miss Sally replied. "The problem is that she made an idol out of your father. I don't think she realized it until he was gone."

I wrinkled my forehead, "What does that mean?"

"It means," Miss Sally said, "Your mother didn't realize she had the chance to choose between love and forgiveness. She chose unforgiveness and her choice made her bitter."

I moaned silently. "Why was her rage directed at me all the time?" I felt tears welling in my eyes.

"Dear heart," Miss Cecelia answered, "You are everything that your mother yearned to be. When she sees you, she sees herself once upon a time. You look just like her and seeing you must be a hard reality to accept on a daily basis."

"The truth is," Miss Sally handed me my coat. "The woman your mother was supposed to be hasn't forgiven herself, and that's not your fault. What matters is how you respond to her moving forward. When you stand before God and give an account of your life, you answer for your actions, not hers."

Miss Ceceilia added, "Life is like skating. You have to use your core to balance yourself. Just put one foot in front of the other and roll with the rhythm of the music. Come on, let's go." For the first time in my life, I was the younger sister. It felt wonderful, I didn't have to worry that I was going to be punished for something that someone else did. And I didn't have to stay up for hours cleaning and recleaning to meet unrealistic expectations.

I had never been to a party before, so I changed into a modest brown swing dress with long sleeves. For good luck, I put on my purple silk scarf. Even though I was away from Mother, I had morals and values to uphold. I was finding myself, but I had limits, too.

I stood on the wall for a long while. I watched people whiz by me on their skates. Some fell on their butts and others held hands as they floated past. It was a wonderland until a hit song came on, and Miss Sally and Miss Cecilia came over to me.

"Give me that cup," Miss Sally said taking my lemonade and setting it on a table.

They both grabbed one of my hands, and led me to the center of the floor. "This is the place newbies learn how to find their footing," Miss Sally had spun around. "After tonight, you will be a true skater."

I was so moved by the music that I didn't care who was watching me fall down, stand up, or miss a beat! The music gave me power, and I began to skate without their assistance. The music moved me, I didn't feel like I was looking foolish in a room full of strangers. Nobody cared about who I was or who my mother was. Skating gave me my power back. On my wheels I felt like I was flying!

I was treated like a young adult by Miss Sally and Miss Ceceilia. We sipped hot tea from antique China and shared meals family style. We had Bible studies that helped me to understand God and what I truly believed about Him. We shared testimonies, and I was able to express my curiosity. We delved into conversations about gratitude, and I especially loved sitting with them at the kitchen table.

We had many heart-to-heart conversations and girl talks around the dinner table about love, womanhood, God, and even sex. I took copious notes in my journal so that I could share what I was learning with my sisters and my brother. One thing Daddy always told us was to take our thoughts and put them on paper. These unacceptable topics that we were discussing were valuable gems, and I didn't want to lose them.

There were so many life skills that had not been passed down to me by my mother. I felt layers of heaviness being peeled off of me, like the skin of an onion. I knew that once I left their house, I was going to be prepared for whatever God had in store for me.

After many of our conversations that transversed from late night into early morning, I thought about how they knew a side of my mother I never met. I made sure to ask Aunt Portia as many questions as I could about my parents. I wanted to tuck as much information into my heart as I could for days when I needed to remember their love.

A few days before I was to cross the stage, shake the president's hand, and get my college degree, I caught a glimpse of Mother coming out of the thrift store from a distance. I wasn't close enough to speak to her, nor did she see me, but my heart started to race. Then I lost my footing, stumbling.

I stopped in my tracks, unsure of my next move. I wanted to run down the street and cower in an alley around the corner. I wanted to hide behind a tree. Surprisingly, I also wanted to run after her screaming, "Mommy! Mommy!"

Instead, I leaned against the deli and caught my breath. I watched my mother as she cradled her thrift store treasures and climbed into her car. She lifted her right leg in first, and turned slightly to lift her left leg. Then, she straightened her skirt and closed the door behind her, as she sat parallel to the steering wheel.

I recalled her teaching me how to get in the car that same way. She had demonstrated what to do and said, "This is how a lady gets into a vehicle."

I watched Mother pull off, slowly, hands on ten and two. She liked to ride that way so people could see her. "Why didn't you say something?" I grilled myself. "That was your chance to make things right with her." Honestly, I couldn't find a good reason. I pivoted on my heels and started running back to Miss Sally's house.

I burst through the door, huffing and puffing, tears streaming down my face. I expected to unfold my pallet and rest to keep the clouds from forming around my head and keep the headache at bay, Instead, I saw Miss Cecelia sitting on the floor, reading her Bible.

"Oh Joyce," she looked up when the door banged open. "What happened?" I hesitated, and she stood up to lead me in the door. "Is everything okay?"

I shook my head, and she turned me into a tight embrace. Through the clouds, I could hear the sound of her praying for me. I couldn't make out her words through the sound of my own blubbering tears. I cried until my emotions knocked me down, I fell to my knees.

"Father," I heard Miss Cecelia praying, "Give her peace through this storm. She feels overwhelmed. Adonai, we know You are in control. Jehovah Jireh, provide peace. Jehovah Rapha, be her healer. El Roi, we know You see Joyce."

I don't know how long I was on the floor, but when I came back to myself, Miss Cecelia was sitting cross legged across from me, holding tissue, and nursing a cup of tea. "I made you some." She pointed to the tea set on the end table. I picked up some new hibiscus tea from the farmer's market, and it tastes delightful."

I sat up and crossed my legs, putting my hands under my thighs. I had a queasy feeling in my stomach and a cloud floating over my head. Seeing my anxiety, Miss Cecelia slid over to me and placed her arm around my shoulders.

"Now," she said, squeezing me, "Do you want to tell me what's got you all upset?" She handed me the tea and said, "Sip your tea."

I cradled the hot tea cup in my hands then put it to my lips. I savored the hibiscus flavor on my tongue and let the liquid swirl around my mouth. I closed my eyes and breathed in the scent of Miss Cecelia's perfume.

Through closed eyes I murmured. "I saw Mother."

Miss Sally dropped her arm and scooted in front of me. "What happened? Did she strike you again?"

"Oh no, it was nothing like that. She didn't see me, I just . . . I couldn't face her today. She was so close to me, yet so far away." I relaxed and let out a breath. "I wish Mother could see my accomplishments. I wish she would celebrate with me and be proud of me."

"She is proud of you, honey." Miss Cecelia sipped her tea. I noticed how she cradled the saucer and slipped her fingers through the ring. She was so feminine, holding her pinky finger straight up. I never could do that.

"How do you know she's proud of me?"

Miss Cecelia straightened her spine and said, "She talks about you every Sunday."

"She does?"

Miss Cecelia let out a hearty laugh, "Your parents and I were high school classmates. She's guarded, because she's a good person who has been hurt."

I felt myself getting defensive. "Miss Cecelia do you tell her anything about me?"

"Don't worry," she patted my knee. "I have never betrayed your confidence. Your story is your story. Your mother's story is hers to tell you. One day you'll be able to remember your strength since you've written it down. When the time is right, you'll share it with the right people." She patted my leg and said, "Unforgiveness is a burden you carry, let it go."

Ms. Cecelia took a deep breath and said, "I have seen Annabelle changing. She's kept her guard up for so long." She sucked her teeth. "Your mother is strong, but she feels weak. She's struggled with self-confidence for a long time."

"I never knew that." When she sang hymns, mother's rich alto voice would outshine everyone in the room and they would be still, almost frozen in time. Mother's voice was so beautiful, it arrested everyone's attention. I couldn't fathom that she lacked confidence. "Maybe that's why she sang with her eyes closed," I said aloud.

Ms. Cecelia countered me, "Maybe, she sang with her eyes closed to ground herself and find her power."

I thought about how LJ, Enid, and I always sat behind her at church. We'd pass notes and try not to snicker too loud at something funny. If we accidently let out a sound, Mother would swing her arm behind the pew and discipline us with a hard pop on the leg. That made us stifle our laughter more!

Enid and LJ would blend with her in a harmony that transported me to peace. Mother sang everything as a soulful plea, making every song a demand for worship. I felt myself laying down at the feet of God, and all of my worries melting away. In those moments, I loved being at church when Daddy was our pastor. Mama set the atmosphere, and Daddy made learning the Bible fun.

My community was built in church. My friends were in church. My skill development and confidence was built in church. As I got older, though, the judgmental eyes of some of the church mothers bore holes in my soul. I could feel their laser eyes scrolling up and down my body when I walked passed. They looked at everything from the part in my hair, to the fit of my clothes and the color of my stockings. I could hear their whispers.

If I didn't speak to certain women, I got a tongue lashing. One woman said, "I have known your family before you were born, you need to speak to me." It was their sense of entitlement that made me feel like an outcast. I felt like I could never escape the scrutiny of people who despised me because they despised Mother.

Being a pastor's kid wasn't easy, but I understood the assignment. My siblings and I were living under a calling from God to be an example of His love for our generation. My siblings and I were proud of our parents and how they served God, but at times, we wanted to live like normal kids.

When our friends were at football and basketball games, we were at church. At church picnics LJ would play pick up football, but Mother didn't let me or Enid anywhere near athletic activities. And, of course, we couldn't go to any dances. Enid is the only one of us that she relaxed the rules on. The cause of this whole breakdown between me and Mother was because of Enid's Sadie Hawkins' dance.

Mother was my first introduction to fashion. Every Sunday she'd meticulously lay out her outfit, accessories and hat. Clothes, suit skirt, suit jacket, blouse, went on the bed. Stockings and shoes on the floor. All of her accessories matched. She'd dress her side of the bed up first, then coordinate Daddy's outfit with hers on his side of the bed. She'd hum and pray while taking her shower, and I'd be in my room, mesmerized by her worship.

At the last possible minute Mother would call out to Daddy, "Eldridge Sr, come on and get dressed. We're going to be late."

"I'm talking to the Lord," he'd respond.

Because it was my responsibility to get everyone else ready for church, I got up early. I hung my Sunday best on the bedpost, and my accessory was usually a piece of silk either tied around my neck or in my hair. In my room, I would sashay around, twisting my hips and pivoting on my heels like Aunt Portia had showed me from her modeling days. I always imagined myself modeling like the women I saw in the magazines.

Sometimes I'd sit on my bed listening to Mother sing. Her soulful voice would lure me into her bedroom. When she'd open the bathroom door wrapped in her towel,. I'd be sitting at the foot of her bed with my eyes closed. Mother was much happier then.

She'd sweep me out playfully, "Get out of here, girl and go get ready for church!" I'd take a whiff of her baby powder fragrance in the air and say, "Mother you smell good," before I scampered out to check on my siblings. Closing her door, I often wondered, "If Mother would let me, I'd love to give her clothes a little bit of pizzazz. She'd be the most beautiful woman in the room. Those dull brown lips and pink rouge against her chocolate brown skin don't compliment her."

I wanted to help Mother be classier and more poised, like the models in magazines. She slouched her shoulders and walked with her head slightly bowed with an air of confidence, but a touch of trepidation, just enough to look humble.

Mother's hair was so long back then, she could have sat on it. I wanted to stand behind Mother as she sat in her vanity chair. I imagined what it would've been like to smile over her shoulder as she took her time in the mirror to paint on her foundation and blend it all over her face. Also, what it would have been like to grease her scalp and braid her hair.

I wanted to see the woman, Annabelle, outside of a tight bun that she never let down in front of us. She was always put together as if being dressed to the nines would prevent people from really seeing her. I always wondered if God allowed women to spread their wings and explore life without limitations. I didn't want to run into the darkness anymore.

Mother didn't teach me that.

Chapter 14

Daddy's fall from grace.

I knew that Daddy had been framed by one of the Deacons in the church who wanted his brother to be the pastor. It might sound far-fetched, but Deacon Hent spiked Daddy's tea with some kind of drug. He left him alone in his office and invited Hannah's mother, an escort, to take advantage of him. When she got pregnant, she decided to make my Daddy her ticket out of that lifestyle by using blackmail. Daddy stepped down to keep things quiet.

Ironically, when the search for a new pastor was initiated, Deacon Hent's brother didn't even apply for the job!

I saw how people treated Daddy in church. I heard how they talked to him at church meetings, but he never retaliated or defended himself. That made me so angry! I wanted him to yell at the top of his lungs, "Sister So-and-So, you are being dumb," but that wasn't in his nature.

Some people had the nerve to confront me and my siblings when Mother wasn't around. (They didn't like her, either). They would try to correct us or rebuke us about any little thing we did. I never told Mother what they did, but I wish I had. I needed to feel protected and I wanted her to scratch them with her bear claws on my behalf. Maybe we'd be in a different place with our relationship if I had been honest with her. I needed her to mother me.

As a teenager, I wasn't rebellious like other preacher's kids. They called us, "PKs," and I hated that term. Daddy's allegiance to God, and the way he served Him is not how I was called. I hated that church people put pressure on us to be a certain way without letting us enjoy our childhood.

"Pull your dress down, girl," someone would rebuke me. "Straighten your tie, young man," another would scold LJ. "That is not the way we dance in this church," someone would grab Enid during service. It was a constant merry go round of negativity, from every corner. I was so tired of it, I got a job and started working on Sundays to get out of going to church. That caused another rift between me and Mother.

Daddy died of cancer in 1968, the year I graduated from high school. It took several years for the church to get a new leader. Pastor Jones was selected, and he moved to Xenia from Springfield, Illinois. I don't know why he brought his family to our small town, but I'm glad he did.

Although we only got to be friends for a few months before she graduated and went away for college, hanging out with Olita made me hopeful. She was older than me by two years, and I imitated her confidence. She imitated my style. Mama made me go to service when they came, "You need to find your way to service two Sundays a month," she had said.

Olita and I instantly clicked. When we were introduced, I met someone who got me, and I got her. On Sundays and at special services, my siblings and I sat with Olita. She made me laugh, and she always told me, "Don't let this church stuff get under your skin. Do everything you do for God, don't worry about the people."

When I was trying to make the adjustment of being without my father and getting to know her father as my Pastor, Olita would drop little nuggets into my ear. "I'm so sorry your Daddy died," she said one Sunday, leaning over so much that her head was practically in my lap. I heard my Daddy say that he was a good man."

That made me feel good. "My Dad, on the other hand," she said, sitting back up, "needs Jesus." I looked at her sideways. "He enjoys a little honey dip on the side."

"Whaat?" I whispered in disbelief.

"If you ever see him with a blue cup," she looked over her glasses, "It ain't coffee."

"I love my Daddy," she said watching him in the pulpit, "But he doesn't live what he preaches. Why do you think we left Springfield? And" she whispered in my ear, "Daddy gets a little too close to women in the congregation." She winked. "If you know what I mean."

"I don't know what you mean."

"Girl," she threw up her arms and fell across the pew snickering. She chortled so loud that Mama popped us on the leg. "Shhhh!" She said over her shoulder.

"You are so naïve." She whispered, "Your Mama keeps you so secluded that you don't know nothing about nothing. You hurried up to finish high school, but she won't let you go anywhere. You're book smart but you don't have common sense. I'm going to have to teach you everything I know before I leave in the fall."

I never got to learn those lessons. Mother didn't let me anywhere near Olita because she heard rumors that she was caught smoking marijuana in the park.

"You are forbidden to be around Olita," she said, pulling me away from her at church while we were talking with friends one day. "I heard that she has been smoking the devil's grass."

"But she's my best friend," I whimpered.

"Not anymore," Mother dug her fingernails into my wrist. "And another thing," she huffed, "That little girl got hussy tendencies. I heard she let that reprobate football player boyfriend of hers take her virginity." As Mother pulled me away, I looked back at my friend, feeling ashamed that Mother dishonored her publicly.

Miss Cecelia cleared her throat, capturing my attention. "What are you thinking about over there?"

I stretched my legs and said, "I was wondering how Olita is doing these days. She was my best friend until Mother made a scene at church."

Miss Cecelia beamed with pride. It took her only seven years to finish college, her master's, and her Doctorate in Psychology. She is Dr. Olita Dumont now." I sucked in air and smiled. "And you know what, we went to her wedding. She was still wearing the promise ring her mother gave her when she was 12." Miss Cecelia leaned back and finished her tea. "You know what that means?"

I did. She had saved herself for her husband. "Hmmph, she proved Mother wrong," I thought.

"I know what you're thinking," she said, refilling her teacup and adding a little honey to the water.

"You do?"

"Why haven't Sally or I gotten married, right?"

"I had wondered, but I didn't think it was appropriate to ask."

"Well," she cleared her throat. "Sally and I have had plenty of prospects throughout the years, but neither of us have ever felt butterflies in our stomachs about any of them."

"I've never had a boyfriend, Miss Cecelia."

"I know, honey. Your mother's watchful eye kept many of the fellas at bay, but I've seen sparkles in the eyes of a few young men when it comes to you."

I clutched my pearls. "Really?" I blushed.

"Especially Ernie, he was really sweet on you."

"Ernie? I asked incredulously. "I've never thought about him that way." Ernie, Deacon Joe's son, was a quiet, thoughtful young man. "What I always remember about him, his remarkable dimples and light brown eyes."

"Did you ever notice how he would be the only escort whenever you needed to get to your seat?"

I laughed. "I thought that was just because he was an usher."

"He wants to usher you, alright?" We cackled at her witticism. "He's courting a nice young lady out of Columbus, I think. She's a dancer and a college student."

I felt sad in that moment thinking about the missed opportunities in my life. "Good for him," I purred. "If only I could explain to Mother how much I long for a male companion." That made me cry.

"Neither I, nor my sister have ever been married. Although we both have always wanted to be wives."

She stretched her legs and leaned back. "I think our Father taught us that we didn't need to depend on anybody else, but God and ourselves." She stretched her back and leaned forward, staring at the floor, "I think we internalized that lesson and buried ourselves in our work. We didn't open our hearts to love, but we'd sometimes pretend we were getting married by walking down the middle aisle at church."

"Oh wow, Miss Cecelia. I didn't know."

"These are things we don't talk about in church enough. My sister and I are in our fifties, and we have never been touched by a man. I am willing to give up my career as an educator so that I can have a respectable relationship and support my husband."

"Miss Cecelia, have you ever felt sad about not being able to have children?"

"Oh, yes! But you know that Sarah was 90, I still have hope." We fell back laughing and slapped hands.

"I hope that I can have a conversation with my mother about how much I long to know what it really means to be a woman. I don't even have a real definition of what it means to be Annabelle Turner's daughter. What did sitting in that second row of church really do for me?"

Miss Cecelia shrugged. "Keep praying, God has a plan for you, Joyce. A plan that you can't even fathom right now. With your skills, talents, fashion sense, faith, and beauty . . ."

I swept my hair behind my ear. "What else, can you say?" I teased. "Keep the compliments coming."

"I have no doubts that some lucky guy will sweep you off of your feet. What you are looking for is looking for you, too. Love will always find a way. God will always find a way. You just have to trust the process."

"Thank you, Miss Cecelia." I know Miss Sally likes having her sister close. Do you think you'll live with her if she gets married first?"

"Oh, girl, no! Sally says that, but she is hoping to retire from the library soon. Deacon Leroy has been courting her, and she is smitten with him."

"Well, maybe Deacon Timothy will follow in his footsteps and ask for your hand in marriage, too."

She swooped her hair back, straightened her bosom and said, "I'm ready for my wedding night!" She patted her thigh to the rhythm of her laughter.

"To change the subject," a smile spread across her face as she said, "Joyce, you only have five days till graduation, are you excited?"

Chapter 15

Graduating to the next level.

On December 13, 1974, I crossed the stage and received my college diploma in front of most of my favorite people. My siblings were there, Aunt Portia, Miss Cecelia, Miss Sally, and both of their Deacon boyfriends. I was celebrated by everyone, but my mother, who stood on the other side of the fence, watching. When they called my name, I saw her as she walked back to the car.

Getting my college degree was one of my greatest accomplishments. At the end of the night, I disrobed and looked at myself with pride. My throat was clogged with tears of joy and grief, but I looked forward to getting up the next morning and getting on the bus with my sister and my nephew heading to Cincinnati.

Because I was diligent, I had saved enough for a bus ticket to spend a few days with Hannah and Elijah, another ticket to Toledo, and a few months of rent for a boarding house. I had graduated a semester early, and I was scared and excited to leave town. I bid a tearful farewell to my big sisters when they took us to the bus stop. Mother drove Enid and LJ to see me off, but she didn't get out of the car, or even look my way. She sent an apple pie instead.

The first thing I did before I got on the bus to Cincinnati was to stop at the drug store and buy myself a tube of bright red lipstick. Once the driver announced to the riders, "Next stop, Cincinnati," I pulled out my lipstick, applied it and kissed my compact mirror. "You've got this, Joyce."

Sitting in the window seat, I watched the only city I knew pass by me. I stayed awake for most of the ride, writing in my journal, praying, and watching my back. Hannah and Elijah, on my right, slept peacefully. I settled into my seat and allowed myself to embrace the unforeseen future.

When we arrived in Cincinnati, Ms. Nancy was waiting for us. "Come here, Graduate!" I breathed in the fresh air and hugged her back.

***

I loved everything about being in Cincinnati with my sister. Riding up the hills in a car and flying down the hills in a sled. We went skating, to the Zoo, and to see Christmas lights. Some of the houses we saw blew my mind. By the time I boarded the bus for Toledo, my confidence was strong, and my mind was wide open. I was 21 years old and green around the ears, but I was motivated to make myself and my loved ones proud.

I knew I had to set a standard for myself that exceeded the small thinking my mother placed on me. When I did call to reconcile with her, I needed to give her some good news, to show evidence of my success, so I could make her proud.

It was hard to leave everything behind, but I knew that I had to put that small town in my rearview mirror. Being under Annabelle Turner's thumb for the rest of my life was not my lifelong dream.

Hannah rode the city bus with me to the Greyhound station after I shared a tearful goodbye with my nephew. "Get a seat a few rows behind the driver," Hannah had instructed me. "If you can see him in his mirror, he can see you, and that's the safest place to be on the bus."

I was one of the first people to board. I chose a seat next to the window behind a beautiful, brown-skinned woman snoozing with a baby. There were several seats filled with people sleeping. The ticket in the young mother's lap let me know that she boarded in Louisville and was going to Cleveland. "That's a long ride," I thought putting my bag under my seat.

The mother looked to be a few years older than me, and the sight of her with her child warmed my heart, but made me sad at the same time. "I wish Mother could have come see me off to start my next chapter." Hannah stood in the terminal with her hands on her hips like a watchdog. I fought back tears thinking about everything we had been through as a family. I affirmed myself, "You're on your own now, Joyce."

Hannah communicated with hand gestures telling me to smile. I cackled loudly, startling the baby who started to whine softly. I tapped the mother and whispered, "I'm sorry."

She turned her body and leaned her head back, smashing her thick afro against the window. "It's okay," she said rubbing her baby's back. "She's slept through much worse." That's when I noticed the bruises under her eyes and the band-aid under her chin.

I watched the young woman nurture her child. I tried to think of a tender moment with my own mother, but I couldn't. The woman's baby nestled in the crook of her mother's neck, sucked her thumb, and rubbed her mom's ear until she fell back to sleep. "It's amazing how a mother can be a safe place for her baby to break even when she needs her own pillar to lean on."

An older white woman with silver gray hair pulled into a bun shuffled down the aisle holding several bags. I turned my attention to her and asked, "Do you need some help, Ma'am?"

She pointed to the seat next to me and said, "Good morning, Darling. Is this seat taken?"

"No ma'am," I said, "Sit here." I took two of her bags and held them while settled into the seat. I felt the warmth of her hips spilling under the arm rest.

She leaned in and whispered in my ear, "Riding on these buses is so scary for me." I wanted to lean my head on her shoulder and tell her I was nervous too. "I'm Lainey. What's your name?"

"I'm Joyce," I said, extending my hand to shake.

"Nice to meet you, Joyce. Are you a model?"

"No ma'am. I'm not a model." I blushed.

The driver made his safety and instructional announcements and I watched him readjust his hat and seat. I waved goodbye to my sister and we pulled away from the station. The bus was silent for about thirty minutes, then everyone seemed to come alive at the same time. It was so loud with chatter, even the baby in front of me started to babble.

The lady next to me opened one of her bags and said, "Would you like a piece of pound cake?" I could smell the sweetness, and before I could answer, she pushed the treats toward me. I removed a piece of cake from the bag and felt the warmth of the foil. She handed a piece of cake to the girl in front of me, put a piece in her lap, and closed her bag.

"I shouldn't eat this," I warned myself. "I don't know this lady, how she made this cake, or what she put in it." Against my better judgement, I broke off a piece and put it in my mouth. I was pleasantly surprised at how good it was. "This is good Ms. Lainey, did you make it?"

"I did, just this morning. I got a recipe from a dear friend." She paused to swallow tears. "I'm traveling to Toledo to help her daughter clean out her house."

Lainey dropped her head and started to cry. "My childhood friend Peaches passed a few days ago. She left me her car and her cat." Ms. Lainey pulled a handkerchief out of her pocket and wiped her eyes. "I didn't keep in touch with her as much as I should've once I moved away."

I folded my cake back in the foil and rubbed her shoulder. "I'm so sorry, Ms. Lainey."

"Life has a way of humbling you, Joyce." She blew her nose. "I did everything I could to forget where I came from. Even though we promised to keep in touch, I never returned her letters or came home to visit." She looked at me, patted my leg, and said, "Wherever you go, always remember you can't run from the past, nor can you control the future. Be present in every moment of your life. Home is always where you are."

Lainey closed her bag, put her head on the headrest, and closed her eyes. After a few seconds she said, "Life is for the living. It's too short to live in regret."

"I understand," I said, returning to nibble on my cake. "This is so good, what did you put in it?"

She opened her eyes and smiled, "You wanna know the secret?" I nodded. "Peaches told me to whip the eggs for 15 minutes and add a teaspoon of sour cream."

"What!" I said chewing, "I never would have thought of that."

"Peaches and I used to cook with our moms. Growing up across the street from each other, we became very close. Our parents were good friends, and for a little white girl, and a little black girl growing up during a tense time, we formed a solid bond." She sniffled, "I let my friend down."

"Ohh Ms. Lainey, why do you say that?" I adjusted my bag on my lap.

"I left after high school and never looked back. I tried to get Peaches to go to college with me, but my friend fell in love with a man who sold her empty promises from the bottom of a bottle and knocked her around."

"Oh no," I moaned.

"Our life is about choices, Joyce." She wiped her eyes again. "Changing the subject, are you traveling for business or for pleasure?"

"Well, it's a mix of both. I'm going to Toledo to take a job with Ms. Alfreda at her shop."

"That is wonderful!" She cheered, collecting looks from other passengers on the bus. "Sorry," she whispered. "She is amazing. Will you be one of her models?"

"I haven't considered that, but I'm her apprentice."

"I don't mean to intrude, Joyce, but consider every possibility in this life. If the door doesn't open, it's not for you, but knock whenever you see a door." She adjusted her coat, snuggled into her seat and said, "I'm going to rest for a bit." The rest of the way to Toledo, I listened to Ms. Lainey sleep as I and digested our conversation.

When we arrived in Toledo, Ms. Lainey slipped me her phone number on the back of her ticket and said, "Keep in touch with me."

I opened my arms to hug her and said, "Take care of yourself, Ms. Lainey. Thanks for sharing your heart with me."

Chapter 16

Breaking new ground.

My first day at Ms. Alfreda's shop, I was extremely nervous. I caught the bus and arrived a half an hour early in the cold because I didn't want to be late. I stood under the awning of the door holding my bag full of thread, needles and scratch fabric. I had samples of my work, a sketchpad full of ideas, and all of my favorite magazines. I had even worn my favorite dress and a matching beret—the one I made from Daddy's ties.

By the time Ms. Alfreda arrived and opened the door, I had gathered the pieces of my confidence and built a strong tower. When she hopped out of the passenger side of the car she captured me in a firm embrace. "How was Cincinnati?" The driver pulled the car close to the curb and parked it.

I held my hat. "It was nice. I enjoyed every minute of it." I lifted my bag, "I brought some nice fabric for us."

Ms. Alfreda turned to look at the car and said, "We have to wait for my son, Doug, to let us in. My keys are in the ignition." Doug promptly exited the car, jumped out and said, "Let me get that for you, Ma." He unlocked the door and held it open for us. I watched him watch me, and I felt something weird on my stomach. "Is this what love feels like? I don't even know this man." I pondered.

I recalled a conversation with Miss Sally and Miss Cecelia when Miss Sally said, "Romantic love doesn't always reveal itself like you see in the picture shows. Sometimes it sneaks up on you."

"It sure does," Miss Cecelia added, "When you know, you know."

In that moment I knew. Doug did too, he shouted to Ms. Alfreda, "Ma, this here is my wife!" I was a quiet girl then, too bashful to flirt back, but I knew he was right.

Ms. Alfreda grinned from ear to ear. Two weeks after I moved to Toledo, I met the love of my life. Before I knew it, he had replaced my promise ring with an engagement ring. Even though we moved quickly, I had no doubts that I loved him, and he loved me. There were no strings attached. I was longing to be loved earnestly, deeply, intentionally, completely, and God was showing me through people that His love was real. Doug was one of his representatives.

Ms. Alfreda insisted that Doug and I join her church and that I move out of the boarding house. Doug was hard working and always doing odd jobs, starting businesses, and making sure that I was his number one priority.

For years, I had yearned for a taste of freedom and to be away from Mother's house. Working with Ms. Alfreda and meeting her son Doug, I was forever changed as a person, and most importantly, as a woman. For the first time in my life, I felt hope. Being with people who were kind, compassionate, and creative restored me. Even though I had always known God, I came to love Him for myself because of them. I no longer feared the God that Mother pushed on me, I was in awe of the God that loved her, me, and my new friends.

Toledo was far enough away for me to feel like I was in another country, yet I was close enough to Mother if I wanted to get to her.

Chapter 17

Surprise.

A few weeks later, Doug gripped my hand as we walked along Dorr Drive from my bus stop. "Joyce, I have something to tell you, but I don't know how you're going to receive the news."

I clutched Doug's arm and pulled him close to me. "Just as long as you're not telling me that you have a secret girlfriend, I'm fine."

Doug looked at me sideways and said, "Joyce, the first time I saw you, I knew you'd be the mother of my children."

"Oh," I lowered my eyes and let him go. "What if I don't want children, Doug? Will you still want to be with me?"

"Of course!" He pulled me back to him. "I want to have children, but I want to be with you, Joyce." He stopped walking and looked me in the eye. "I really love you. I can't imagine my life without you."

That made me blush. "Okay. Do you understand that you're the first man I have ever been close to like this?" He nodded. "Miss Sally, Miss Cecelia, and Aunt Portia told me to open myself up, but this happened so fast, I couldn't even be scared." We chuckled.

"I can't wait to meet them."

A gust of wind blew Doug's hat off and he caught it without losing his stride. We chuckled as he put it back on his head. "Go ahead, and finish your story," he said, leading me across the street.

"We haven't known each other long."

"Exactly 22 days," he added.

"Yup. And I've told you everything there is to know about me. The good things, the horrific things, and the dreams I have dreamed since I remember dreaming." I put my head on his shoulder. "So, what do you want to tell me?"

Doug took a deep breath and said, "Do you remember me telling you that I applied for a job as an elevator salesman?"

"I do. You didn't talk about anything but that interview for days."

"I got the job!" He grinned.

I put a skip in my step. "Wonderful news, Dougie!" I clapped. "When will you start? Where will your office be?"

He cleared his throat. "I only have a few weeks to get everything together before I leave Toledo." "Leave?" I stopped walking and dropped Doug's hand. I turned my body away from him and covered my face with my scarf to hide my tears. With my heart in my stomach, I said, "What does that mean for us?"

Doug looked at me with sympathy, "I guess we have some decisions to make." Without realizing my speed, I jogged the last block to work, heels and all. I was so far ahead of Doug that I crossed two streets, leaving him on the sidewalk. "Lord, why would you expose me to love and then strip it from me?" I prayed. "I'm just getting to really know him."

When I reached the shop door, I wiped my eyes, fixed my hair and popped my lips to adjust my lipstick. I had to be stoic so that Doug, his mother, or no one else in the shop would see my emotions. I felt a cloud forming around my head, and I didn't care to wave it away. I had to carry myself as a strong woman, stoic, as if my heart wasn't the texture of curdled milk.

I flung the door of the shop open, startling everyone in the room. I waved with embarrassment and walked slowly to Ms.

Alfreda's office to put my coat and lunch bag away. I settled at my machine and started on my tasks for the day.

I kept my distance from Doug, finding a reason to cross the room whenever he came near me. I couldn't stand to be near him. I wanted to forget everything about him. "He can go live his life in Texas," I fumed, pinning a sleeve together.

It was a busy day of final preparations for Ms. Alfreda's winter show. We were bustling with activity, fitting models, making alterations, and ripping out seams. Around lunchtime, in the middle of half-dressed models, and unfinished garments, Ms. Alfreda called me away from my sewing machine. "Give me one second, Ms. Alfreda," I said without looking up. "I'm finalizing the details on the blue knit dress for scene five."

"Joyce," she called again, "Take a break from that and come try this on for me."

I finished my seam and let the pedal of my machine return to my foot before I let it go. I stood up, wiped my hands on my apron and walked over to Ms. Alfreda. I looked in her eyes, still trying to mask my pain. She was holding the gown I had designed for the final scene. "Ms. Alfreda," I protested. "I'm not in that scene. Miranda should be here soon."

"I know, honey." She spoke with kindness. "I think this will lift your spirits, you seem down today." She patted my hand. "Are you okay?"

"I'm okay." I lied.

"Well, why shouldn't the designer be able to try on her own gown? You envisioned and pieced together this beautiful garment. I need you to put it on so that I can fix the zipper." Ms. Alfreda handed me the dress beaming with pride. Light reflecting from the white sequins shined across her face like a disco ball.

"Are you sure, Ms. Alfreda? I mean, there are several other models who are Miranda's size that can probably do it for you. I have so much to do for the show next week."

"Yes, I'm sure Joyce!" She smiled showing all of her pearly whites.

I felt like I was carrying a ton of bricks. I carried the dress into the dressing room and sat on the stool for a few minutes trying to compose myself. Between feeling lightheaded and heartbroken, I felt numb. I stared at myself in the mirror and asked myself a question that moved me to tears, "Will I ever get married?"

I changed, stepping gently into the dress and making sure no sequin was disturbed. Turning to face myself again, I said, "You look gorgeous, and you did a damn good job on this dress, girl. Somebody is going to be extremely happy."

When I pushed back the curtain of the dressing room, Ms. Alfreda covered her mouth in amazement. Everyone in the room gasped for air, making statements like, "Oh my God!" "You are beautiful." "Okay, Joyce, I see you!"

Doug, the staff, and every model in the room were standing in front of me. I was the center of attention, something I had never been before. I noticed that Doug was on his knees raising flowers above his head and I asked, "Why are you on your knees?"

"Joyce," Doug said, "I know we've only known each other for a few weeks, but I need to put the bait on this hook before a bigger fish comes along and steals you away from me." He stood and held my hand. "I'm ready to give up anything and everyone that is not you. I told Ma the first day that we met, there is no one else in this world for me but you."

There were some oohs and ahhs from ladies in the room, that warmed my heart. "Joyce Turner, will you marry me?"

One model, whom I did not recognize, huffed and stormed out of the shop slamming the door behind her. No one turned to take a second look.

Doug was crying. I was literally watching him melt into a puddle of emotion in front of me. Tears soaked his shirt; seeing his vulnerability mended my heart, I was putty in his hands. I threw all of my inhibitions to the wind. There was no record of time, no explanation of space, and no need to wait for anyone else to love me.

I had no other answer but a resounding, "Yes!" that billowed out of my soul. I wrapped my arms around him, as Doug stood, squeezing me like it was the last time he would ever see me. Now I know you may be thinking I rushed into something I had no business jumping into, but like Miss Cecelia had said, I knew he was the one!

Out of the other dressing room popped LJ, Enid, Hannah, and Elijah! I lost all my marbles in that moment, seeing my family. I covered my face and dropped to my knees. I was overtaken by the beauty in the moment. "Doug made sure to think about everything and everyone who was important to me."

Ms. Alfreda looked so happy seeing me and Doug together. She kept giggling and hugging Doug. "My son is marrying one of the best designers I've trained. This is a marriage made in heaven." Ms. Alfreda pulled us into a hug and said, "We have a wedding to plan!"

She scampered over to her desk and lifted the receiver on the phone. "We need to call your mother right now and tell her the good news. What's her number?"

My heart palpitated in my chest. I went from being heartbroken about losing the love of my life to being engaged to the love of my life! And now I'm being given the task of having to call my mother. I hadn't spoken to her in six months. I asked my siblings, "How can I call Mother and let her know I'm getting married? I can't call her. She won't understand."

They encircled me, taking their positions on both sides and behind my back. Elijah reached for me, and I held him closely. Enid spoke up first, "Doug called all of us? Mother knows because he asked her permission to accept your hand in marriage."

"As your little big brother," LJ squeezed me from behind, "Doug and I have had numerous conversations over the phone about you. He's not playing when he says that he has loved you from the first day he saw you." He stepped from behind me and gave Doug a high five, "I also gave my approval after checking him out. You told me through your letters that he reminds you of Daddy."

Hannah said, "Yes, you told me that he has restored your hope in love."

"But I'll have to move to Texas." I protested. "I'm worried that the distance would change our relationship."

"Sissy," Enid led me to the phone. "We all live in different places. As long as we write and call, our bond will always be as sold as a rock."

Ms. Alfreda insisted again, "Joyce, you really need to call your mother and let her know you're getting married. I know you haven't spoken to her in months, but I want to meet her. I want her to know that you are in good hands with me. I want her to help us plan this wedding. I know as a mother, she would appreciate this from you."

I looked at Doug and dialed the number to my mother's house. My heart felt like a whole ensemble of drummers marching in my chest. I imagined what she was doing on a Tuesday night. "Is she studying her Bible? Is she in the middle of a prayer circle?" Questions zipped across my mind. I started to feel a cloud forming. Ms. Alfreda waved everyone out of the room.

Mother answered on the first ring. "Turner residence." Her voice sounded kind, melodic, and sweet. That made me whimper. "Joyce? Is that you darling?" I had no words. I could only shake my head up and down in response.

"She can't see you, honey." Ms. Alfreda took the phone from me. Doug took me into his arms and led me to a chair nearby. "Hello Ms. Turner? This is Alfreda Davis. We met several years ago at your church. Your daughter, Joyce, has been here in Toledo working with me since right before the Christmas holiday."

Ms. Alfreda turned her back to talk. "Uh huh. Well, I wanted to let you know that Joyce is doing a fine job here. She has helped my business grow by leaps and bounds. I'll show you some designs when you come to visit. She's a beautiful model and furthermore, she's teaching me a few things. Did you teach her how to sew?"

I shook my head fast, bringing back some slight dizziness. Ms. Alfreda paused. "Oh, I see. Well, from what I can see, her eye for fashion is a God given gift. Her enhancement of my designs along with her own ideas are growing through this town like a dandelion weed."

I took a deep breath and watched Ms. Alfreda, a woman who mothered me as she engaged in conversation with the woman who birthed me. I hoped that my mother would be happy. "Well, Ms. Turner, my son and your daughter are an item. He just proposed to her." She looked at me. "It is wonderful news, isn't it? Of course," she handed me the phone and mouthed the words, "She wants to talk to you. It's okay."

She patted me on the back and led Doug to take a few steps back for privacy.

"Hi Mother," I squeaked. "Have you been well?"

"My Joyce, it's such a pleasant surprise to hear your voice." Mother seemed genuinely happy to talk to me. "I hear that things are going well for you, do you agree?"

"Yes Ma'am. I'm sorry I haven't reached out to you."

"We didn't leave each other on the best of terms, baby. I understand your reasoning, but God has answered my prayers and brought you back to me. I do apologize for my behavior. I am truly sorry."

"I'm deeply apologetic, too."

"So, can you have your wedding here before you move to Texas? I want to see you and meet your new husband. He sounds nice."

"Ms. Alfreda told you everything," I chuckled. "I'll check with Doug, I'm sure he'll get us there soon."

A few weeks later, we had a small ceremony in the park. My siblings, Aunt Portia, Miss Sally, Miss Cecelia and both of their deacons came to Toledo. Ms. Lainey came. We all huddled together in the small shelter, trying to keep warm. I pinned Daddy's picture to my bra and made a boutonnière out of his old ties for Doug. I wanted to honor Daddy, too.

We had a few friends and coworkers join us for a cake reception. Mother scoffed when we told her that after the cake reception some of us were going skating to celebrate. "I see you're still up to your old antics." I didn't take her bait, and she said nothing more, which showed growth in both of us.

That night we consummated our marriage. However, it wasn't our first time together and we were careful not to reveal that information to anyone.

At the skating rink, Miss Sally and Miss Cecelia put their arms through my arms and skated with me. It reminded me of the first time I was introduced to skating, by them. I was much more confident on my feet, thanks to them. Miss Ceceila leaned over and whispered in my ear, "Doug was a nice surprise, wasn't he?"

"Yes, he was." I blushed.

"I'm happy to know that you opened your heart, Joyce. You didn't sit in rejection. I told you God had a plan for you."

Miss Sally leaned over and said, "You've inspired me."

"I have?"

She beamed, "Deacon Leroy has asked me to retire with him to Florida. We're getting married!"

I hugged her and said, "I'm so happy for you!"

Coming up behind her, Deacon Leroy grabbed Miss Sally's hand and said, "This is our song, my love." She giggled as they zoomed off for a couple's skate.

The next morning, I said tearful goodbyes to my family before beginning my life with Doug as a married woman.

A few weeks after we moved to Texas, Mother called in the early hours of the morning. When I answered the phone she said, "I had a dream about a little chocolate baby sitting at my feet playing with two knitting needles bigger than her. She was a cute little thing."

"Mother?' I blinked and caught a glimpse of the red numbers on the alarm clock. I whispered, "Why are you calling our house at 5:00 in the morning?"

Doug was a light sleeper, he flipped the blanket back and asked, "Who is it?"

Mother continued. "Darling, I'm sorry. I've been up praying, and it slipped my mind that you are behind us. Well anyway, I've been on the prayer line with my prayer warriors, and I wanted to tell you the news."

"What news?" I covered my face trying to stay in a resting position.

"Joyce, why didn't you tell me you're pregnant?"

I was so out of it that I looked at Doug and whispered, "I don't want to be pregnant." Then I hung up on Mother, threw the quilt back over my face and fell back to sleep.

Doug told me later that he sat straight up in the bed, and Mother called right back. "Mother-In-Love?"

"I had a dream about the baby."

"What baby?" Doug said, he was confused.

"Do you and Joyce have wax in your ears? Why didn't you tell me that my baby is going to have a baby?" Doug recounted that she was so excited, that when she dropped the receiver to worship, Doug heard it crash against the floor. "Mother-In-Love? Hello?"

He always recounts the call was fuzzy with static, but he heard Mother singing "Amazing Grace."

There is no doubt that Mother was a praying woman, and she did hear from God. "Doug, I'm so happy." She cheered, "I'm about to have my first grandbaby! It's a girl. She's going to be chocolate brown like me, have long fine hair, curly eyelashes, and dark brown eyes."

He tried to get her off the phone. "Mother-In-Love, can we talk about this in the morning?"

"No baby, unh, unh. I know I woke you up, but we need to talk about it now. I know you like your little elevator sales job down there, but it's time for you to pack up the apartment and bring your little family back to Ohio. I want to be near my grandbaby. I'm gonna tell my prayer warriors to start praying for you and Joyce to come back home. Don't you want to be close to your Mom?"

"Mother-In-Love, we haven't been married long enough to make a baby." It didn't occur to him that the baby probably was implanted BEFORE the wedding, but he wouldn't dare mention that to Mother.

"I can't believe I'm having a grandbaby. I am so excited. God told me the baby is going to be special. I saw her holding two silver knitting needles. She was sitting on the floor in front of your mother, and I was singing Amazing Grace over her." Then she started singing our family hymn.

"She is going to be a bundle of love," Mother squealed through the phone, "bringing the joy back to our family. Good night. I'll call you tomorrow." Mother hung up, and Doug went back to sleep, dazed at the news he was about to be a father.

That evening, over dinner, Doug asked, "Do you remember the call from your mother this morning? Is there something you want to tell me?"

"Mother called?" I said stuffing a forkful of chicken and rice in my mouth.

Doug played with the food on his plate and said, "Mother-In-Love called early this morning rambling about you being pregnant.

I clutched my hand to my stomach, "Baby, no! I'm not pregnant. I don't want children."

"Why, baby?" Doug asked, pushing my hair behind my ear.

"What if I'm not a good mom? What if I yell at the baby? What if I hurt her?" I started to cry, "What if I'm like my mother?"

"You won't be, Baby. You're not your mother."

"But I . . .," my voice trailed.

"We are in this together. I'm excited to be a dad, and I'm scared as hell, too. But we have the prayer warrior gang on our side. How can we fail?" We laughed. "Your mother had a dream during her prayer warrior meeting, or whatever she calls it, that you're having a girl."

"That really scares me." I clutched my heart and shook my head left and right. "I can't have a girl; that's too much responsibility." I patted my heart to make it stop fluttering, "I'm scared."

"If you are pregnant, and if it is a girl, I want to name her Anita Joyce." He grinned, and the gold crown on his front tooth shined. "I thought about that name all day while I was at work. I believe God gave it to me."

"It has a nice ring to it."

"Yes, Anita means grace. Since your mother hears from God, and this may be one of her prophecies, I want to make sure we give a nod to God's presence in our little baby's name. She may be a little cantankerous, but she loves us. I do believe she hears from God."

"Well," I searched my brain for something. intellectual to say, "I guess we'll have to find a doctor. It doesn't make sense because I am still having my cycle."

"We'll have to find a doctor to confirm it."

"Doug, if I am pregnant, do you really believe that we are ready to be parents?"

"Babe, we're going to take one day at a time." Doug squatted next to me. "Stop worrying. We're ready when God says we're ready. You must let God be God. No one ever makes a mistake unless they refuse to learn."

"Well, thank God we are married. I definitely don't want Mother-In-Love to be embarrassed about having a bastard grandchild. You know how she feels about that."

Doug laughed. "You're right, but I think Mother-In-Love will be fine. Babies have a way of bringing people together." I thought about how my nephew had softened Mother's heart. "I hope so," I said, finishing my dinner.

"We need to call Ma and tell her."

"We don't even know yet," I teased. "But this is a bet I'm willing to make."

"Well, you know Mama is going to be ecstatic either way." He went to call her, and I cleaned up the kitchen, pondering my life change.

Later that evening, I opened a new journal to write down a list of things I was grateful for. It was a habit I had adopted from my father. Every night, I listed things that made me smile, laugh, or feel good. That night I wrote a letter to my unborn child. Curled up on the couch under a quilt given to us as a wedding gift from my mother, I let the moment soak in. Everything I had prayed for, dreamed about, and hoped for, God had blessed me to be living in that moment. I couldn't help but cry tears of joy.

I sketched out a dress for the baby to come home in, and I wrote down my hopes for my baby . . . filling pages with my prayers and hopes. I wrote until I was free of apprehension and full of hope.

My Dear Baby,

Our lives are a result of the choices we make. I have not always chosen to see the beauty around me, or to recognize the beauty I contribute to the world. I may not be perfect but knowing that a beautiful flower could be growing in my belly, I am a bit nervous and humbled, yet excited.

The first thing I want you to know about me is that I promise to always give you what I believe you need and listen when you tell me what you want. You will never have to question my intentions. I will always be open and honest with you, never keeping secrets.

Second, I will make mistakes, but I will never do anything intentionally to hurt you or strip you of your dignity. Your Daddy, uncle and aunts will hold me accountable, they know my story.

Finally, you will never have to doubt me or my love for you. My love carries you now, and it will carry you long after I am gone. You will be one of my greatest gifts to cherish.

Your Daddy and I are making room for you. God knows your name, and He knew it before you were formed in my womb. I am thankful for the opportunity to be your mother, and I promise to follow the path of faith that led me to meet your father and to trust myself. I have had to fight for my life, and I promise to fight for you.

My wish for you is that you internalize what an incredibly strong person you are. I want to see you believe that you are incredible, and you deserve everything God has for you.

I already love you so much,

Mommy

When I was empty, I handed my journal to Doug. "Baby," I said, turning to him as he read the newspaper, "We need to write down our wishes for our child." He put the paper down and gave me his full attention. "I want the baby to know that as parents, we have good intentions. I need them to know that even though they may be coming to us as a surprise, we're happy about them and will dedicate our lives to shepherding them into greatness."

"That's such a good idea." He took my journal from me and started to hum "Amazing Grace." His deep baritone voice lulled me into his arms, and he rocked me as he hummed. "You know, Joyce," he said, "When I saw you standing outside of Mama's shop the day we met, I had hit rock bottom."

I lifted my head to look at him, but he didn't look at me. "Doug what happened?" My husband started to sob. For a long time, I held him in my arms as he cried out whatever he'd been holding. "Hang in there, baby," I said, rubbing the waves in his hair. "We're gonna see this through, I promise."

He never told me what made him feel so broken, but somehow, I knew that love had broken through his pain. He started to hum again, this time putting words to his tears.

Dear Anita, (I believe you're a girl)

Being loved is a special gift from God. I'm a man of many faces. I've been involved with things that I'll never speak to you about, but I know that I'll protect you from anyone who has ill intentions toward you. When you look at me, I want you to know that I was changed by love. I was healed by love. I was restored by love.

My mother, your grandmother, is one of the sweetest women you'll ever meet. She loved me when I was belligerent and didn't love myself. I've seen this world through rage, but there has always been something keeping me grounded. For you, I vow to keep my feet rooted in truth. I promise to be a good man for you and your mother.

I didn't always believe in coincidences or happenstance, but when I met your mother, I knew I had to make a change. She was standing on the corner, waiting for my mother to open her shop. She looked so innocent, so pure, and confident. I didn't know anything about her, but the world around me stopped. She arrested my attention, and I felt something change. My mother got out of the car, and I brushed her wheel on the curb trying to park the car.

I knew when I walked past her to hold the door, that your mother was the one. Something clicked in me whenever I was around her. I know now that she sees the good in me, she's the woman my mother prayed for, and the woman I need. As I watch your mother give everything to serve others, I want to make sure to restore her treasure chest with gems, and you baby girl, are one of those treasures.

Your mother pours her heart into everything she does, and I have no doubt that she'll do the same for you. She's a little scared right now, but be patient with her, we're all new at this thing.

You are coming into a world where many people have open arms, waiting for you to arrive. The village surrounding you is a fortress.

You're already the greatest thing I've ever accomplished. I promise to give you the world on a silver platter. You'll never have to worry about anything as long as you trust that your Daddy has your back. As I hold on to God's hand, your mother's hand, and your hand, I've found my reason.

Wish on every star that you find, and when you feel like a dandelion, run until you get to your resting place, my love. That's where you'll find your strength. Whenever you feel tired and like you can't go on, you're almost there.

Love,

Daddy

By the time our baby made her way into the world, Texas had become home for Doug and me. We joined a new church, I established some clients to sew for, and Doug had settled into his job, becoming the top elevator salesman within his first two months. I made sure to keep in touch with my family, and everyone was excited. Ms. Alfreda had come to stay with us for a few weeks to help me with my business.

I was so tired all the time. I could hardly keep my eyes open, I was always falling down or stumbling over my feet. I didn't want to eat anything but oranges all day. My belly was so big, I couldn't see my feet. I loved being pregnant, it was the only time I didn't have headaches!

The baby came early. Several weeks before her expected due date, she shocked everybody! A few days before her arrival, I was feeling unsettled. "What are you doing?" Doug asked one day when he opened the door of our apartment and found me lifting up the couch.

"It would look better over here by the window," I grunted, sliding the couch into position.

"Go sit down somewhere before you hurt yourself girl!" He looked around. "You've changed everything in this house." He inspected the living room, kitchen, our bedroom, and then came back. "Why didn't you wait for me?" I had started nesting, moving furniture and getting rid of clutter to make room.

The day Anita was born, I was scarfing down my fifth orange of the day, and chugging water. I started feeling woozy, tried to stand, but fell back into my chair. I felt terrified. I wanted to call Mother, but I didn't know what to say. Doug wasn't home, and I couldn't call Aunt Portia. I felt so alone, and I just wanted my Mother.

I felt the cloud forming around my head, and I started to cry. The pain in my head and heart were in sync. I tried to stand, but couldn't get up. The baby decided for herself it was time to arrive, I felt water splash on my chair and down my legs. I couldn't handle the pain the baby's impending arrival was causing me. I screamed for help, and my neighbor came over, unlocked the door with her key and everything is a blur after that.

The baby was born on the way to the hospital in the back of her grey station wagon. I learned later that her umbilical cord was wrapped around her. "I messed up, and my baby isn't even a day old." I cried to Doug, "How am I going to do this?"

I felt so guilty about my baby being born under those circumstances. I was scared to be a mother, then I birthed her into trauma. I started chewing peppermint gum to calm my nerves. Mother used to eat peppermint candy, I hated that candy, but loved the smell. That smell, and cleaning with lemons helped me stay focused.

When the baby was born, Doug called my siblings to share the good news and Mother flew to Texas the next day. I was so nervous to be a mom.. It was good to have her and my mother-in-law, Ms. Alfreda with us.

My baby had to stay in the hospital for ten days. I cried for thirty minutes in the hospital garage, when the nurse rolled me in the wheelchair to the car. I just kept screaming, "My baby! I don't want to leave my baby here!" I gripped the arms of the chair and planted my feet on the ground, preventing the nurse from pushing me forward.

Mother kept singing "Amazing Grace" while Doug, the nurse, and Ms. Alfreda pried my fingers off the wheelchair. When they finally got me in the car, I fell asleep to my mother's singing. I clutched my belly; I was in so much pain in my body and in my heart, all I wanted to do was sleep. Mother rubbed my hair while I slept for the thirty-minute ride home.

That first night, Mother and Ms. Alfreda served me. I didn't have the strength to get up and do anything. Doug and our mothers tickled each other with jokes about the prophecy of the baby. "Did you interpret your dream correctly, Mother-In-Love?"

"Boy, I hear from God," she tapped him on the shoulder. "The baby is caramel brown with a hint of white cream. I know she was supposed to be chocolate."

Doug said, "She does have a cute little birthmark on her right cheek that looks like a heart, probably the most chocolate thing about her."

"I also thought that her eyes were going to be dark brown, but they are hazel." Mother opened the oven and checked the casserole, "Since you named her Anita, can we call her Nitty?"

"That's a nice nickname," Ms. Alfreda stirred the lemonade. "Why do you want to call her that?"

Without hesitation Mother said, "Her purpose in this life will be to bring people together. I think she's the hope and second chance our family needs." Mother winked at me. "She can call me Nini!"

"You know," Ms. Alfreda said, "I wonder why her little feet were hot?"

"She has hot feet like her Grandpa Turner," mother smiled at the ceiling. "Eldridge Sr. would have loved his little grandbaby."

"And you know what?" Doug had a revelation, "When she came into this world, her fists were balled up like she was ready to brawl. I love Muhammad Ali and I'm going to teach her how to box. Ain't no daughter of mine gonna be no punk."

When she was three, we found out about her hot feet and balled fists, when she started running everywhere she went. A few years later, when my son, Grayson was born, her feet cooled down so he could keep up with her.

PART 3 – WE ARE, BECAUSE I AM

Chapter 18

Bye, Y'all.

My family arrived on Cotton Street Commons in Dayton, Ohio during the winter of 1982. It was an extremely cold day of misery for me and I think my mother, Joyce, felt just as bad as I did. Neither of us talked much during the four days we traveled. She was deep in her thoughts and so was I.

Why my Daddy wanted to live in a neighborhood called "Cotton Plantation," always stumped me. Back then, I worried because we'd just watched a movie about Black people on a plantation. All I could think about for days after watching it was how slave masters with whips and chains treated Black people. I was scared something was going to happen to us.

By the time I was in my late thirties, knowing what I knew about Black History, I would never have let Daddy buy a house on any street with the word "Plantation" in its name. I don't care how cheap it was . . . I didn't want to be reminded of anything that represented the trauma our people had to endure over the years.

I remember Daddy laughed so hard when I asked him, "Am I a slave?"

"No baby." He beat the steering wheel laughing.

"Well, why do we have to move to a plantation?"

"Nitty," he chortled, "We're not moving to a plantation. That's just the name of the place where our house will be.

"Oh," I said, watching Daddy drive. We were out shopping for a few things for my birthday party. I was so happy I was turning thirteen whole years old! Two entire months before my actual birthday, we planned my party as a family.

Mama had said, "You can pick eleven of your friends from school, church, and the basketball team to come to your party at the house."

Thankfully, that was just enough people because including me, it made an even number, twelve. I had my whole party planned out, we'd eat ribs, drink pop, and dance to Micheal Jackson. Mama said we could play games, and she was going to buy vanilla birthday cake and make ice cream.

Mama let me pick out pink decorations with strawberries and my favorite cartoon character on them. We hung the decorations in the yard, and Mama let me stand in a chair to hang them in the places I couldn't reach.

Daddy and I danced together as we blew up balloons and set up chairs in the backyard. Grayson, my three-year-old baby brother, ran around us, giggling.

When she tucked me in bed Friday night, Mama leaned over to kiss me on the forehead. She put the blanket under my chin, and said, "When you wake up in the morning, make up your bed, take your shower and put on lotion. I laid your clothes out for you on the dresser. Make sure that you take your stocking cap off, before you come downstairs. And don't forget to grease your scalp."

"Okay, Mama," I nodded.

"I love you, Nitty."

"I love you too, Mama."

I woke up the next morning, around 9 a.m., giddy, like it was Christmas. The music rising from the speakers downstairs added to the soundtrack of my excitement. I threw back the covers and jumped out of bed, stumbling over a big suitcase under my feet. *"Where did that come from?"* I wondered, as I grabbed my towel and washcloth from the closet.

Snapping my fingers to the beat and dancing around my room, I bobbed my head and made my way into the bathroom. I took my shower, singing along to the songs Daddy was playing on his record player. I ripped the price tags off my new clothes and got dressed.

My braids were crisp with designs this time instead of straight back. Mama had grabbed all my baby hairs into the braids. My eyes were pulled back to my brows, but I didn't care!

When I took my stocking cap off I saw my perfectly lined up braids, I shook my red beads and listened to them clack against each other. I felt so pretty as I smiled at myself in the mirror. I put some grease between my cornrows and gave myself a chef's kiss.

Walking down the stairs, I noticed that the house felt different. I stopped in my tracks, when I saw the stacks of old newspapers and cardboard boxes. Half of the furniture in the living room was gone, and there were piles of dirt all over the floor. "What's going on?" I questioned myself, as I slinked down the stairs.

I saw one of Mama's staff members, Miss India, sitting in the middle of the floor wrapping newspaper around some glasses. "What's she doing here?" I thought.

"Hey Miss India," I said, tapping her on the shoulder.

"Ohh, Nitty! You're up! Happy birthday," she said jumping up and scooting to the other side of the room, retrieving a pink bag. "I got something for your birthday."

She handed me the bag, and I peeked inside. There was a card, some hair bows and a bouquet of lollipops. "Thank you, Miss India," I said, giving her a hug. "Do you know where my mother is?"

She pointed. "She's in the kitchen."

"I'm going to miss you, Sugar Lump." She looked at the bag and said, "There's enough for you and your friends." She handed me a few pieces of peppermint from her pocket. "And I put a little something extra for you in your card."

"Oh, thanks, Ms. India." I wanted to say, "What are you doing here? I didn't invite you." But instead, I hurried into the kitchen looking for my mother, passing a few other ladies.

"Mama!" I said, pushing the kitchen door forward. The door hit someone's feet, blocking me from entering. I heard feet scampering, and from behind the door my Aunt Enid appeared. "Happy Birthday, Dollface!" She said, sweeping me into her arms.

"Auntie!" I jumped up and down. "I'm so happy you came for my birthday! When did you get here?"

"I got here around midnight and we've been working all night, Dollface."

Mama has two younger sisters, Aunt Hannah and Aunt Enid. Aunt Hannah lives in Cincinnati, I don't get to see her or my cousin Elijah a lot. Elijah and I talk on the phone and write letters sometimes; he's three years older than me.

I idolized my Aunt Enid. To me, she was the most beautiful woman in the world, with her chocolate brown skin, shiny round afro, and long slender legs. Watching her gave me confidence to be myself no matter where I was, what I was doing, or who I was with at the time.

I loved to sit with her, while she told me about how she traveled all over the country singing and dancing. She was in plays, on magazine covers, and even sang with people who had hit records! Mama said that she was famous on, "The chitlin' circuit" and Aunt Enid always brought me gifts from her trips.

"Let me look at you." She held me by my shoulders and said, "You are growing up so fast. What happened to the little

Dollface I used to hold in my arms?" I shrugged. "You are so pretty, just like your Auntie." We shared a laugh. Aunt Enid bumped her hip up to mine, like we were dancers in the Soul Train line.

"When I got here last night you were knocked out, so I didn't wake you up. I slept in your room, you didn't even notice I was there."

"I didn't know you were coming."

"You know I like to keep the people guessing." She picked up a glass and took a sip of water. "There are some more surprises for you, Nitty."

I clapped my hands, "I love surprises!" I turned on my heels, Aunt Enid said, "Be careful, honey!" Before she could catch me, I stepped back and bumped into Mama who was standing on a stool emptying a cabinet full of glassware. Mama dropped the plates she was passing to one of her friends.

"Damn it, Anita!" she shook her head as she stepped down. "Those dishes were part of my Grandma's dinner set."

She kicked the stool out of the way, "What were you thinking running in here like that?"

"Sorry Mama," I said eyeing the shards of glass. I could smell Mama's gum. It was a comforting scent, a strong reminder of how she fought for me, stood her ground for me, plus changed because of me. I wanted to hug her and get a whiff of her scent, but I stood still.

The spearmint scent always settled something in me, when I was in her arms. I watched my mother bend over the mess, visibly upset with me but trying to hide it. "Those dishes are irreplaceable," she grunted under her breath, "This is the last thing I need right now."

"Mama?" I said playing with my hair.

"What, Nitty?" Mama murmured.

"What are all of these people doing here?" What I really wanted to know was, "And are my friends still coming over today? Am I still having a party?" I felt so small in that room full of adults.

"Why would you ask me that!" Mama fussed. "Of course you're having a party. Why do you think we're doing all of this!"

"But Mama," I looked around. "There're lots of people here, but my friends aren't here."

"These are my friends," she tapped her chest. "I invited them here to help us pack up this house so we can move." Mama sighed, "Your friends will be here a little later for your party."

"Pack up the house?" I repeated.

"We have to leave for our long drive to Ohio on Monday morning."

"Monday?" I swallowed a lump of tears forming in my throat. It felt like a giant gumball was stuck between the back of my tongue and the roof of my mouth. "But I thought we didn't have to leave until the summertime."

"Things have changed, Anita. We're leaving in two days! You heard what I said." As she knelt down and started picking up glass again, she looked away from me. "Now, please, step back. I need to get this cleaned up before somebody gets hurt."

Mama pointed at Aunt Enid and said, "E, grab that broom out of the pantry for me, please." Aunt Enid winked at me, and I watched her slide across the kitchen floor in big lunges like she was on a stage.

Mama kept fretting about the mess I'd caused. One of her friends handed her a stack of newspapers. She opened the paper and started putting the big pieces in the middle of it. She mumbled, "Shit!"

"You need to pay attention to what you are doing, Anita. I don't know how you can be so reckless at times." She blew out a hard breath, "You just need to slow down and pay attention to your surroundings."

"Are you talking to yourself or to Nitty, Joyce?" Aunt Enid asked, from across the room.

Mama fired Aunt Enid an unkind look and kept cleaning. I felt guilty that Mama was so grumpy.

I bent down to help her pick up the glass, "No, Nitty!" She pushed me back with her arm, "Get out of the way before you get hurt." She shooed me back, "I got it, I just need you to take a few steps back."

My heart thumped in my chest, and I took a deep breath. Aunt Enid handed Mama the broom and put her arm around me. Mama started sweeping, slamming the broom wildly, and hitting it against the floor.

Aunt Enid tried to take the broom from Mama who wouldn't let it go. Aunt Enid gently nudged Mama to the kitchen table. "Be careful before you wake up the baby." She nodded to the bassinet in the kitchen corner.

I looked at my baby brother and thought, "I didn't even realize Grayson was in here." It amazed me how my brother could sleep peacefully in the midst of the storm brewing around him.

"Take a break for a few minutes, Joyce." Aunt Enid put her hand on Mama's shoulder. "You've been up cooking and cleaning since 6:00 a.m., and you said you didn't sleep much the night before."

Mama sat at the table and leaned the broom toward Aunt Enid. She wiped her forehead and squeezed her lips together before saying, "I feel foggy and lightheaded. I feel a headache coming on." Mama put her head in her hands. "Shit!" She said quietly. "This is all happening so fast." She shook her head without looking up, "I don't know if I can do this."

Aunt Enid, still holding the broom, turned me around and said, "Nitty, why don't you go on outside and see if any of your friends are here?"

"That's a good idea," Mama grunted.

There was a knock on the screen door followed up by a deeper, "Knock. Knock."

I knew that voice from anywhere! It was my friend Althea's mom, Ms. Clementine, whose voice I'd heard boom through the screen door like a bass drum! She stepped into the kitchen saying, "The calvary's here, and we're ready to help."

Ms. Clementine stepped back, seeing the shattered glass, "Uh, oh. What happened here?"

Mama spoke through her hands, "Nitty bumped into me, and I dropped some plates."

Ms. Clementine gave me a hug and said, "Happy Birthday, Nitty!" She squeezed me so tight between her big bosom, I could hardly breathe. After a few seconds, she let me go, I gasped for air. "I'm sorry baby, I didn't mean to hug you so tight."

Ms. Clementine playfully pinched my cheek, "That girl has been worrying me about your party all week. She's been begging me to take her to the store. Yesterday I walked in her room, and she was standing in front of the mirror practicing her dance moves."

That made me smile, "She was?"

"I didn't bother her, but I told her it's your birthday, so she has to let you win the dance contest. You're the queen of the day, and you deserve it." Ms. Clementine looked through the screen door my eyes followed hers. "Althea is out there waiting for you. Why don't you go find her and your other friends?"

I couldn't see my friend through the screen door. "Where's she, Ms. Clementine?"

"Around the side of the house, sitting in the shade. Your daddy put out lemonade for them and chips to nibble on."

Aunt Enid put a bowl of dip into my right hand. "Take this out there to share with your friends."

I stood at the door leaning back and forth on my feet. "It's okay, Dollface." Sensing my apprehension, Aunt Enid reassured me, "Go ahead, honey. We'll help your Mama clean up the mess in here, and we'll be out in a little while to eat."

Aunt Enid urged me to go outside. "Don't worry about the mess." She opened the door, I looked out, but I couldn't get my feet to move.

"How can I have fun when Mama is so sad?" I asked myself.

I felt Aunt Enid's hand on my back, "It's okay," she said as if reading my mind. "Dollface, go outside and greet your friends."

Mama said, "And don't you let my door slam, girl." Aunt Enid pushed the screen door open wide for me, and I stepped onto the porch. She held the door handle until it rested on the door frame. I took a step forward and Aunt Enid stopped me. "Wait, Dollface." I kept my feet planted, but rotated my waist to look back at her.

Aunt Enid stepped away from the door and came back with a big plastic bag of ribs from the fridge. She put the food in my left hand and gave me instructions, "Take this bag out to your Daddy."

I held on to the food and remained on the porch holding the cold bag ribs against my leg. I moved to the side of the door to get some relief from the sun, but that's as far as I could move.

I stood there, dazed, listening to Mama as she talked to the women in the kitchen. I heard the chair slide against the floor, "I can't deal with this shit right now."

Aunt Enid said, "Joyce, why did you have to talk to my Dollface like that? It's the baby's birthday, give her a break. She's a sweet girl, Joyce, she was only trying to help you."

"She was in the way, E."

"Mother put you through hell for years! Now here you are doing the same thing to Dollface. You always said that Mother didn't know how to talk to people. You're the main person who should be able to show grace."

I leaned against the house and closed my eyes, listening to the sounds in the kitchen: More clacking of plates; The gas stove turning on; A can opener; Water running; My brother cooing. The light buzzing; The refrigerator running; The fan vibrating on the floor.

I heard Mama exhale hard. "You don't have children of your own, stay out of this." After Mama said that the world froze in time and everything was silent.

I switched hands. The food was heavy, but it felt good on my leg. The bowl of dip on my stomach was starting to get uncomfortable.

Aunt Enid started to hum softly. I recognized the song, "Amazing Grace."

Gradually, I started to hear again: Birds singing; Daddy and his friends making jokes; Cars driving by; Oil crackling; Newspaper being wrapped around objects; Tape being stretched against box tops.

Aunt Enid's voice seeped through the screen door. "That's a low blow, Joyce. Why would you even say something like that to me?"

"I'm sorry, Enid."

"Excuse me ladies," Ms. Clementine tried to lighten the mood. "Joyce, where did you put your spices?"

"Everything should be in a grocery bag in front of the stove," Mama said.

"Oh, I found it!" I heard her rustling in the bag. "Oooh, you have some good spices in here."

Aunt Enid, unphased by Ms. Clementine's efforts to change the subject, kept talking. "I acknowledge your apology. Thank you."

"Anybody want some coffee?" Ms. Clementine asked.

"Girl, don't nobody want no coffee. It's hot as hades outside." Ms. India said.

"Back to you, Joyce. Remember that promise we made the night you left Mother's house after the argument you had with her?"

"I do." Mama blew a breath. "Promises made. Promises kept."

"Right. Promises made. Promises kept. Are you keeping your promise right now?"

Mama let out a slight sob. Aunt Enid consoled her. "It's okay, Sissy. You can make it right with her. We made that promise to each other because when we had children we said we wanted to do things differently than Mother had done with us. We even wrote it in a letter to Hannah."

"That was a long time ago, E."

"It doesn't matter. You pride yourself on being a woman of your word, but you won't keep the promises you make to yourself for yourself."

"You're right." Mama sighed. "I don't mean to be that way towards Nitty, but I always believed that because I had to be strong, I wanted to raise a strong daughter."

"Not this way, Joyce." Aunt Enid said.

"I'm just so stressed out with this move and everything." Mama confessed.

"How do you think she feels?" Aunt Enid defended me. "You're moving her away from everything she has ever known. Did you ever stop to consider that she might be just as scared as you are."

"What can we do to support you, Joyce?" Ms. Clementine asked, trying to show support.

Mama cleared her throat trying to push the emotion away. "All of this picking up to move in a hurry to follow Doug's dreams and leaving mine here is frustrating. I have worked so hard to build up my shop now I gotta let it all go."

The sun blinded me. I held my hand up to my face and shielded my eyes.

"Again, what can we do to help you, Joyce?" Ms. Clementine inquired.

I heard the sizzle of hot oil, "My list is taped to the fridge, Clementine," Mama said, "Once I get this chicken fried up for the road I need to pack it up in coolers. Doug wants to grill all the meat we have in the freezer. If there's any left over, take it home."

I heard Miss India's voice, "You don't have to worry about the shop. We'll keep it going and send you your share every month. Thank you for trusting me to take over for you; I won't let you down."

"I know," Mama said. "I know, India."

"Clementine," I thought of something else you can do for me."

"What's that?"

"I promised Nitty that I'd make her some vanilla ice cream. Do you mind putting the mixture in the ice cream maker for me and watching it?"

"I'd love to do that."

"Do we have someone else bringing ice?" I heard Mama ask, cracking the ice cube tray. "Once we use this for the ice cream we won't have enough for the food."

"I can go get some," Ms. India said.

"One second," I heard Aunt Enid say.

"Dollface!" She called out to me, in a stern voice. "I see you still standing there. Get away from that door before you get yourself in trouble."

I turned and saw her pointing at me through the screen. "I told you a long time ago to go play. If you're standing there because you're trying to be nosy, you're just going to upset your mother even more."

"Auntie. . ." I shook the words away.

I wanted to tell her that I wasn't trying to be nosy. I wanted to say, "I am standing there because my feet are burning. I am standing still and grounding my feet on the porch to keep myself from relinquishing control of my body to my hot feet and jetting off into the country, away from everybody.

"Nevermind," I conceded, dropping my head. The sound of the beads clacking together didn't bring me joy anymore. I felt the heaviness of them against my scalp as the sun beamed down on my neck.

I saw Mama walk past holding Grayson who was grabbing at her shirt. "She must be going to feed the baby," I reasoned.

Aunt Enid stepped outside with me. "Nitty this is not the time to be in grown folks' business. Go find your friends."

"Auntie," I said, starting to cry. "I don't want Mama to be so mad at me."

Aunt Enid squatted down to meet me at eye level. "Dollface," she said wiping a tear from my eye, "It's not your responsibility to take care of your mom or make her feel better when she's upset." She wiped sweat off of my forehead, "Your job is to love her through the changes she goes through."

"I can't leave her." I started to cry. I was hot, bothered, and starting to feel sick. It felt like God had reached His hand through the sun, put His finger on my head, and seared His fingerprint into my third eye, or whatever people say.

"Oh baby. You're too young to be carrying the weight of the world on your shoulders." She hugged me and I put my head on her shoulder. "When you recognize that something is different about her, don't always jump to the conclusion that what she is going through is your fault. Don't blame yourself for something that has nothing to do with you."

I felt better hearing Aunt Enid say that, but I didn't really understand what she was saying. I lifted my head from her shoulder, leaving traces of my sadness on her shirt. I wiped my eyes and stood up straight, aligning my spine like she had taught me to.

What I knew at that moment was that there was a circle of grown women having a healing conversation and my mother was at the center of it.

I had a deep longing to go back to the kitchen. I wanted to sit on the floor between Mama's legs and lean my head on her thigh. I wanted to be in that circle and listen to them pour into her. I needed to lean on those women, to let their words fill my cup, and let their hands prop me up. I was feeling hollow and I didn't know why.

Aunt Enid wiped my tears. She stood up, waved her hands in the air and looked toward the sky. She looked so regal in her yellow dress with bell sleeves. "Give it all to God," she said. "You have the power to push the water and move the sky, just let go of what doesn't belong to you, Dollface."

I watched my aunt wave her hands gracefully as if the air was water and she was lying in a pool of it. She hummed, calming me and cooling my feet. The theatrical way that Aunt Enid swooped her arms, fluttering like a butterfly intrigued me.

"After we eat," she said, straightening her shirt. I'm going to show you some new dance moves. And, tonight," she said winking, "We'll have girl talk before we go to sleep."

That made me smile. "Okay, Auntie." I bumped my hip against hers. "It's a date."

Chapter 19

Is this my party?

I walked down the steps one at a time, clasping the bag of food in one hand and the dip in the other. I let my nose lead me to the grill where Daddy was standing. Once I got to him, I wiped new tears that were blinding me with my forearm.

I heard Daddy's voice before I could see him, behind the grill smoke. "That's the truth . . . ." He had his friends laughing with his outlandish storytelling.

When I walked up, Mr. Walt said, "There is the birthday girl!"

"Excuse me." I said, interrupting Daddy's story. "Daddy," I grunted, lifting up the heavy bag of food to him, as he poked charcoal. "Aunt Enid told me to bring this to you."

"Come here my baby," Daddy said, stepping back from the grill and pulling me into an embrace. "Happy Birthday."

"Thank you, Daddy," I said, using my shirt to remove sweat beads. "Hi, everybody." I said timidly, standing beside Daddy, who made me feel safe.

"Hey Nitty," Althea's dad spoke in his gruff voice, sounding like he was talking through a megaphone. "We're all going to miss you around here." He patted me on the shoulder. "Especially Althea, she's been so sad."

I wrinkled my lips and gritted my teeth.

"Alright," Daddy said, breaking the ice. "Go on around the side of the house and look for your girlfriends." He kissed me on my forehead and pushed me along. "I started cooking early. The food will be ready for you in a bit!"

I walked through the grass to the side of the house. As soon as she saw me, Althea jumped out of her chair and started moving toward me with the speed of a freight train. "Nitty!" She collided into me, almost knocking me over, "Happy Birthday!"

She grabbed my hand and led me to a row of chairs along the wall, I put the dip on an empty chair.

"We got you something for your trip to Ohio." She plopped back where she had been sitting. "I hope I can come visit you."

"Me too," I said sitting on a lawn chair, its plastic poking my skin. I picked up a stick and dug it into the dirt drawing a heart.

Althea handed me a brand new copy of, "*Are You There God? It's Me, Margaret*" plus a few pairs of socks and a basketball! "Thank you, Althea! I love them all." I threw down the stick and held everything in my lap.

Althea said, "That's the game ball, from us winning the championship last year." She started cackling so hard, she couldn't catch her breath! "That's from the game where you defended that girl. You put your hands up, and she tripped you. You slapped her so hard that my face hurt!" She laughed.

Althea slapped her leg laughing, "I'm sorry, but it was funny. For a minute, it looked like you fell asleep standing, then remembered you were in the middle of a game!"

Benetha said, "I felt so bad when Coach made you ride the bench for two games. That didn't stop anything, you just yelled at us aggressively from the sidelines." I couldn't find a thread of humor in the conversation, but I smiled and faked a few chuckles as they cackled.

Looking around at my friends, I felt a sadness I couldn't describe. Me, Althea, May, June, Debbie, Lynn, Maya, Joi,

Mona, Felicia, Gladys, and Nedra have been friends for years. From basketball to church and school, we've been together! "I'm going to miss ya'll." I held back tears.

I watched Daddy fiddle with his grill, that was his happy place. "Will I ever be able to find my happy place again?" I questioned.

Daddy bopped to the music and poked at the meat, moving it around like he was a master chef. "Joyce," he yelled. "The dogs are ready. You got the buns?"

"Be right out," Mama said. "Just finishing up the fried chicken and baked beans."

He hollered back, "You got potato salad, too?"

"Just like you like it, with a little smoked paprika sprinkled on top."

Daddy smiled. "My girl be looking out for me," he slapped hands with Uncle Walt.

A few minutes later, Mama came out of the house carrying my brother. Aunt Clementine held the potato salad, Aunt Enid had my cake, and Miss India carried the baked beans. Someone I didn't know held the buns for burgers and hotdogs. I watched the parade of women, admiring their beauty and poise.

"My baby," Daddy smiled at Mama, pulling her into a hug and giving her a love tap on the butt. I will always remember how he showed affection to her publicly. He wasn't ashamed of their love.

Holding Mama's waist, Daddy whistled, "Come on everybody, let's eat!"

We stood in a circle holding hands as daddy's friend, Uncle Jimmy, Lynne's dad, prayed over the meal. I listened to his heartfelt prayer for protection and family, but I was hungry, and he prayed so long I had to open my eyes. Some of the women in the circle were crying. Mama was leaning against Aunt Enid, who was crying.

Some of the men, Uncle Fred, Uncle Will, and Uncle Marv, looked somber. My friends were crying too, Althea wailed, as her mother held her close. When the prayer was finished, I quickly closed my eyes again. I knew Mama would fuss, if she saw I was peeking.

Daddy pointed to the table, and said, "Elders first." He looked at our neighbor, Ms. Ava. "I made a special sauce for you, Ms. Ava." He held up a cup and winked at her, "I know you like it hot." She gave him a high five.

"I'm going to miss you, and your beautiful family, Doug." She choked back tears. "Who will look after me when you're gone?"

Daddy waved his hand at his friends. "You see these men?" Ms. Ava nodded. "They have instructions to look out for you. You don't have to worry about your grass being cut, a window being washed, or even missing my sauce." He winked at her, pointed at Uncle Jimmy and said, "He's the only one I trust with my sauce recipe."

Uncle Jimmy raised his finger and said, "I gave him my word, Ms. Ava. Me, my wife, and our kids are going to look out for you."

"Aww thank you, baby." She smiled, poured sauce on her ribs, turned to the ladies behind her, and teased, "Don't ya'll touch my sauce now. This is for me!" Ms. Ava carried her plate to a table to enjoy her feast.

"Make your plates," Daddy directed the group. "I didn't stand over this hot grill making all this food for it to go to waste."

A few ladies made plates for their small children, others followed. Mama sat at a card table with Grayson, fanning her face. One of daddy's coworkers sat on a blanket under a tree with his family. He smacked his leg, "Oh baby, we're sitting on a red ant hill!" He jumped up and took his wife's plate. "We gotta move this blanket." She grabbed the kids by one arm and ran after him.

"Come on, fellas," Daddy rounded up the men. "Let's pack some more things in the truck, while the ladies eat." The men stepped back from the table, and followed Daddy into the house. Meanwhile, the women took seats by the grill, replacing where the men had been. They chatted between bites, continuing to talk about soap operas, or whatever it was, they were discussing inside of the house.

Even though my parents had turned my birthday party into a packing party, I knew everyone in our yard was there because they loved us. Our village was strong. There were so many people all around, and the music had everybody's head bobbing and legs tapping. There was joy all around.

My friends and I acted like we hadn't eaten in days. We all piled food on our plates, and it was funny to watch everybody scatter to their respective corners to eat. My friends and I returned on the side of the house to devour our pickings.

I felt happy to see people all over the place. We often had cookouts, but it felt different that day. "I love my parents so much," I said out loud.

"Mmm hmm," Althea agreed, stuffing baked beans in her mouth, "This food is so good."

"This is a good day for a birthday party," I smiled. "I can't wait to dance and play games later."

That feeling didn't last too long. A little boy almost tripped, as he ran through the backyard ripping all of the balloons down from the fence. Joi's little brother took a handful of my cake and smeared it all over his face. A lady I didn't recognize helped her little girl, make a plate with potato salad and a hotdog. She tried to pour yellow mustard on her hotdog but it was too heavy from the mustard so she dropped it. Mustard splashed all over her and she started screaming, "My hotdog!"

I watched ants line up and march toward their treasure and that disgusted me. The mother picked up a hotdog, put some mustard on it and led the crying child into the house.

After the men set up their assembly line and finished loading the truck, they came back, sweaty and famished. By that time, I had already eaten two burnt hotdogs topped with relish and potato salad. I had three ribs, and was going for more when Mama stopped me, "Save room for cake, Nitty," she reprimanded me.

My stomach was full, but I was hungry for something. I kept nibbling on anything I could find to fill the void. I watched as flies feasted on the plates in the garbage can. I knew I couldn't fit anything else in my belly, but I needed something, anything that would help me take my mind off of the move.

I thought about my cousin Elijah and how much I missed him, as I scanned the yard, looking at plates of uneaten food. "Why are they wasting Daddy's food?" I wondered as I watched flies land on mounds of beans and that disgusting mustard mess. Elijah had told me at the family reunion last year, "Hey Nitty. Never eat or drink anything a fly has landed on."

"Why?" I asked drinking my lime pop.

"Because it spits on it."

"Eww" I had said, spewing out my drink. "Why did you tell me that?"

"'Cause as your big cousin, I have to make sure you know what to watch out for. There are a lot of things in this world that can be harmful to you."

"Thanks Elijah." I tucked his weird fact of the day into my heart for safe keeping. Sitting there, I realized how much I missed him. "If Elijah were here," I thought. "He'd probably want to go play basketball and have Daddy run drills for him. "That boy loves to play basketball."

It felt like I was sitting in a sauna, sweat beads rolled down my cheeks, but no one else looked as miserable as I felt. "It's so hot out here," I complained.

Althea said, "Nitty, it's only 70 degrees. It's not that hot out here."

I wanted to be in my room rubbing ice on my face to cool down. "I'm burning up!" I said, trying to fan myself with a paper plate. It was thin and I didn't feel anything when I waved it across my face. I folded it the plate in half to make it heavier, but it didn't help. From the inside out, I was melting.

Me and the other kids moved from our location on the side of the house to the barbeque pit, where the adults had been sitting. Half empty beer bottles and red cups of wine were hidden under lawn chairs. I rolled the basketball under my feet and knocked over a little bit of wine in a red cup.

I watched the liquid soak into the ground and dry up, as I listened to the sounds of the party and tried to get myself to relax. Sitting in that sun, with its sweltering heat, not only was it melting the ice cream on my cake table, but it was slowly melting my resolve, too.

I opened my eyes in time to see the "hotdog girl" snatch one of my presents off of the gift table and run. Her mother dashed out of the kitchen and pulled it from her. That little girl threw a temper tantrum and started screaming at the top of her lungs. Her piercing screams lasted for about ten minutes! I didn't know that little girl, who her mama was, or why she was at my birthday party.

I put my hands under my thighs and crossed my legs to keep myself from running over to her and screaming, "I wish you would just shut up!"

"Wanna jump Double Dutch in the street?" One of the twins, May asked. "Me and June brought our ropes."

I didn't know how to talk about how I felt at that moment. I didn't want to double dutch. I didn't want to do anything but bury myself in a plate of food. My friends got up and ran to the front of the house. Me, I got up slowly, annoyed that I wouldn't see them again. I didn't feel like pretending, I just wanted my birthday to last forever.

I walked slowly as I followed May to the front of my house. June came back and grabbed my arm, skipping beside me as we walked.

We played "speed," (counting our steps to see who could get the most in two minutes). When it was my turn I kept calling out, "Faster!" They would twirl the ropes for a few seconds, and I would call out, "Faster," again. Since my feet were burning, I let them lead me, and I beat everybody out there with 235 steps before Mama called my name from the front door, "Yes Ma'am?" She broke my concentration and I got out.

I heard her say, "Watch your brother for me."

"Ugh!" I threw up my hands. "Can I just have one day for myself?"

Mama opened the door and Grayson ran out, into my arms holding bubbles. "Nitty!" He was so happy to see me that I couldn't be mad for too long. sat down on the sidewalk and played handsy with Grayson. His cute little smile and affection toward me softened my heart.

Joi came and sat with me. "Your little brother is so cute," she said playing peek-a-boo with him. "I help my mom take care of my brothers, too."

I held Grayson as he played with Joi for a while. When he got tired of that game, Grayson jumped from my arms and ran to the side of the house. I chased after him, making him run even more. "Grayson, come here," I said, now sitting on a lawn chair. I opened his bubbles, blowing some out.

"Bubbles" Grayson giggled, waving his hands trying to catch them. I loved hearing him laugh.

Althea came and sat with me. "You okay, friend?"

I shrugged. She nibbled on the last of the chips from the bowl. "Moving. . . on . . . Monday?" Her eyes started to water.

"Don't cry Althea." I said, patting her hand. "I can't take it."

Althea swallowed her emotions and kicked a dandelion. I scooped up chip crumbs and dropped them into my tilted mouth. A few tears leaked from my eyes. I wanted to melt into a puddle of tears at that moment, but I knew I had to keep my emotions in the vault. My meltdown couldn't happen right away, I had to wait until Daddy wasn't around, so he wouldn't see me crying. "Don't cry in public," he had told me when I got the technical foul, in the championship basketball game. "Never let them see you sweat."

Inside of my heart, I was so sad. When we went to church on Sundays, I would pray so hard that they would change their minds. I prayed that Mama would say she didn't want to move. I prayed that Daddy would say it was an April Fool's joke . . . But it wasn't. Watching Althea trying to hold back her emotions, I started to feel heat in my body again. In that moment, I knew that as a child, I had no say in Daddy's livelihood. Taking a job in Ohio and making his family move away is what he needed to do.

"Go with the flow." I told myself.

Chapter 20

Rolling and running.

People passed through my party all day long. There was a slew of more friends, family, and neighbors who came to see us off. My favorite basketball coach, Mr. Lewis, pulled up with his family in the car right before everyone went home. "I can't stay." He yelled out of his window.

"Get out of the car, man, and come speak to my family." Mr. Jackson parked his car. He and Daddy did their handshake and a few of their other fraternity brothers gathered around to greet him. I loved watching the way they slapped hands and patted each other on the back. It was a display of how much they cared about one another.

"I'm going to miss you, man," Mr. Jackson told Daddy. "You're an amazing coach, and the girls are going to miss you." He chuckled, "Well, everything except making them run laps!"

Daddy laughed, "That's one way to teach them discipline, right?"

Mr. Jackson said, "As long as it helps us win championships." They slapped hands again. "Where is Nitty? I want to see her before I go." Daddy pointed to the side of the house where I was watching them talk.

Mr. Jackson started walking over to me, "Happy Birthday Nitty!"

"Hi Coach." I stood and put Grayson on my hip. "Thank you for coming to my party."

"You know I had to come see my star player! I can't stay long, I have another picnic."

"Why don't you and your wife grab a bite to eat before you go?" Daddy asked, "We have plenty."

Mr. Jackson turned and looked at his wife in the car. Mrs. Jackson waved at me, I waved back. "No thanks. Her mother cooked, too." Coach looked at Daddy and said, "You know how that is." They chuckled.

Mr. Jackson took a wad of money out of his pocket and give me several dollars. "Happy Birthday, Nitty."

I took the cash from Coach Jackson and Daddy pinned it on my shirt alongside the rest of my birthday money. Daddy took Grayson, and Mr. Jackson gave me a hug. When he let go he asked, "Are you gonna keep playing ball?"

I shrugged my shoulders. Coach said, "Don't stop running, Nitty. Your feet are going to lead you somewhere."

"Where will my 'hot feet' take me?" I wondered.

As Daddy and Coach Jackson walked away, Coach said, "Let me get out of here, man, keep in touch." As Coach got in his car and sped down the street, the streetlights came on, signaling to me that it was getting late. It wasn't dark yet, but as the day turned to night, I could feel mosquitoes feasting on my ankles.

The task of the day was completed. The house was packed up, and I saw that Mama was more relaxed. The adults, seated around tables, played games and Mama finally cracked a smile playing dominos. She sat with a blanket wrapped around her shoulders, but I was still hot.

I looked away from Mama for a split second and out of nowhere I got hit on the shoulder with a water balloon! The cool water felt good as it splashed on my body, but I didn't know who had thrown it!

I looked up, Daddy was laughing maniacally, and my friends had balloons! Daddy handed me some balloons! Wide-eyed, I chased him, breathing hard and laughing. My friends and I splashed each other with balloons, it lightened my mood.

All of a sudden, Daddy stopped laughing and spoke in slow motion . . . , "Oh shit!" He dropped his water balloons and darted off towards the front of the house. "Help! The truck is slipping." Several men, from all over the yard, looked up and scrambled after Daddy.

Running behind them, I took off too. I don't know what I thought I was going to do, but I jumped out of my chair and started running like I had the strength to move the truck.

"Nitty! What do you think you can do with your little self?" Mama yelled after me. She stood up, bumping the card table where she was sitting. "Get back here, girl!" Mama turned to Aunt Enid, "Is this a sign that we're not supposed to move?"

"I don't think so, Sissy," she shrugged.

I heard Mama calling after me, but I couldn't stop myself from running. All my pent-up emotion from the day had seized me, and I had to follow its lead. I ran down the block and passed the truck! Every step against the concrete relieved the stress my body was trying to absorb.

"Nitty! Where are you going?" I heard Mama calling after me, "Nitty!"

The commotion of people congregating and calling instructions rang in my ears. "Catch it!" Somebody called out.

"What do you think I'm trying to do?" A man answered.

"Jesus help us," somebody prayed behind me.

"Did he forget to put the parking brake on?" Another person asked.

"Stop talking and help me catch it, old man," Daddy said. I heard their feet on the pavement. As the truck rolled, the men were running as fast as they could. Hats were flying, pants were sliding down, and those middle-aged men were all sweating profusely, trying to be superheroes. None of them were strong enough to stop a moving truck of heavy furniture!

I heard the voices of my friends, along with some adults, calling my name. Still, I didn't look back or miss my stride. "That girl needs to go to the Olympics!" Somebody whistled, "She is booking."

I felt free as I ran with the wind against my face. I breathed the way Daddy taught me to, and I swung my arms with intention. The street light shone a spotlight on the ground, highlighting my ordered steps. I was in the zone.

It was Aunt Enid's call that captured my attention. "Dollface," she said calmly. "Cool your jets and come on back home." I took a deep breath and cut across a corner, taking a shortcut home through a field of dandelions. I passed Daddy and Uncle Fred bickering, as they ran beside the rolling truck.

"How did you let this happen?" Daddy huffed through his breath.

"I don't know what happened, Doug!"

"You were the last one out here, Fred."

"Thankfully, you live on a short street, the truck didn't get too far." Uncle Walt huffed.

I focused my attention on Mama and Aunt Enid, they were standing in the middle of the street, with their arms outstretched, waiting for me. I ran hard into Mama's arms, like she was the finish line. I closed my eyes as she wrapped her arms around me. "I got you, baby," she whispered in my ear. Mama rocked me and the smell of her spearmint gum made me appreciate I was home. She rubbed my back, and said, "It's going to be alright."

Mama always told me to hug until the other person lets go. "That's how you know they got what they needed," she had said. In that moment, I held on to her for dear life—clinging to what I knew, gathering what I needed. Mama held me until I let her go. With my head on Mama's chest, I listened as she and Aunt Enid hummed, "Amazing Grace" over me.

When I regained my composure, Mama and Aunt Enid stood on either side of me holding my hands. We watched the men scramble to secure the truck. I busted out laughing when Daddy's friend laid down in the middle of the street with his arms and legs stretched out. "I can't run no more," he gasped.

I knew what was at stake if they couldn't stop the truck, but at that moment, I couldn't help but laugh. Everybody started to see the humor of the situation.

"This is as funny as it is scary," Ms. Clementine said, between chuckles. "Get on up, Leroy!" She giggled at her husband bent over trying to catch his breath.

The truck jolted to a stop, at the end of the street where the curb was broken and cracked. It bumped against the curb giving Uncle Fred the ability to climb inside and put it in park. Somebody shouted, "I can't believe he climbed in there like that. He's so agile!"

"Thank God nobody got hurt!" Ms. Clementine said waving her hands in praise.

"I know that's right," Ms. India agreed. "That is something I'll never forget."

Ms. Clementine, in her booming voice said, "Now who's ready for some ice cream and cake?"

Hands went up and most of us said, "I am!"

Ms. Clementine led the way to the back yard. We followed her like she was the Pied Piper.

I heard Daddy fussing, "We need to secure the parking brake this time, plus find branches to brace the tires."

Uncle Fred said, 'Well thank God your brother-in-law is coming to drive this truck to Ohio for you."

"Yeah," Daddy grunted.

I looked at Mama with my eyes as big as saucers. "Did he say that Uncle LJ is coming?"

"Surprise!" she grinned. "Your Uncle LJ will be here in the morning to help us drive the truck."

I was starting to feel joy again.

Chapter 21

Becoming strong.

When Daddy and the fellas were finished fiddling with the truck, they came back to the backyard looking like they'd just worked all day chopping wood. Mama gave Daddy a glass of water and asked, "Doug, what've we gotten ourselves into?"

He looked at her and shook his head, "Baby, I don't know, but something big is about to happen for us, I feel it."

"I hope so," Mama said sitting next to him.

Daddy downed his water, stood up and said, "Is this where the party is?" He pulled me up from the chair I was sitting in, and we had a dance battle right there in front of everyone. "Come on, Enid," Daddy gestured toward her, "Show us what you got." Aunt Enid joined us, and everybody moved to the dance floor to cut a rug with me!

Ms. Clementine carried my cake outside and lit the candles. I stood still as the group sang the birthday song to me, clapping and swaying. Ms. Clementine put a plastic crown on my head that read, "Birthday Girl." When she put that crown on me, it felt tight, but I wore it with pride, soaking in the love directed towards me. I stood tall, ignoring the heat in my body and the pain in my head.

It was so hot to me, but the cool air of the night had everyone else putting on jackets and cuddling under blankets. I didn't know what thirteen was going to bring, but I was ready for it! I ate a piece of cake topped with cool ice cream and let the comfort of my treat hug me from the inside.

I wanted to snatch the crown off of my head, but I stood there and took the pain. I wanted the attention more than I wanted to feel comfortable. Keeping the crown on, I locked myself into a behavior where attending to my needs became second priority. That came back to bite me later in life.

We spent the rest of the night dancing to Daddy's music, singing at the top of our lungs and enjoying each other's company. At the end of my party, when everyone started to leave, I wasn't feeling well at all, but I didn't tell Mama I felt sick. The feeling of wearing that crown became a part of me. Whenever I felt overwhelmed or anxious, I felt it tighten.

As soon as I could, I snatched that crown off and tossed it in the trash, then I crawled into bed, covering my face with the blanket. I was asleep almost immediately. Aunt Enid and I didn't have our girl talk.

When I woke up, my headache was gone, but the smell of bacon and eggs almost made me gag. I didn't even notice that only thing left in my room was my bed. My dresser had been moved, and there was nothing hanging on my walls.

It was real . . . we were moving.

Chapter 22

Car sick.

Sometimes when I ride long distances, I feel the heartache of my thirteen-year-old self when we moved from Texas. Riding in the back of Daddy's car, cramped together for four long days wasn't pleasant. Sleeping was the only way I could stop myself from kicking and screaming. That, and eating Mama's cold food wrapped in foil. I ate so much that I stopped eating chicken and ribs. I played with the foil so much that my hands were scratched up.

I stared outside as we sped past places I'd never heard of, or cared to know about, anticipating a future I couldn't foresee. Moving away from my friends definitely wasn't the birthday present I wanted. I cried for three of the four days that we drove across the country. I didn't have any words to describe what I was feeling about leaving everything I had ever known and mostly everyone I had ever loved.

My Uncle LJ and his wife, Aunt Naomi, followed us in the rented moving truck. Daddy sang love songs at the top of his lungs, and Mama occasionally checked on me through the passenger sun visor mirror., "You okay, baby?" She'd ask every few hours.

I was so hot, sweating and miserable. I propped my pillow against the car door and curled up as tightly as I could. Between the nausea from the curvy roads, I didn't know if I was coming or going. There was nothing to do in that car. I tried to read my book, "*Are you There God? It's Me Margaret,*" but I couldn't get past the first page. Althea and I wanted to read it together.

Mama had packed coloring books and crayons for me, but I didn't feel creative at all.

When the adults got tired of driving, we slept in a hotel. Me, and Aunt Enid in one bed, Mama, Daddy and Grayson in the other. Uncle LJ and Aunt Naomi had their own room.

We arrived in Dayton, Ohio, on Valentine's Day. "Wake up everybody." Daddy tapped me from the front seat. "We finally made it!" I wiped sleep from my eyes and followed Daddy's finger to the house. When he finally pulled up to the yellow house and clicked the gear shift into park, the butterflies in my stomach wouldn't be still.

Aunt Enid shook my leg. "We're here, Dollface. Look at your new house!"

"I see it, Auntie," I whispered, wiping sleep out of my eyes. I gulped down the truth. "It's nice."

Daddy clapped his hands. "We finally made it."

I looked away when he kissed Mama. "I was worried, Doug, but I like the house. I'm so proud of you, honey!" She slid her arm through the crack between the door and patted my leg, "Wake up Nitty, we're here."

"I see it, Mama." I knew not to say anything negative, but I thought, "Who makes a house with one window in the front?" Wind blew across the car so harshly it shook us like a roller coaster.

I exhaled on the window and my breath froze. I shivered and zipped up my coat. I'd never seen snow or felt that kind of cold.

Uncle LJ knocked on Daddy's window and said, Come on man, can we get inside? It's cold out here." He shivered.

"Ya'll ready?" Daddy switched the ignition to stop the engine of his beloved black 1980 Cadillac Brougham and then turned to face Mama. Aunt Enid handed him a blanket and

Daddy tossed it over my brother's head. He flung open his door and said, "The hawk is out tonight!"

He looked back at me, still frozen in my seat. "Come on, Anita, let's get out of this cold!"

Mama walked slowly across the ice, as she carried Grayson. I don't know how she could see where she was going with that scratchy wool over her face, but she made it to the porch just fine.

There was a big red bow on the front door. Daddy fumbled with the keys, and I was surprised to see my NiNi open the door. "Surprise, Joyce,!" Daddy said. Mama didn't look too happy to see my grandmother.

NiNi took Grayson from Mama and disappeared into the house, Mama, Uncle LJ and Aunt Naomi followed her.

Aunt Enid placed her hand on my leg and said, "You ready?" I nodded. She opened her door, ran across the street and to the house. "Come on, Nitty," she motioned for me.

I scrambled to open the car door, a gust of wind grabbed me by the hood, slammed my door, and threw me into the street. Every time I tried to tiptoe back up the hill where Daddy was waiting on the porch, I slid right back down.

Just when I thought I had the hang of walking in the snow, I heard a loud bang and turned around to look. I slipped on some ice and slid down the street on my back. I heard the laughter of a male, but I didn't know where it came from, later, I learned it was someone from the Dinkins family!

I opened my eyes to see a pink mitten reaching out for me. "Are you okay?" I hadn't been around a lot of white people in Texas. Seeing her startled me, but I reached for her hand, and the girl helped me stand. "Hi! I'm Sandy."

"Hi," I said, wobbling as I stood. "My name is Anita, but everyone calls me Nitty."

"Hi Nitty." She pointed to her house across the street, one house over to the right of ours. "I live in that house right there with my Dad, and Great Aunt. We have two dogs and three fish. I'm adopted."

"Ohh," I responded, wondering why she felt the need to tell me all that information. Sandy looped her arm through my arm and led me back to my house. "Tilt your body sideways and put your weight on your toes. That's how you walk in the snow."

I saw people in a house watching us through the window. I could tell they were laughing, and I wanted to run back to Mama and Daddy, but I was focused on getting into our house. My back was already hurting from the fall earlier. When we passed the house Sandy whispered, "Stay away from that house, they're all bad news. My auntie calls them fire starters."

"They start fires?"

"Nooooo," Sandy giggled, "They cause problems for people in the neighborhood."

That tickled me, "Where I come from, they'd be called nosy!" Sandy and I shared a laugh as we walked up the steps to my house.

She greeted Daddy, "Hi, sir," she stretched out her hand. "I'm Sandy, and I live across the street."

"Hi Sandy," Daddy said, shaking her hand. "What are you doing up this late? Who are your people?"

"My Daddy is Mr. Cornwallis Jones. He's a city councilman, my mom used to work for him and when she died he took me in."

"Oh really?" Daddy lifted his brows. "Tell Mr. Cornwallis Jones that his old friend Doug Turner just moved back to town!"

"You know her father?" I looked at Daddy.

He smiled at me, "Baby, I grew up in this town, and I know lots of people here! I know you didn't want to move, but it looks like you're gonna be alright."

Sandy was cheesing, "Can I give you both a hug?" Daddy opened his arms for me and Sandy, and we walked into his embrace. As sad as I was to be living on Cotton Street Commons, Sandy was equally as happy. She said, "God has sent me a new friend. I've been so lonely."

"Go on home and get in bed, girl. You can come over tomorrow."

Sandy skipped across the street. I watched as she closed the door and turned off the porch light. Since that day she's always been the yin to my yang, and so far, nothing has been able to upset that balance.

Little did I know how vindictive the Dinkins (fire starter family) would be over the next few years. They tried to tear up my family, Sandy's family, and everyone else's who didn't conform to their matriarch's demands and commands. It was like living in one of those soap operas that Mama used to watch every day.

We weren't assimilating. My parents stood ten toes down in the face of Ms. Dinkins and her meddling. When she died, her fire-starting family picked up the gasoline and matches, but they couldn't ignite anything. It was determined, no family could dictate who lived here, how they lived, or why they stayed, regardless!

Daddy knew his history and he was confident. Ms. Dinkins and her family learned, the hard way, not to mess with us when Daddy started speaking.

Chapter 23

So much change.

Moving to Ohio changed my family, but not in a good way. We all became like zombies, seemingly stripped of our joy. After a few months of living there, Mama became surly without explanation. She was never mean to me, but she had a sharp tongue with Daddy. She spent the first few weeks on the phone talking to her siblings or watching soap operas.

I can't really explain it, but we were different. I was thankful Mama put me in the same class as Sandy, that way we could walk to school together; otherwise, being alone might have consumed me.

Sandy and I left for school early in the morning, sometimes when it was still dark, yet Mama always made sure we had a hot breakfast before we left.

Daddy was hardly home, he was working so much trying to save money. "We're going to open a barbeque joint," he told Mama, one day over dinner. "I don't want to work for the man anymore." He said making air quotes and dropping his fork on the plate.

"Doug, what about that promotion at work?"

"I've been working there for almost ten years, and I keep getting passed up for the promotion."

Mama put her hand over Daddy's and said, "I'm so sorry, Baby."

"There ain't nothing to be sorry for. I'm a hustler, or shall I say, an Entre-po-negro. I have dreams and goals for us."

"I have dreams too, Doug." Mama pulled her hand back. "I feel like I'm losing myself here." She slid her chair back from the table, and said, "I never wanted to move back here to Ohio. You got me out here working all these odd jobs to help us make ends meet. You know I wanted to stay close to home and have a flexible schedule for our kids." Mama looked at me.

I watched her stand up and storm into the kitchen with her plate. She came back holding her head, "I'm going to lay down, I feel foggy."

"Baby," Daddy called after her. "It won't always be this way. Just be patient with me."

Mama huffed. "I've been patient with you, honey, but I'm not used to living like this. I don't see you, and I need a break from the kids sometimes."

I kept my eyes and head down, finishing my food. "May I be excused from the table?" I asked.

"Yes, baby," Mama said. "Take your brother with you." I lifted Grayson out of his chair and led him by the hand out of the room.

"Just a few more weeks, Baby." I heard Daddy say. "Sit and let's talk about this." Mama sat, scraping her chair against the floor. "I'm doing everything I can, selling rib dinners and telling people about your sewing services."

"I don't have time to sew right now, Doug. I hardly have time for myself." She looked at me, "I never wanted Nitty to be a Latchkey kid."

"Nitty," Daddy said, "Go on up to your room."

My feet started to burn and I wanted to hit the pavement.

I heard Mama say, "Mother thinks you lack motivation. The other day she said, 'Doug wouldn't take a job if it was in in a pie factory tasting pies.' I don't know how to get her to back off about it."

Daddy laughed, "Give me some time, Joyce. I'll give Mother-In-Love something to brag about."

I closed my door and ran in place.

Chapter 24

Fire starters.

Daddy was always walking the perimeter of our house. He would stand by windows to listen, watch, and observe. One night he came into my bedroom and said, "Keep your curtains closed. I think Ms. Dinkins has her tribe of grandsons watching our house." That scared me, but there was no way I could reconfigure my furniture to get my bed away from the window.

So, let me tell you about Ms. Dinkins. She was an elderly woman who had lived on Cotton Commons Street for forty years. Her house, a white duplex, was six doors down from ours. Cotton Commons was probably a few thousand dollars over the poverty line in the Eighties. Ms. Dinkins and her husband were one of the first families to move into the neighborhood.

Ms. Dinkins walked up and down the street like she owned it. She was petty, and when she did something crazy our neighbors took notice. One time she watered a neighbor's grass, because it was too brown, for her. She remained there for so long, hosing someone else's lawn, that she drowned, the owner, Ms. Harper's garden.

Another time her grandson shoveled her car out of the snow, he dumped the excess snow in front of another neighbor's car, blocking him in. He asked Daddy to help him shovel, so he wouldn't be late for work.

Everyone tolerated and respected her, but she respected nobody. I think when her husband died, she just stopped caring about people other than herself. When we moved in, Daddy became the target of her ire.

I often wondered if Ms. Dinkins took after-church naps to recover from church or to gain energy to unleash her anger on Daddy about the abandoned field next to our house. She would bang on our door every Sunday, whether it was raining, snowing, or sunny, at 4:00 p.m. like clockwork. We knew it was her, because she didn't knock with her knuckles. She banged like her hand was a hammer, and our front door was an unsuspecting nail.

No matter who opened the door, she'd be standing on our porch wearing a flowery snap-up Moo-Moo that peeked from under her robe, with her hands on her hips, ready to start an argument.

Her fuzzy blue bathrobe would be tied to the side, pink rollers under a red bandana, and she'd be in her torn and dirty house slippers that exposed her ashy feet, but she didn't care. I never understood how she felt comfortable walking down the street in night clothes. Daddy always said, "We represent the family when we go outside. Always look your best." I guess the Dinkins name didn't mean anything to her.

Ms. Dinkins would bang on the door, and if Mama answered she'd say, "Tell your husband to call the city tomorrow." She'd slither her way home without looking back.

If I answered she'd ask, "Is your Daddy home?" I'd shake my head no, and she'd squawk at me, "Tell him to cut that grass in that field, or I'm calling the city on him. I don't want to see them dandelions." She'd make a two-point turn and walk away waving her hands as if she had just passed a law.

For a few months, Daddy was kind to her. When we heard the knock, we'd all chuckle, and he'd say, "Here we go," as he walked to the door. Daddy would always stay calm, no matter how loud or disrespectful she was to him. She would rebuke him like it was his fault the house was torn down and an empty lot remained. "You live next door to that lot, it's your responsibility to keep it mowed."

After a while, their interactions became more intense. Ms. Dinkins' talk changed to entitlement, and she'd say things like, "I worked hard to save money to buy my property and my land. I fully intended to keep my house in the family for generations, but you are bringing the property value down."

"I don't own that lot, Ms. Dinkins," he'd retort. "You can call them yourself, or perhaps, get one of your grandsons to cut it for you."

She'd raise her voice, "You live here, you have to take care of it!"

"That lot was vacant before I moved my family here. Who took care of it before I came?" Daddy would say, "Goodbye, Ms. Dinkins." Then he'd gently close the door and walk away.

After about six months of them going back and forth, Ms. Dinkins took matters into her own hands. What she did changed everything for everybody on the street. She started a war!

One Sunday I was in my room listening to the radio. I had my feet up on the wall and was singing at the top of my lungs, when I heard the infamous knock on the door. Ms. Dinkins' squeaky voice cracked up our steps and into my room, which was up the stairs from the front door. "They don't care about what happens over here," she grumbled.

"Hello to you too, Ms. Dinkins."

I heard the front door slam, and Daddy shouted, "Did you cut my bushes!?" I sat up straight in my bed, but I knew not to go downstairs. Mommy ran past my room and trotted down the steps.

"Ms. Dinkins!" Daddy said, "Those are my bushes on my property. You had no right to touch them!"

I slipped off of my bed and crawled over to the doorway where I could hear better.

Mama's voice was soft, "Doug, come inside."

"She done cut my damn bushes, Joyce! Nobody told her she could cut my bushes!"

"I couldn't see the field," Ms. Dinkins responded.

"You live six houses down, Daddy yelled! Why do you need to see the field next to my house?"

Ms. Dinkins screamed, "Your bush was too high."

"Who are you, the tree police? Go home, Ms. Dinkins. I don't want to disrespect you, but you're really pushing my buttons."

"Now you listen here!" Ms. Dinkins was loud and indignant. "I've been living on this street longer than you've been alive, young man."

"And?"

"The likes of your kind don't lay down roots anywhere, you don't know anything about stability!"

"Oh really?" Daddy laughed incredulously. "You have overstayed your welcome. Leave my property, now. You're not welcome here."

"I'll leave when I good and well please!" I heard Ms. Dinkins say. "We need to get this straight. You and your ghetto ways are wracking my nerves." She added.

Mama said, "Did she just call us ghetto?"

Daddy shushed Mama. "What do you mean by that?"

Ms. Dinkins continued, "I don't want to hear your loud music or see you and your friends on the porch drinking beer. When it gets dark, you get drunk and cuss each other out. We live in a respectable neighborhood and that is ghetto."

Daddy laughed. "I'm a grown man and I pay the bills in this house. Get out of here with that. Nobody around here is getting drunk. We don't say anything about them boys you got living in your house who litter and harass our kids. Worry about your own household."

I could hear more voices in the yard besides Mama's, Daddy's and Ms. Dinkins'. My heart started to race because I couldn't see what was happening, and it was getting loud. "You're out of line, Ms. Dinkins!" I heard Sandy's dad say. Mama was humming ,and I knew she was getting upset too.

There was a voice I didn't recognize, "I see your grandchildren dumping bags of trash in people's yards and hiding drug paraphernalia. When the police come on our street, they're after your grandkids, not our kids!"

Ms. Dinkins rebutted, "You don't do anything but stand around smoking cigarettes and tinkering with your raggedy car. Don't talk to me."

"Nitty," Mama called my name.

I stood attentive at the top of the steps. "Sandy is here. I want ya'll to go into the basement and close the door." I guess Mama didn't want us to hear what was going on outside. I only went to the basement to do my laundry. It was Daddy's space.

Sandy carried Grayson downstairs. She didn't speak until I closed the door behind us. "It's crazy out there, Nitty."

"What happened?"

"Ms. Dinkins cut the tree in front of the house." She sucked her teeth. "Your Daddy is so mad."

I plopped on the couch with my legs crossed. "How did she cut it?"

Grayson laid his head on Sandy's chest and started falling asleep. "She cut it, cut it!"

"Are you serious, Sandy?"

"You know how tall it was, right?" I nodded. "She chopped it so low," she leaned into me and put her hand parallel to my calf. "Now, the tree is here."

"Daddy planted all those trees. I can't believe she did that." I watched Sandy lean back slowly.

"Most of the neighbors are outside. They're all upset, because you know how Ms. Dinkins is!"

"I'm scared, San."

Sandy rubbed Grayson's back. "No need to worry, God's got us, and karma will get Ms. Dinkins!"

About an hour later, the adults joined us in the basement. Mama was still humming, and Daddy just kept pacing. Sandy's Dad was scratching notes on a pad.

Daddy said, "I can't believe that lady had the nerve to cut my bushes. Talking about, 'Don't you disrespect me.' Ugh! She disrespected me!"

"Amazing…" Mama started singing and it woke up Grayson. Everyone got quiet. "It's going to be okay, everybody," Mama said, after she finished her song, "We can't let the antics of one disgruntled woman make us lose our character."

She opened her eyes and Grayson reached for her. "Girls," Mama said, taking the baby into her arms. "Go up to Nitty's room for a while. We need adult time."

In my room, Sandy and I looked at magazines and listened to music. "I can't wait till this summer, Nitty," she said holding up a magazine. "We're going swimming, playing kickball, and going to festivals. We gotta have fun before freshman year!"

"I know, I can't wait!"

What neither Sandy nor I knew was that when Ms. Dinkins went home, she twisted the story and made herself the victim.

Her family plotted for weeks to retaliate against our families, using me and Sandy as bait! It was going to be a long summer.

Chapter 25

Ready for a fight.

A couple of days before summer break, Sandy and I got off the school bus and started walking to my house. I don't even remember what we were talking about, but we were laughing and chatting. We passed one of the abandoned houses on our street and out of nowhere, we started getting pelted with rocks!

"Ow!" Sandy said.

"Oh shoot!" I crouched down. "I think somebody is throwing rocks at us."

"Yeah!" Sandy agreed. I just got hit in the chest.

"Come on, Sandy. We gotta run!" I insisted, letting my burning feet take over. Immediately, my burning feet took over! I blasted off like a rocket towards my house and didn't look back. It reminded me of when I ran after the moving truck in Texas, I ran off without thinking.

I didn't realize Sandy wasn't behind me, until I was halfway down the street, two houses from home. I heard her shouting, "Nitty!" I turned around just in time to see Sandy falling. She tripped over her shoelace and toppled over, shoulders weighted from her book bag. "Nitty, help me!"

Several of Ms. Dinkins' grandsons and their friends were waiting to ambush us! The boys attacked Sandy, jumping on top of her, calling her out of her name, punching, and kicking her. I ran back as fast as I could. She was shrieking and the whole scene chaotic.

"Get off of her!" I said, swinging my arms wildly.

One boy grabbed me and put me in a headlock. He punched me in the stomach incessantly, and pulled my hair. I was doing my best to fight back, but he was much stronger. Although the crown on my head was starting to get tight, I didn't let him take me to the ground.

Out of the corner of my eye, I saw another group of boys running towards us. "Oh no," I thought, "There're more of them?"

One of the new boys said, "Let her go!" The bully squeezed my neck and released his grip, I landed, gagging on my knees. I gasped for air, as I tried to gather myself. My voice was hoarse, "Sandy, are you okay?" I whispered. She didn't answer. "Sandy?"

I could hear her crying, and a boy said, "You are punks for hitting on girls. Who does that?" I wiped my eyes and stood up, slowly. I had never seen the boys before, but they had on basketball jerseys from a neighborhood school.

Ms. Dinkins' oldest grandson taunted the boy, "What are you going to do about it?"

One of the boys squared up, planted his feet in a Muhammed Ali stance and said, "I can show you who I am better than I can tell you." He looked Ms. Dinkins' grandson in the eye and said, "My mama doesn't like when I fight, but this is justified. You deserve an ass whipping for what you did. Now step back and let her through."

The bully didn't back down. He said, "Ain't nobody scared of you."

The boy's twin said, "Harold, you might need to let them know who you are. Harold stayed focused and locked in his position. The boys stepped aside, and I inched my way through the crowd. I knelt down and watched Sandy's body rock from her silent sobs. She was bloody, her face was puffy and her hair was dirty. I brushed the leaves off of her, tied her shoe and helped her stand up. "Let's go home, San."

I picked up Sandy's backpack and put my arm around my best friend. As we started to walk away, I looked the bully in the eye, wrinkled my nose and gritted my teeth, "I. Hate. You. So. Much." I rolled my eyes, continuing, "You, your cousins, your mama, and your dumb Grandma, too."

"Shut up, welfare queen!" He retorted. "I think the big brown WIC truck is bringing your powdered milk, cheese, and cereal tomorrow. Doesn't it come every Wednesday?" He and his friends laughed. "We watch you carry those heavy boxes in the house."

I was pissed. "What did you just say to me? My parents work hard, and they're not ashamed of asking for help." I pointed at him, "You need to go to the loony bin because you need help!"

The boy who had squared up with the Dinkins' put his hand on my shoulder. I instantly felt calm, and the burning sensation in my feet stopped. He spoke softly over my shoulder, "I'm Harold. Don't waste your energy on hate." I turned to look at him, I saw tenderness in his eyes. "And" he winked, "I know your parents taught you to respect your elders. Dude ain't going anywhere in this life. I heard he dropped out of school because he couldn't pass fourth grade. Don't get distracted."

"But…"

Harold interrupted me, "This dude isn't worth your hate. But" Harold raised his fists in the air. "If he bothers you again, come find me, and I'll handle it." I felt protected when he moved to stand between me and Sandy. With his shea butter moisturized hands, he grabbed both of our hands and held them. "Take your little friends and bounce, dude."

One of Harold's friends started bouncing a basketball. Ms. Dinkins' grandson sucked his teeth, "Man this is dumb. Come on, let's go to my house and watch the tube."

Harold's teammates stood like soldiers in front of us as they walked away. Harold's twin, asked, "You good, bro?"

"Yeah. Ain't no thang, Harem. You can go home. I'll be right there."

Harem protested, "I'm staying with you, bro. I want to be here in case they come back."

"They know what's up. Dude always got a bunch of little kids following him around. He's seventeen, playing with ten and twelve-year-olds. I'm not threatened by him. If he doesn't change his ways, he'll fall by the wayside by suicide, drugs, gangs, or jail, but I pray that doesn't happen."

Sandy started crying again. "He's always bothering me. They've been picking on me for years." She sniffled, "He's been throwing rocks at my window every night since Ms. Dinkins cut down the tree."

"Someone has been throwing rocks at my window, too." I said. "There was a dead bird on my windowsill. He must have used a ladder to put it up there."

I could see fire in the eyes of one of the basketball players, "Ugh, he is atrocious. I'ma beat his . . ."

Harold put up his hand and shook his head. "We're not going there, Reg." Reg dribbled his basketball with fury. I wanted him to pass me the ball so I could shoot it like a three-pointer and swish it against Ms. Dinkin's grandson's head. My feet started burning again.

Sandy said, "Nitty, we need to tell our parents."

"Nitty?" Harold laughed.

"People close to me call me that."

"Why they call you that?"

"Long story."

"Can I call you Nitty?"

"Maybe one day." I directed my attention back to Sandy, "I think Daddy will break his arms or something."

Harold took a deep breath. "You have to tell your Dad to make him stop. Let your father handle it. I will go with you to tell Coach Turner."

"Wait," I looked at Harold suspiciously, "You know my Daddy?"

The guys started laughing. Harold smiled, "He and my Daddy are fraternity brothers. We all know him." He blushed, "Plus, he told me to keep an eye on you."

"Why is Daddy going behind my back telling a cute boy to look out for me?" I thought frowning. "I'm glad he did, though. Good lookin', Daddy." I blushed.

"I'll walk you home." We started walking, all three of us holding hands. "You live in the yellow house, right?"

Sandy snickered and winked at me. "He's cute," she mouthed. To Harold she said, "You act like an old man. I like that. Thanks, Oldie."

"Is that my new nickname?"

Sandy smiled, "It's like the bat signal. When I call you Oldie, I need you to come to my rescue." They gave each other a high five. After that day, Sandy and I were always surrounded by Harold, Harem and their friends. Harold was always a fierce protector and a nurturer for me. He became my high school sweetheart and husband.

Chapter 26

Eating my anxiety.

Something changed in me after Sandy and I were attacked in the neighborhood. I started eating anything salty and crunchy that I could find. Even though Daddy called the police and the boys got in trouble, Sandy and I were pretty shaken up by the incident. We didn't talk about it for years, because it was so emotional for us.

One thing was true, though, the WIC truck made a delivery once a week, and it brought many treasures that helped me eat my anxiety away.

It was effortless for me to consume a whole pack of saltine crackers in one sitting. Where this habit came from, I can't remember, but I do know that I usually felt a sense of comfort eating my cares away.

The only thing I could cook when Mama wasn't home was grilled cheese sandwiches. I'd cut a huge chunk of cheese and slather some butter on the bread. The cheese would melt around the sides of the bread making a crunchy crust. It smelled so good, and I would be salivating cutting sandwiches for me and Sandy into triangles. I'd make us some red Kool-Aide and we'd be in heaven. She usually stayed for about an hour until her aunt got home. Mama came home around the same time with Grayson from the babysitter.

I always made a big bowl of tuna fish to keep in the fridge. That's how I could open the crackers and hide a stash in my room. I carried crackers with me everywhere I went. I'd put my feelings on reserve, only dealing with them while I was alone in my closet, singing and crunching on crackers. I ate crackers with anything that a cracker would hold: soup, potato salad and lunch meat.

Eating crackers was the ultimate reward for enduring long days of school, especially math, fourth period. Math was so boring, I hated it. I would probably have chosen to sweep a dirt road in 100-degree heat over listening to my teacher talk, sounding like a dull pencil sharpener.

I became a mindless eater, without even understanding what that was. My eating habits got so bad, I could eat an entire box in a day. Usually I was putting the entire cracker in my mouth and half chewing it. Incidentally, seeing Ms. Dinkins make me shake.

One time I ate some crackers while walking through the house and left noticeable crumbs in the kitchen, dining room, and living room. Daddy wasn't happy about the mess I'd made. "Where did these cracker crumbs come from?" He asked me with a puzzled look on his face.

"I don't know," I lied, looking away.

"Well, vacuum it up." He pointed to the chunks and inspected the rooms, "This carpet is a mess!" Daddy gave his directive and went upstairs, clueless to my addiction.

Later that summer though, I went to visit NiNi in Xenia for a week. She came into the bedroom while I was snacking and fussed at me. "Is this why you're getting so fat?" She said, snatching a sleeve of crackers from me. She stormed out of my room and called my mother. "Joyce, that girl ate a whole box of crackers! Did you know she eats like that?"

I wanted to say, "NiNi, I don't like your church, the kids are mean, and Sunday School is boring. I eat crackers because I didn't have friends here," but I didn't.

I waited for my punishment while she talked to Mama. I imagined her standing at the dining room counter rocking on both legs with the phone against her left ear and a pen in her right hand doodling. I could see my mom sitting on her bed, looking over at my dad, wondering how she would explain their child ate an entire box of crackers.

NiNi came back in my room after she hung up with Mama. "That's why you got crumbs in your hair!" It was like the light bulb turned on for her, "Take a bath and get ready for bed." I didn't get a punishment, but I gave up my cracker-eating habit cold-turkey after that.

Chapter 27

Pause.

Nothing significant really happened in high school. I won some awards, graduated as valedictorian of my class, and Sandy was Salutatorian. We worked hard in school, Daddy set the bar high for us. I ran track and went to every basketball game to support Harold and our friends, but I never felt the urge to play again.

When it was time to go to college, a whole group of us from the neighborhood went to Wilberforce, even Sandy. We started a marketing business in college, making flyers and doing resumes. We kept it going after we'd graduated from college. We married our high school sweethearts, Harold and Reggie, and Daddy died right before Sandy had her second son.

It broke us all, but his sudden death from a heart attack became a battery in our backs. We knew he had overworked trying to hustle to make his dreams come true. We knew we had to run hard after our dreams, "Make it happen," the lesson he taught us became a beacon of light, but we promised to live life, too, not making work our focus all the time. Although Harold and I tried getting pregnant early, my body kept rejecting the pregnancies. Nevertheless, I buried myself in my work, focused on my five-year plan and my goals with Daddy as my motivation.

***

When I'm in the zone, I need things a certain way. First, I need my door closed and my window opened for a free flow of fresh air and sunshine. Second, I need some good musical vibes like the sounds of Stevie Wonder, Angie Stone, Bobby Brown, Erykah Badu, or Fred Hammond. I can tie a song to every event, season and important moment of my life. When I can't speak the right words, there's always a song that can verbalize what I can't say.

As usual, I was jamming to one of my playlists while working that night. I had my candle burning, a cup of hot blueberry tea, and I was sitting in my favorite position, my right leg curled under me. I was working diligently to meet a hard deadline of midnight, November 12, 2022. This deadline was designated for our newest client, Dr. Carlene Brooks, a veterinarian. Sandy and I wanted to make sure we could meet her demands and get her project finished. Although she was kind and compassionate, Dr. Brooks was a difficult client.

Personally, I was tired of her double-minded decision making, her self-deprecating attitude, and her constant project changes Each always a contender in her continuous cycle of, "I don't like this; change it." to "Put it back, I like it that way."

We were helping her launch her mobile veterinarian business, which I thought was a good idea initially. After so much back and forth, I didn't want anything to do with dogs, cats, fish, gerbils, lizards, or any animals people adopted!

Something told me to tidy up my desk, which wasn't even cluttered. I was feeling off, but couldn't put my finger on what was happening to me. "Get up, Anita." I willed myself to move, but gravity and the spinning room held me down. My eyes were watering and my vision was blurry.

"I need to stand up, maybe that'll help," I exhaled. Next, I took everything off my desk and piled it on the floor. My head was spinning as Charlie Wilson crooned through my speakers. "Why does my head hurt like this?" I thought.

Feeling lightheaded and nauseous, I reached for my water and accidentally knocked it over. "What's going on with me?" I watched the water splash all over the floor and grabbed a paper towel from my beverage cart. I scrambled furiously to stop the fast-rolling water beads from reaching the extension cord under my desk.

I stooped under my desk to clean up the puddle and bumped my head against the beverage cart door. "UGH!" I screamed. "Why'd I leave it open?" My head progressed to throbbing, and surprisingly, a few drops of blood escaped from my nose.

I pressed my fingers into my temple, but it didn't help the tap dancing in my head. Scrambling to cover my blood droplets and organize the chaos on my floor, Sandy opened my office door.

"Oh," she stepped back, seeing me on the floor. "Are you okay?" I waved off her concern. "Why don't we go to my office for the meeting?"

"Nah Sis," I looked up at the clock and motioned for Sandy to set up the Zoom, "It's 5:50 and you know Dr. Brooks is going to be prompt."

"Don't worry about the mess." I changed the subject, "I was rearranging my desk. You know I like things a certain way." I don't know why I felt the need to lie to Sandy, I didn't want her to know I felt terrible.

"Are you feeling okay, Nitty? I can call Deb to come in for the meeting. She knows the plan for Dr. Brooks." Sandy crossed over the office and turned down the music.

I shook my head too fast and felt like rocks were banging against my skull! "I'm okay," I tapped my temple. "Deb left early today, remember?"

Sandy set up the Zoom, silently. As soon as Sandy entered the room, we saw Dr. Brooks in the waiting room. I noticed immediately that something looked different about her, she wasn't her usual chipper self.

"Good afternoon, Dr. Brooks, how are you today?" I greeted her with a smile.

"Hi sweetheart," Dr. Brooks responded, voice sounding heavy with grief.

"Dr. Brooks, you look so pretty today," Sandy complimented her as she adjusted the focus on the projector.

"Thank you, baby. I don't feel pretty. You see all this gray hair? I couldn't get to the hairdresser this week."

"There she goes with her self-deprecating tone," I thought. "I hope she doesn't go on a tangent today.

"Oh Dr. Brooks," Sandy sang, "My aunt used to say, "If you're having a bad hair day, put on some jewelry and a nice blouse—no one will notice your hair. You look beautiful, like I said. Let's get into your presentation."

For forty-five minutes, Sandy and I presented slides, audio files, photos and brand identity sheets to Dr. Brooks. She smiled, nodded her head, complimented us and applauded at the end. I high fived myself in my mind and thought, "We nailed this!"

"So what do you think Dr. Brooks?" Sandy switched between slides, "Which color palette do you choose, navy blue, teal, or black and white?" I beamed with pride because in my mind, this project, as hard as the past six months had been, was one of our team's best displays of effort and teamwork!

"Well," Dr. Brooks took a long pause. "I think we need to pause for a few weeks." Sandy and I looked at each other. My mouth got dry. I shook my head in confusion.

"Excuse me," Sandy cleared her throat, "I didn't hear you, what did you say, Dr. Brooks?"

"You two ladies and your team have been so kind, but I can't finish this project right now. I need to pause for a few weeks. I have a lot going on in my life right now." When she turned her camera back on, she was holding and petting her shih tzu, Buttercup.

"Um, give us one second, Dr. Brooks." Sandy turned the camera off, muted us, and flopped on the couch. "What are we going to do, Nitty?"

"I don't know, San," I shrugged, "I can hardly contain my anger, right now. My head is pounding like a bass drum and I can't hardly think. I want to go for a run."

"You can't run just yet. Let's hear what she has to say." She glanced at the duffle bag I keep under my desk, "after the call you can change your clothes, and hit the pavement." I gave Sandy a thumbs up and rubbed my eyes, forcing a smile as San turned the camera back on.

"Sorry Dr. Brooks," Sandy smiled as she turned the camera and audio back on. "We needed to discuss a few things on our side of the camera. What do you think your timeline will be?"

"I don't know when I'll be ready to proceed." Dr. Brooks turned her camera off for a few seconds. "I'm so sorry ladies," she said, shuffling across the microphone. "I just have so much going on in my life. I can't focus on anything but my precious dog right now." Hearing the emotion in her voice softened my heart, but I was hurt by her decision.

Before I knew it, I stood up and blurted out, "Oh my God! I can't believe this!" Immediately regretting that statement, I tried to retract it, but it was too late.

"Oh my!" Dr. Brooks said, literally clutching her pearls. "I'm sorry you feel that way, Anita."

"I'm sorry," I took a deep breath and blew it out hard. "It's not my intention to be disrespectful to you, Dr. Brooks. I must admit though, I feel gravely disappointed. We've all worked tirelessly to get you ready to launch your business." I stood, and moved in front of the camera while bouncing on my toes. I had to keep moving, my feet were burning as they often did when I felt anxious. "Is there anything we can do to change your mind, Dr. Brooks?"

As she often did, Dr. Brooks put her head down and said, "I'm so sorry you're disappointed in me."

"That's not it, Dr. Brooks" I protested, "I'm disappointed that we've come this far with only a few things to finalize, but you don't want to proceed. Our team has done everything you asked every step of the way, this feels like a slap in the face; I have to be honest. Half a year's work, six month worth, feels like a waste."

"Oh no, honey. I don't mean to make you feel like that. My baby is having surgery next week, and I can't think straight." I could hear the pain in her voice.

Sandy, the diplomatic one between the us two, took over the conversation., "What's going on Dr. Brooks? Are you dissatisfied with our services?" Behind her back, Sandy motioned for me to sit. I sat, swinging my right leg over my left. I'm glad San took over the conversation, I think the only thing remotely that would've made me feel better was to scream at the top of my lungs! I was so frustrated that all I could do was rub my forehead. "*I must go for a run*," I thought.

"Oh no, honey." Dr. Brooks broke my thought, "You all have done beautiful work. I just need a couple of months to get things together, everything is moving too fast for me."

I stared at Dr. Brooks trying not to show my emotions on my face. It took everything I had to maintain my humility and professionalism in that moment, as she spoke. I wanted to give her a mean mug plus a side-eye, but I chose to bite my tongue and hold my breath. I could feel the crown on my head tightening and my head began to hurt. I thought, *"We've spent half of 365 days working with this woman, and now she wants to quit? We pulled out all of the stops and made so many changes to appease her double mindedness, and now this!"*

I watched as Dr. Brooks was pressed for more information. Sandy was compassionate and kind, which is her strong suit, "Is there something going on we should know about Dr. Brooks?" Listening to San speak was soothing for me, but I was concerned.

"Buttercup is having leg surgery next week." She kissed and petted her dog. "He's my baby and I can't think straight right now."

"This is about her dog? Did she just say that she wants to stop her business launch because her dog is having surgery?" I held my notebook in front of my camera and screamed silently for a few seconds. I could see a smile spread across Sandy's face. I know she wanted to laugh, but she held her composure. Behind my notebook I pretended to take notes, but I was gritting my teeth!

Sandy cleared her throat and said, "As a dog mommy myself, I understand what you're going through completely." Sandy continued to console her, "My first dog, Lily, was only five months old when she had liver failure. We had to put her down several months after we got her."

"Oh no!" Dr. Brooks gasped. "I'm so sorry."

"Thank you." Sandy swallowed her laughter at me, displaying her sadness over losing Lily. I remembered how sad she was about losing her dog for weeks. I put my notebook down and watched Sandy in action. Watching her with Dr.

Brooks, I felt like I was transported into the lens of a movie. Sandy was standing with poise and leaning into the camera. Her voice was soft when she said, "How old is Buttercup, Dr. Brooks?"

"My baby is twelve."

"Aww, she's made it to such a good age." She clapped, "That's something to celebrate! We love you, Buttercup."

"What happened to Lily, Sandy?"

Sandy took a breath and said, "The breeder didn't tell us that she was sick when we adopted her. When she died," Sandy wiped a tear, "I was heartbroken and angry, to say the least. My sons loved her immensely, it was challenging for me, as a mother, to see them in so much pain and anguish. They brought her to us…" she gulped, "she was limp and crying."

"That is terrible, Sandy. You should've sued the pants off of them."

"I wanted to, but my husband wouldn't let me."

Dr. Brooks was asking so many thoughtful questions that I wrote on my notepad: "She's compassionate. Dr. Brooks really cares, and I like her." I looked up when she asked, "May I ask why your husband didn't want to sue the breeder?"

"He said it wasn't worth it to go through the trouble. We prayed about it and chose to leave them in God's hands; He will give them the consequence for their wrongdoing, whatever He deems is necessary. Suing them wasn't going to give us Lily back. For my husband and I, starting the Lily Care marketing push was our way of honoring Lily. We partially funded the $10,000 scholarship for you and nine other business owners. Anita and her husband funded the rest."

"Eureka!" Dr. Brooks exclaimed, "I see the connection now."

Sandy nodded, "You got it now Dr. Brooks?" She and Dr. Brooks laughed with the clarity of revelation. "We believe it is necessary to help animal parents start and sustain businesses for their pets because for so many pets are service animals or companions that keep hope relevant."

"That's part of the reason I wanted to join the program, you're both so caring. I knew that ElnaHue was the right place to bring my business."

I envied Sandy's patience and compassion with Dr. Brooks. I was starting to feel balanced again. I sat up straight on the couch and crossed my legs, giving both Dr. Brooks and San my undivided attention.

Dr. Brooks kissed Buttercup, "How did you handle it? How did you handle the grief?" I could see and feel the love emanating from Dr. Brooks. I studied her background and saw things I'd never noticed before: photos of her with her deceased husband and other family, fresh flowers, and smiles.

A beautiful African painting behind her intrigued me. It was a captivating, colorful image of a woman in a red dress carrying a basket. The setting was a dirt road . . . the crown on her head, silver, beaded, ornate, provided texture and commanded my attention. "I see your crown, Queen," I thought. "Hopefully, it isn't too tight."

I looked back at Sandy, "I dove myself into my work with Anita to help business owners like you. Helping entrepreneurs embody their purpose is important to me, I take it seriously. That's what we do here, at ElnaHue."

Dr. Brooks turned her attention toward me. She looked behind her at the painting. "Isn't she captivating?"

"Yes ma'am," I looked at Dr. Brooks and smiled. "The crown especially. I was just thinking about her journey, how she walks through the dust, going about her daily life, wearing a crown but her circumstances might be hell. No one would ever know."

"That's an interesting perspective, I've never thought about it that way. You are so insightful, Anita, you see the big picture, I appreciate that about you."

That was my que. I inhaled deeply before I spoke and I made sure to speak slowly and watch my words. "Are you sure you want to push back your launch, Dr. Brooks?"

"I do appreciate what you've done for me." Dr. Brooks sounded like she was about to cry. "I don't think I can do anything right now."

"Can you explain why? I truly don't understand. We have only a few small steps, photo approvals, color schemes, things like that." I continued my breath work, pressing through, trying to get to Dr. Brooks' reasoning.

"I just don't have time to do anything. I can't imagine my measly business doing the great things like you ladies are trying to show me." It was her lack of confidence that caused this barrier. I wanted to transport through the projector, into her office and shake her shoulders.

"I can't look at anything or think about anything but the doctor's instructions right now. After my late husband died twelve years ago, I got Buttercup because I needed a companion, and I can't bear another loss right now." It broke my heart when she started to cry. I understood Dr. Brooks, but the disappointment of her giving up on herself outweighed my sympathy for her.

Sandy started to turn red. She spoke steadily, almost as if she was blowing bubbles, "Dr. Brooks, help us understand what we could've done differently. Your business is going to do well. Adding the product line is next."

"Everything is so good," Dr. Brooks nodded.

"You scheduled the pop up shops and we've secured a venue for your Donuts with Buttercup event. You helped us collaborate with six nursing homes to sponsor the cost of service dogs for their residents." Sandy sighed. "The ball is already rolling, and it'll pick up momentum once you approve your photos and videos."

Sandy pointed to the brand stylesheets on the screen. "Dr. Brooks, which color scheme do you prefer? All you need to do is choose a color, everything else has already been approved, by you. Why stop the launch now? You're so close."

I was screaming inside. "*So many excuses!*" I thought. "Okay, Dr. Brooks," I exhaled, taking over the conversation, "Let us know when you're ready, we'll hold your files for up to six months."

"Are you upset with me?"

"Oh no!" I lied. "We understand that you don't want to continue right now, I just don't want to hold you if you have other things to do."

"Dr. Brooks," Sandy smiled, changing the tone. "We will be here when you are ready to finish the project. I hope Buttercup heals quickly."

"Thanks for understanding." Her phone started to ring, "I gotta go," she said eyeing the caller ID, "This is the vet calling." Dr. Brooks left the meeting without saying goodbye.

I lost the battle with the headache I'd been fighting earlier. It came back, tightened my crown, and stomped on my head with cowboy boots and sharp spurs.

Chapter 28

Something's wrong.

Speechless, I shook my head at Sandy. Dismantling the laptop from the projector, I said, "All she has to do is look at her branding photos, approve them, and we can launch. We've invested so much. I don't understand why she wants to quit."

I could see the confusion on San's face. "I don't know, Nitty. Maybe we'd stop everything if it were our husband, parents, or child."

"You know we wouldn't bring the whole train to a stop so close to the station. When you told Dr. Brooks that you dove into your work, that's what we do to work through our pain . . . she sits in hers. Why do you think she is always putting herself down? Somebody said something to her a long time ago, and she can't let it go."

"It's unfortunate. As disappointed as I am, I understand that what Dr. Brooks is displaying is the fear of success."

I sighed, "It's hard to see someone, as seasoned as Dr. Brooks, being so hard on herself." I stood up and danced on the ball of my feet.

"Feet burning, huh?" Sandy asked. I nodded and she continued talking, "Like your mom taught us, we have to give her a different level of patience because she is our elder. Her generation bent their backs to create a step ladder for us. Perhaps, she doesn't digest rejection well." San packed up the ring lights, "We'll be here when she's ready and her promotion will be awesome."

"Maybe, but one thing this whole situation confirmed for me," I waved my hands in a circle. "Is that we're cut from a different kind of cloth." I rubbed my forehead. "First off, we were raised to never waste anyone's time. Second, our parents wouldn't tolerate us speaking to ourselves the way she does. I get so confused watching elders put themselves down."

"Dr. Brooks is so amazing, I don't know why she can't see it in herself, a woman with two doctorates and two MBA's can't see her authentic greatness." Sandy zipped up the ring light bag, put it on the shelf and sat on the couch.

"Me either, girl," I flopped down on the plush rug, laid on my back, and put my feet up on the ottoman, the only thing I could do to keep my feet from burning. I closed my eyes and said, "When Dr. Brooks turned her camera back on and she was holding her beloved Buttercup, I knew she was up to something. Yet, I would've rationalized that she was about to put her project on pause." The burning sensation in my feet was incredibly intense.

I inhaled then exhaled slowly, but it wasn't really making a difference. "Yeah," I agreed. I can't imagine being seventy-five and putting myself down like that. It really breaks my heart." I felt myself calming down. "I really love Dr. Brooks, and I want her to be ready for personal transformation, but we can't force it on her." I could feel my heart thumping in my chest. I kept breathing and started to massage my scalp.

"Nitty!" Sandy called me with concern. "You okay? You don't look so good."

"I'm just trying to push back this headache. I don't get them often, but when I do, you already know what happens." I sat up and reached for my water bottle, but got dizzy, so I laid down and closed my eyes.

"Here," I could feel Sandy putting my water bottle into my hands. I took a few gulps, but for some reason, couldn't quench the thirst that was tickling the back of my throat.

Unaware of the sun storm brewing in my head, Sandy kept talking, "Dr. Brooks reminds me of NiNi in some ways."

"How so?" I managed to whisper through my desert dry throat.

Sandy's voice sounded like she was standing in a box. "Dr. Brooks has a demeanor like your grandmother, stoic, yet she's wearing a mask and everyone knows it."

"Don't . . . like . . . change." I rubbed my temples.

"Right, some people like the idea of change, and the notoriety of accomplishment, not the process, or the time it takes to transform. Going back to school to get two doctorate degrees at fifty-five is a major accomplishment. She doesn't even acknowledge it."

That was a dose of reality for me. "I haven't even had the chance to go back and get one doctorate, and this woman has two!" I got upset all over again, and I could feel the crown tightening on my head. I whispered, "We could've helped somebody who was willing to complete the work needed to launch. Dr. Brooks has been putting herself down, complaining and ruminating on her failures. That irritates the hell out of me! Excuse my French." I grunted, "This can never happen again. ElnaHue is a business, not a charity."

San started laughing, "But what's funny is," she said between chuckles. "When you slowly put your notebook in front of your face and covered the camera, I knew you were silently screaming."

I laughed too, "Yeah, girl, I'd had enough of her. Dr. Brooks has plucked my last nerve."

Sandy cracked up for a few seconds. "In all seriousness," she said when she calmed down. "We do good work, friend. We have to trust God that there's a lesson in this. Let's give her a couple of days before we check back in. I have a feeling she'll change her mind and come back to us once her dog, Buttercup is in recovery."

"If I had the energy, I'd change my clothes and go for a run, but I just want to lie here and I gather myself."

"You want me to take you home, Nitty? You don't look like you can drive right now."

I opened one eye and looked at San. "Let me lie here for a little while. Follow me home, I'm not leaving my car here, no way!" We laughed, our office is located in a great neighborhood, but there are no cameras.

"I'll go back to my office, but before I let you go I wanna say this," San squatted behind my head, leaned over and looked me in the eye. She hesitated before she said, "I think you should consider seeing the counselor Harold, your own husband, found. You don't seem like yourself, Nitty. You got a little snippy with Dr. Brooks, and we can't represent ourselves like that."

"I agree, San. I tried to calm myself. Something is off with me, I just can't figure out what it is."

"I think you have more in common with Dr. Brooks than you care to admit. Deep down, Nitty, you know what you need to do."

"I agree that there is a lesson, and I will pray about it. Now, leave me alone for thirty minutes, Sis." San stood up, walked to the door and turned off the light. Before she closed the door she quietly said, "I love you, Sis."

"I love you, too." I pulled a blanket from the couch onto the floor and curled up under it. I closed my eyes, blew out a breath of defeated exhaustion, and imagined myself tearing my dress off to change into my running clothes. I wanted to hit the pavement running to make my headache cease, but I fell asleep thinking about the woman in the red dress, in Dr.

Brooks' painting. I wondered if that woman, wearing her crown, had to run anywhere.

"The headache crown on my head is so tight," I thought. "Lord, relieve this pressure."

Chapter 29

What is happening to me?

I felt a little better when Sandy woke me up thirty minutes later. She called me from the doorway. "I'm turning the lights on, cover your eyes, Nitty." I put my hand over my face and slowly adjusted to the light. "You ready?" Sandy jingled her keys.

"Give me a few minutes to get my stuff." I stood up slowly, to ensure that I didn't get dizzy. I grabbed my bag, keys and phone. "Let's go."

On the twenty-minute drive to my house, I kept my head on the headrest determined not to swivel right or left too quickly. My hands were at ten and two, pressed and locked on the steering wheel. Thankfully, the route to my house from our office is mainly backroads with no sharp turns or bumps.

I listened to a smooth jazz station, set to a low volume and drove mindlessly home. On cruise control in every way, "I just need to get to my couch!" I coached myself. I glanced at the clock on the dashboard, unbelievably, the numbers were blurry. "Is it 8:00 or 9:00?" I wondered.

Through the rearview mirror, I could see Sandy behind me. Her hands were firmly on the steering wheel at ten and two also, and she looked vigilant. "I wonder what she's thinking," I said aloud. "She looks so intense right now." I crawled through the darkness counting the turns. I saw a deer peering out at me when I got to Stony Trail Way. I rolled to a slow stop and let him pass. Behind me, Sandy tapped on her horn to let me know that no other deer were coming out.

I accelerated with a jolt and continued on my way. When I got to Cornerstone Parkway, I relaxed and thought, "One more mile." Pulling into our subdivision, I put on my signal to let Sandy know I was going into the garage, and she could go home.

As I pushed the garage remote and pulled into the driveway, I cut the wheel too closely and caught the curb. "Oh shoot," I gasped. "I told Harold to fix that light, it's too dark out here!" I grumbled. The bumpy sensation of the left wheel running over the curb made me laugh. "Straighten up, girl," I said to myself as I turned the wheel, chuckling.

I pulled into my spot, stopped abruptly and turned off the car. I jumped out and waved Sandy on, tapping on the garage door, but she pulled in behind me and came running, activating the remote sensor on the garage door, sending it back up.

"Nitty! Let me help you into the house." She closed my car door and put her hand on my spine to steady me as I walked up the steps. "On second thought," she grabbed my arm turning me around, "Maybe I should take you to the hospital, you don't look so good."

I shook my head and pulled my arm away, "Unh, uh, San. No hospital. I just want to lie down." I dropped my purse, keys, and phone by the door and walked to the couch. I flopped down and closed my eyes. Sandy hung my keys on the key rack and picked up my phone.

"I'll be okay in about an hour. I didn't eat anything today, remember? Usually when I don't eat I feel like this." I knew it was more than just a hungry headache, but I didn't want to go to the hospital.

I watched Sandy go to the basket and retrieve our favorite blankets, mine a red and white one with hearts, and hers a black and white one with polka dots. "Usually when you feel like this you eat too much." She tucked me in the blanket and said, "This is something else." I took the blanket and covered my face.

"Can you turn the lights off?" It was too bright and everything on my head started to ache, even my eyebrows. Sandy curled up next to me on the recliner couch. "What are you doing?" I said with my eyes closed. She turned on the relaxation playlist on the t.v., and I settled under the blanket to calm my body.

"I'm not leaving until I know you are okay." I heard her dialing her phone. "Oldie," that is her nickname for Harold. "I'm here with Nitty and she's not looking good." She covered the phone and whispered something. I wondered what they were discussing.

"Okay, I will, Oldie. I'll stay until you get home." I heard the phone dialing again. "Hey Babe, how was your day?"

I imagined Reggie blushing at San. Their love story is one for the books. "I'm at Oldie and Nitty's," she said. "I followed her home from work, she wasn't feeling well. There is that leftover chicken and rice if you and the boys are hungry. I'll be home as soon as Oldie gets back from Columbus."

"He's out of town," the words were stuck in my mouth. "He's coaching tonight."

"I know honey," Sandy patted my leg. "What I want you to do right now is get some rest. Oldie will be here soon. Probably by the time you wake up." She kept talking to Reg and I was soothed by her soft voice.

"I'll tell you about it when I get home. Don't worry, I got her." It was quiet for a few seconds. "I love you, too."

I found the perfect spot for my left foot, the spot between cold and hot, and breathed in lavender from the air diffuser. With my eyes closed I asked, "San, what Harold say?"

"Oldie told me to have you lie on your left side and make you a cup of tea."

"I don't want any tea right now," I whispered. "I just want to sleep." Everything went black, and like it does in a movie, darkness turned to light as bright as the sun. As Lionel Ritchie sang about dancing on the ceiling, I saw myself as a sixteen-year-old, sitting in my bed with homework from Ms. Bell, my senior year English teacher. Her class was hard, she used to make us read every day and write a 500-word essay once a week.

Mama walked into my room with a weird look on her face. "*I Know Why The Caged Bird Sings*," was on my bed along with loose leaf paper and some pens. I saw my boombox with detachable speakers, and I was diligently working. I was probably in the zone when Mama frantically interrupted me bursting in my room smelling like lemons.

"Nitty," she said. "I need you to go to the store and get some lemons for me, I need to clean the kitchen."

"Mama, I have to finish my homework."

"Baby . . ." the sound of Mama's voice cut through my headache. Mama had said, "The fragrance of lemons will always lift you spirits."

"I hate lemons now," I tried to say, but it didn't make it through the heaviness in my head. I thought, "My spirits aren't low, I feel sick."

I snapped out of my memory and gripped the couch to center myself. I could feel Sandy's hand on my thigh, but I couldn't verbalize that I needed my mother, my NiNi and my aunties. My head was feeling tight and the room was spinning. I wanted to unlock my phone to call somebody for help, but all I could do was press my eyelids closed. I prayed silently, "Lord, let this pass. I don't have time for this!" I lamented.

Sandy moved her hand, "Rest, Anita."

I thought about Mama again. The imagined the smell of her spearmint, but for some reason, I kept seeing myself chopping lemons.

The world spun around me, as I tried to fall asleep. I questioned my life; I knew something was very wrong with me. I had to ask myself, "Girl, are you about to die because you didn't listen to your mother?" I rolled on my other side, and snuggled into the leather under me. I rolled my spine until it felt just right but I couldn't find my sweet spot. I turned my head and saw San's gaze. "I have to stay awake." The reality of my situation was hitting me like a ton of bricks. For a woman who never let anyone see her emotions, I couldn't help but cry.

"Aww, Nitty," San rubbed my back, "I'm so sorry you don't feel good." I couldn't stop the tears from flowing. "God," I prayed, "I just want to know, what is happening to me right now?"

Sandy watched me like a mama bear watching her cub. All I could do was stare at San. In my mind I was praying for clarity, but my body was numb. I looked at Sandy and asked, "Can hope and guilt exist in the same space?"

That caught San off guard. I asked again, "Can I really have hope and be confused about what I believe? Can I have faith and be mad at God? Do you think He'll forgive me for not taking care of myself?" I wiped tears from my eyes. "San, I'm the effect of my choices, you know that? Will I be able to accomplish my dreams? I want to have a baby."

Sandy threw off her blanket and stood up. She put on her shoes and grabbed her keys. "We're going to the hospital."

"Noooo!" I whined and pointed. "Get medicine from the bathroom." I curled up under the blanket and covered my face. "Taking a nap now."

I prayed. "Now I lay me down to sleep. I thank you for your mercy, and take this headache away, I have work to do." I took a deep breath, "I promise I'll do better, and I'll go back to church. I won't work so much. I'll call Mama more. Just please, loosen this crown on my head. I don't want to miss my blessings, Lord. I believe in You, but sometimes I can't see what you're doing. I guess I need more faith, huh?"

I welcomed the sleep that had been taunting me since Dr. Brooks shut the door on her blessing, but my heart thumped. "Can you hold hell back for me? I must be doing something right, the last six months, hell has sent everything it can to steal, kill, and destroy me." My mouth was dry, "Not this time, devil." I said out loud. "You can't have me, or anyone I love. You can unleash the armies, but I'll fight back."

"Nitty, I'm not playing with you," Sandy said in her stern voice, handing me a cup of water and a pill. "I'm going to take you to the hospital. You're talking in circles, your eyes are red, and you are scaring me." Her phone rang, "I'll be right back." She went into the bathroom and closed the door.

I closed my eyes and a ticker tape of my goals and dreams spread across my eyes: 40 Under 40. Visit India. Film a movie. Scale our business. Be a mother. See my grandbabies. "Lord, please don't let me die."

I drifted to sleep thinking about Mama.

Chapter 30

Flashback.

When I was eleven, before I started my period, Mama tried to talk to me about my womanhood. I could tell she was nervous. She didn't use proper names for body parts, nor did she look me in the eye. "Here," Mama said, walking into my room holding the cordless phone. I'm talking to your Aunt Enid. She held up in one hand, a belt with four strings attached to it, and in the other, a long piece of gauze. "Do you know what this is?" Before I could tell her I didn't, Mama said, "This is a period belt."

"Joyce," I heard Aunt Enid laugh. "That's not what I told you to say. Hey Dollface. How are you doing?"

"I'm good, Auntie. How are you?"

"I'm good too. Your mom and I were just talking about how you will be starting your period soon. Do you remember the talk the two of us had when I was there last?"

"Yes, Ma'am."

"Your mom is just trying to share some more information with you." Auntie chuckled. "Go ahead, Joyce."

Mama sat on my bed, pushed my rollers aside and watched me roll up the ends of my braids. "Your hair looks nice, Nitty." She blew out a hard breath. "Well, you know I don't like talking about this stuff."

"I know, Mama. It's okay."

She held up the tails of the pad, in front of my face. "Put these, into this," she slipped the tails into small metal clips on the belt. "Then you put the belt on like this."

Aunt Enid was cracking up. "Joyce, what are you doing over there?"

Mama stood up and stepped into the contraption. She looked so clumsy trying not to fall. Finally, she got it into the right position. Mama looked at me and said, "You put this belt under your panties. This is how you protect your clothes when your body releases toxins once a month."

"Mama," I said, fastening a roller, "Are you talking about my menstrual cycle?"

"Yes." She said taking off the period belt. "I am talking about when Aunt Flo comes to visit."

"Joyce . . . Aunt Flo? You're so old. You can say period, it's okay."

Mama was exasperated, "Enid, that's what I call my period, silly." I wanted to laugh, but I stifled it because she was trying to be serious.

"Joyce, you don't have to be shy when you talk about these hard topics. We want Dollface to know what she needs to know, right?"

"Bye Enid, go teach your dance class. Call me later."

"Bye Joyce, you've got this." She addressed me, "Bye Dollface. And listen to your mother." When Aunt Enid hung up, there was an awkward silence. "Mama, we talked about this in health class. I feel comfortable using pads, they have different ones now. I think I know what to do."

"I know, baby." Mama said, picking up a roller and putting it around one of my braids. "I want to make sure you know about menstrual cycles and all the things women need to know. Mother didn't have these conversations with me."

"I understand, Mama. Remember I was there when Sandy got her cycle last year and you helped her."

Mama smiled, "Yeah, I'm glad Sandy sees me as a mother-figure. I'm so happy God blessed me with two daughters. I just hope I'm as good a mother as you two are daughters." Mama leaned over and put her arms around me. "I love you Nitty. With everything in me, I love you."

"I love you too, Mama." She got up, walked out of my room and closed the door. She never said anything else about my cycle after that.

When I was seventeen, Mama had another awkward conversation with me. She burst into my room, I recall, with a big bag of medical supplies and a huge yellow plastic cup, with a smiley face on it, full of water.

"We have a history of high blood pressure in our family," she said pushing my legs back and getting under my blanket. "Here, drink this." She said pushing the cup toward me and spilling some of its contents. "I think you might be dehydrated. That's why you sleep all the time."

"Mama! Why do we have to talk about this right now?" It irritated me when she walked in my room acting all suspicious, pushed my legs aside, and sat on my bed. "This is a blood pressure cuff," Mama said, pulling a medical device out of the bag she clutched tightly between her fingers.

"I know what that is."

"Nitty," she said, "If your head ever starts to throb out of nowhere, turn the lights off and lie down on your left side. That feeling means your blood pressure is probably too high."

"What are you talking about?" I was so confused.

"Just listen to me Nitty, this is important. You're about to be eighteen. I need to make sure you know how to protect and take care of yourself. I won't always be around to tell you what to do." She pulled a box of condoms out of the bag and held them up to me. "Don't use cheap condoms."

"Why are you giving me these?" I pushed the box away. "I'm not even thinking about having sex until I get married, Mom. Neither is Sandy."

"Oh," she blushed and looked pleasantly surprised. "Well, that's good to know." She tucked the condoms back into the bag. I didn't need the condoms or the blood pressure cuff; I side-eyed my mother. "Why does she think I'm having sex?" I mused.

"Where is this coming from, Mama?"

Mama cleared her throat. "I'm sorry to disturb your homework." She breathed and said, "I was just thinking about all the things I wanted to teach you growing up. I don't know if I have done enough to prepare you for your future. I want you to know that you have to exercise, practice safe sexual health, and be a productive citizen."

"Huh?" I studied my mother. "You took me to a sex education class at the hospital when I was eleven. Plus, we talk about everything."

I thought, "She's going around the mulberry bush trying to tell me something." I noticed that she looked different, like she had aged overnight. I could see worry lines in her forehead and crust around her eyes like she'd been crying. Mama rubbed my leg. "I just want to make sure you know that I love you and your brother with everything I have in me." She wiped a tear, "Everything."

In that moment something struck me and I saw my mother clearly. Not just as my mother, but as a woman, a daughter, a wife. I saw Mama, flaws and all, and I realized that I loved her deeply. Never had I seen her cry, or laugh freely. She was always so phlegmatic, so dauntless, and untouchable. It was endearing, for sure.

She continued talking, "If you ever feel angry at me, or frustrated about anything I do, please tell me."

"What is going on, Mom?" I closed my laptop and sat up straight. I stretched my legs out and Mom rested her elbow on them.

She sighed, and dropped her head. "Nini had a stroke."

"A stroke?" My heart thumped in my chest. "What does that mean, Mama? Is she okay?"

"She's okay, honey. I'm catching the bus to her and I plan to stay there with her until I know she's okay. I'll be gone for a few days. Uncle LJ is going to pick me, Aunt Enid and Aunt Hannah up from the bus station tonight. As a family, we have some things to work through."

"I need to pack a bag." I moved to get out of the bed, "I gotta tell Sandy."

Mama patted my knee and said, "No. You have to stay here with your dad. I plan to be home by Saturday, but if I need y'all, your dad will drive you up."

I was confused. "We went from talking about high blood pressure and condoms to Mama telling me my Nini had a stroke?"

Seventeen years after that conversation with Mama, I was resting on my couch, in the dark. My body was pressing against the leather, and I focused on the sensation of its smoothness on my skin. The crown on my head was tight and I knew, in that moment, I was trying to control a blood pressure number that was probably too high. "A stroke…am I having a stroke?"

I reached for Sandy. "San, I have been feeling stressed out," I confessed.

I heard the concern in her voice, "What is stressing you out, Nitty? Is it Dr. Brooks that is causing you to feel like this? Compromising your health is not worth it. We can let her go."

I stretched my arm, "Where is my phone? I need to call Mama. She'll know what to do." I felt Sandy put my phone in my hand, but it felt heavy. I didn't have the energy to do anything with it.

Chapter 31

A wake-up call.

When I woke up, Sandy had her head in a Styrofoam container that smelled like a piece of heaven. "Are you eating a turkey burger and sweet potato fries?" I looked at the container and the smell of the food tickled my nose. "Can I have some?" I wanted to grab a few fries and stuff them into my mouth.

Sandy covered up her food and stood up. "Girl, you had me worried sick."

A nurse came in the room to check my vitals. "How are you feeling, dear? Your blood pressure was high when you arrived. It's come down significantly." She fixed my blanket. "Can I get either of you anything?" We looked at each other and shook our heads. "Alright, I'll be back to check on you in an hour."

When the nurse left, I looked at Sandy and said, "You promised!" I looked around the room and felt a wave of emotion. "Why am I in the hospital?"

Sandy closed her eyes and sighed. "I had to call the ambulance." I tried to sit up, but I couldn't move. "Nitty, you were moaning and thrashing in your sleep. Oldie told me to call 911."

"I was? Where is Harold?"

She checked his location on her phone, "Looks like he's two minutes out."

"How long am I going to be here?" I choked back tears. "Are they going to admit me?"

"Apparently you have to stay here until your blood pressure stabilizes." She looked at the monitors. "This is serious, Nitty. It's a reality check for all of us. No more late-night eating, no more snacks. We're cutting everything out."

"No! I need my salty snacks."

She waved her finger at me, "No you don't! What we both need to do is figure out how to decrease our stress. If we need to cut back on our clients, shorten our hours, fast, pray, meditate, or do yoga, we're doing what's necessary to live."

"Sandy…"

"Uhn, uhn. I don't want to hear it. I had to call 911, Nitty! They brought you here in an ambulance." She cleared her throat. "I know your family history. NiNi had a stroke, your mom had a stroke, and you barely escaped one. I had to call Harold and tell him you were going to the hospital in an ambulance. I had to call Mama Joyce to tell her what happened, and you know she asked me 1,000 questions."

"What did Mama say?"

"She called NiNi on three-way, and of course they argued about what natural remedies would work best for you." Her voice cracked, "You can't imagine how hard it was for me to make those bad news calls, or how hard it was to see you like that."

I turned my head in shame. "I'm sorry, San." That's when I noticed I was wearing a yellow hospital gown.

"Girl, you haven't been taking care of yourself. You crashed into the garage door last night, a few weeks ago you fell down the steps and broke your finger. You've been having nightmares, and last month you had a miscarriage." She snorted. "Are you deliberately attracting catastrophes?"

"Of course not," I whispered. "To hear you mention all of this sounds so crazy to me! I guess hell is after me. We must be doing something right to keep getting all of these crazy attacks from hell."

"It's deeper than that. I think you need to go to counseling, Sis."

"What do you mean?" I rubbed my temples.

"I think talking to somebody will help you."

"I don't believe in counseling. Daddy used to say, 'What happens in this house stays in this house.' We didn't ask for help even when we were drowning. So much trauma and no healing. Not after Grandma Alfreda died, not after that girl at our school committed suicide in seventh grade, and not even when the little girl at the community center drowned." I turned my head away from Sandy.

"Nobody talked about counseling back then, Nitty, but something has to give, you are feeling broken."

I turned back to face Sandy, "It could be a spiritual attack that's moving to my physical body. I don't want to minimize what you are saying, but I really don't think it's that serious, San."

"Nitty," Sandy rocked her head back and forth before she spoke. "Something in your heart is crying out for attention and you keep running from it."

I had to digest that thought. "You know what, I remember praying something about that when I was on the floor in my office. I told the devil he couldn't have me."

"At least you had the wherewithal to pray. When I saw you, I panicked first, then I uttered a one-word prayer, "Help!" I had to laugh at that. Sandy usually used her prayer language and gave long soliloquies when she prayed.

"You were at a loss for words, huh?"

Sandy nodded and wiped a tear. "That's the easiest way to say it."

"Sandy, I have a confession to make." I straightened my head and squared my shoulders. "For a few weeks I've been thinking about how we had to fight Ms. Dinkins' grandsons. I recently saw an article about him, and it brought everything back to me. I wish I could go back and . . ."

Sandy interjected, "Go back and do what, Nitty? Harold and Daddy Doug handled it. They tormented me for years, long before you moved on the street. Because of Ms. Dinkins and her family, everybody knew that my mother was on drugs. My Daddy and Aunt shielded me from a lot of the gossip, but the Dinkins clan told me everything."

Sandy turned her face from me. Behind her back she said, "I don't understand what triggered this for you. Is this what your nightmares are?" I nodded. "Does Oldie know that the root of your nightmares is the Dinkins boys?"

I shook my head left and right. "We just talked about how concerned he is about how my insomnia." I sucked my teeth and said, "I think I've been hitting him in my sleep."

"Another reason to go to therapy, Sis." Sandy paused and picked at some lint on her pants. "While we're on this topic, I need to tell you something and I know you won't like it." She sat on the edge of my bed.

"What's wrong?"

"I had to make a hard executive decision," Sandy paused. "I'm doing what's best for ElnaHue, but Nitty, you are officially on administrative leave for four weeks. Stay home and get yourself together."

I blinked at her, "Sandy?"

"As COO I have to do what's best for the team right now. I need my CEO and best friend back to 100% and for now, she's out of commission. I don't want to see you in the office.

I don't want to see you on a Zoom call. I just want to see you better, Sis."

"I hear you." I sighed.

"I hear you, too," Harold said standing in the threshold of the doorway holding a bouquet of white lilies. I was both embarrassed and happy to see him. He inched his way from the door and hugged Sandy. I smiled watching my husband and best friend enjoy a tender moment as if they were siblings. "Twenty years of doing life together through thick and thin solidifies relationships," I guess.

Harold broke from Sandy's embrace and said, "Get her together, Sis."

Sandy looked as relieved as I was to see Harold. She sat in a chair by the door, making room for him next to me. He walked to my bedside, kissed me on the forehead, and looked me in my eyes, "Playtime is over. I don't know what I would've done if I had lost you."

"I'm not going anywhere." I moved my head around. "I don't have a headache. Can we go home?"

Harold spoke sternly, "Nitty, you'll go home when the doctors say you can go home. Now get some rest, while I find a counselor."

I didn't usually get headaches, but that day, the crown I've been wearing since childhood felt heavier. While in triage, I found something funny on the old television and laughed my heart out for two hours. I was released with medication and instructions to rest when my blood pressure came down.

Chapter 32

A lot to think about.

A week after that hospital stint, if you want to call it that, cabin fever started to sneak up on me. It happened slowly, but when I realized I was feeling it, the anxiety of being stuck felt like an avalanche on my head.

I watched our neighbor across the street through the blinds, as he cleaned fresh snow off his car. He saw me looking through our window, I waved because I didn't want him to think I was being a Peeping Tom, but I was caught off guard when he saw me looking. Dan smiled and waved, and then he gave me a thumbs up. I could see the question mark on his face. "Harold must've told him about me being hospitalized," I thought.

I returned his gesture with my own two thumbs up, and he used his broom to brush the heavy snow into the grass. When his car was clean, he shoveled the driveway. Then he went back inside, leaving his wife's car untouched. "That was selfish," I said, closing the blinds.

Other than looking out of the window and watching comedies, I was starting to feel bored like I did when we were in the COVID-19 bubble. I couldn't leave the house, I couldn't go to work. I couldn't even do too much cardio because it spikes blood pressure. During COVID, Harold shopped, but at least at that time I could put on a mask and go if I wanted.

To cope with COVID, I would just mosey between my office, the kitchen, and the bedroom holding a plate of something comforting to eat. Now that I think about it, it was probably all of that comfort food that started the high blood pressure nonsense. It never dawned on me that stress was a culprit, too.

Having a diagnosis of high blood pressure (HBP) felt isolating. I was the sole resident in a bubble of reconstruction. Everything before HPB was wiped out, leaving me as a patient and the lone survivor. Being forced to face myself and the silent killer that stood before me, with a real threat to destroy me had put my life into perspective. My NiNi used to say, "Life is but a vapor," I get it now.

All my family's interactions with me were with a long-handled spoon. They all were acting like HBP was a contagious disease, stepping back and turning their head to grimace. I wanted somebody to hold me in their arms and tell me everything was going to be okay.

I really wanted to hear that I was going to be okay. I sat alone in my room and watched a lot of television.

One day I ran across a movie about a little boy who literally lived in a plastic bubble. Everyone talked to him through the plastic, they slid his food on a tray across the floor. His immune system was compromised and no one wanted to endanger him.

"I can relate, my boy," I said out loud to the movie.

Sandy wouldn't let me do any work in the business. Harold wouldn't let me eat anything I liked or enjoyed. He did all this research about natural remedies and bought an industrial juicer to make concoctions with garlic and beets. He loved everything he made, but I choked down his special juices that tasted like dirt.

I was only permitted to consume raw veggie salads and lemon water for two weeks straight. The fact that I hate lemons made it worse. Mama wouldn't let me rest. She fussed over me, rearranged my blankets, poured me hot tea, and fixed my hair constantly. I think it was her way of showing me love, but it wasn't in my love language—I wanted her to hold me.

It seemed like every five minutes she was calling Grayson, giving him updates. It was an endless cycle of boredom, nasty, unseasoned food, and people telling me what to do, all day long. I was sick of it!

"I was only in the hospital for four hours, they're acting as if I was in intensive care." I thought, one Saturday when Sandy, Reg and their sons, my nephews came to coddle and entertain me. I was so happy to see those little people. The adults were just getting on my last nerve.

In total, Harold and I have eight nieces and nephews between our four siblings. Sandy and Reg have two boys, they are the oldest of the bunch. My brother has three, Harem, Harold's twin, has three children.

Running with Sandy's athletic nine and eleven-year-old boys made me want to get back into my running routine. They play soccer and run track so the stride and precision of their steps is to be admired. Though I had to pause my strenuous exercise for a few weeks, my feet had been burning to hit the pavement. Thankfully the boys were happy to go for a light jog with me, otherwise I would've pulled my eyelashes out from sheer frustration about the whole situation.

Having a diagnosis of hypertension was not on my task list, incidentally, it was quickly becoming the biggest, most unappreciated inconvenience of my life! It felt good to be outside, even if only for a few minutes. I enjoyed the pretty Ohio snow, as my nephews raced me up the block.

I jogged with gratitude. "We picked a nice neighborhood to move into," I thought. "I'm so glad there are no abandoned houses here." I thought about how Cotton Commons had so many abandoned houses. As a teenager, I used to run through the neighborhood watching out for broken glass, high grass, needles and stray dogs. My head was always on a swivel, and I ran when I felt anxious about life. Ironically, when I was a kid, running through my neighborhood made me feel anxious about living.

The boys and I ran around the block a few times. I let them get ahead of me by a few houses, but I put on my turbo jets and passed them, running into my yard. I cackled as Jacob slipped on a piece of ice and Jonah threw a sloppy snowball at me. At that moment, I was grateful for my nephews. I realized how much I missed being around the little people in my life.

I thought about the day when Harold and I would bring our baby home. Everyone we love would be standing around oohing and aahing about our blessing. I can already feel my baby in the crook of my arm and I imagine myself looking around the house feeling it overflowing with laughter, hugs and love. I had a miscarriage last month, and I didn't even know I was pregnant. I'm still getting over that loss.

Me, Harold and Sandy have come a long way from living in Cotton Commons. We only live about fifteen minutes away from our old neighborhood, but the two communities are a world apart. The house I lived in was torn down. Sandy's dad still lives in our old neighborhood, and he's as active now as he was when we were kids.

In the upscale neighborhood that we live in, we don't have to worry about drama. The community is small, yet people mostly keep to themselves. We don't have nosy neighbors poking around our yard or calling the city on us to complain like Ms. Dinkins used to do to my father. Our Homeowner's Association has strict rules about trash cans and the height of our bushes, but they haven't bothered us for the six years we've been here.

I love our house, but I'd give up everything and move into a trailer, if it meant I could give Harold a baby of our own.

Jonah tapped my shoulder, "Punch bug, two times." We cracked up as we passed the neighbor's house, and their two yellow beetle cars parked in the driveway.

Chapter 33

Time to talk.

Harold made an appointment for me to go to therapy because he was worried that I wasn't taking care of myself. I flat out told the therapist, "It's not a good time for me."

I retrieved my planner from my bag and flipped through it. I slowed down when I saw August 2024.. "I can come back in two months."

"Ah," I smiled, "I have some down time after the women's conference at our church in July." Harold cleared his throat. "What, Harold? I'm on the committee, and you know our First Lady is a lot." I blew out a breath, "It takes a lot of work to plan the women's conference, the First Lady of our church has big visions."

Harold sighed, and I looked up from my planner. "Nitty," he spoke slowly, "The doctor told you that you have to slow down."

Ignoring his statement, I took my pen out of its holder and started tapping my lips. "What days work for you in August, Dr. Octavia?"

"Nitty." Harold put his hands on my shoulder. "Did you hear me? You need to take this situation seriously. Make it a priority to talk to Dr. Octavia."

"I'm doing that, Harold." I snapped. "Sorry," I said to Dr. Octavia. Her head was tilted, but she didn't respond. "I usually go to the spa after grant season, but I can make a few appointments with you instead. Mondays and Tuesdays are good for me."

Harold slid closer to me on the couch, clasped his hands together and said to the therapist, "I'm really worried about her."

I furrowed my brow. "You're *worried* about me? You don't have to worry about me. And, why did you have to wait till we came here to say that in front of a stranger? No disrespect, Dr. Octavia, but we could've handled this at home."

"No disrespect taken. You have a good point." She shifted in her seat and wrote a note on her pad. "Harold," she pointed with her pen, "Why did you wait until you got here to talk about it?"

He shrugged his shoulders. "I've been worried about her for months, but I didn't know how to communicate my concern. The hypertension diagnosis is the cherry on top of the cake. She had a miscarriage, suffered from insomnia and nightmares, I don't know what else to do. Ever since. . ."

"Well babe," I cut him off. "You don't need you to worry, I tell you everything. You micromanage my medications, oversee my schedule, cook my food and monitor my sleep. We are in this together, remember?" Harold nodded.

The counselor looked back and forth between me and Harold. "One second," she nodded at Harold, "I heard you say something that I don't want to glaze over. Ever since what?"

I didn't speak. I wanted to melt into the couch or run out of the door. "I apologized about that incident, Harold." I side-eyed him and glanced at her. "You don't need to …"

Dr. Octavia raised her eyebrows and her eyes doubled in size. Harold didn't let me finish. "Dr. Octavia, I have observed Nitty…I mean, Anita, display some behaviors that have become increasingly concerning for me. During her night terrors she hits me."

I looked at Dr. Octavia and took a deep breath before turning back to my husband and snorting, "I'm fine. I really am fine." I crossed my right leg over my left and started kicking it. Harold slipped his hand to cover my right knee and tapped softly with his fingers. Each tap felt like he was turning the volume down on the storm brewing inside of my chest.

Tap. Tap. Tap. I let out a hard breath through my nose, before sucking in more air and letting it out slowly through my mouth. Tap. Tap. Tap.

"Babe," Harold turned his body to face mine. I didn't hear anything he said at first. My eyes drank in every inch of my husband of ten years. I mean, Harold has been fine since I met him in eighth grade. From his shiny bald head, purple Malcolm X inspired glasses and perfectly lined salt and pepper facial hair, I'm still mesmerized in his presence and absolutely in love.

Harold looked delectable in his royal purple button up dress shirt. He coordinated his gray and brown striped suit with a purple and gold tie and brown pocket square that accented his hazel eyes. I remember how he slid off his suit jacket and folded it in half, shoulder to shoulder, and laid it across the arm of the couch when we came into the office. The crisp lines of his pants carefully ironed, were sharp like a razor's edge.

"That's my man, my man, my man!" I thought.

Harold and Harem, were always fashion icons. Maybe it's because their mom was a model when she was in college, and she kept them dressed from treasures she found at the Goodwill, or made. Nobody, and I mean not one single person, would ever dare to say something crazy to them. If they had to, the twins would knock the stick off your shoulder and punch you first, but they were kind, caring people.

"Baby," Harold tapped my hand, snapping me back to reality in the counselor's office. "You promised me you'd do this." I watched worry lines cross Harold's brow.

I nodded in agreement. I gave Harold my word that I'd try this "counseling thing" for six months. I don't really want to be here in this office, with this lady, at this moment. I just don't understand how telling somebody all of my business would help anything. I had to cancel a lot of meetings to be here. I swallowed my emotions. "How can you be so tender with me? I'm not always kind."

Harold wiped tears, "Nitty, you have always been a bridge between people. Your NiNi was right, you were made to knit things together in love." Dr. Octavia hummed with enlightenment at that statement.

"Thank you, baby."

I put my pen away and looked around the counselor's office. From what I could see, Harold did his research. *He considered everything I needed*, I thought. She checked every box I would have listed in my bullet journal. The office was painted in a calming blue, reminding me of a beach I visited in Haiti while on a mission trip. Half of the wall to her left was full of framed certificates and degrees. "I like that about her," I thought. "HBCU educated like me. Go, girl!" A highly educated Black woman is my kind of Sista.

Sorority sister, check.

Natural hair, check.

Calming music, check.

I saw the photos of her family on her desk. "She's a mother," I thought. "She has some similar characteristics to Mama, but a little older." I like her, check.

Colorful, but no bright yellow, big check! I don't trust anything yellow but the sun, sunflowers, and dandelions. These are the only things God made that make sense to me. It seems like yellow is that one annoying thing I see every day and have to deal with. Yellow is like a bee that won't leave you alone, you can't swat it away, you have to learn to deal with it being all up in your face!

Of course I live a life with joy, but I'm not out here all giggly with smiley face emojis and rainbows all the time. I hate the color yellow. Growing up in the only yellow house on Cotton Commons street, the Dinkins clan always had something stupid to say and I hated it! One of the boys used to ride his bike past our house and throw banana peels on our porch. He'd say, "Hey welfare queen!" And ride off cackling.

Yellow irks me. Mama, whenever she was sad or feeling overwhelmed would chop lemons to clean the house. Some days the lemon smell made me gag because it was so strong. She'd say, "The lemon scent lifts your spirits, baby." She was wrong, it might have lifted her spirits, but it was a reminder to me that whenever I got in trouble, it was my job to chop up lemons for her!

Yellow things don't seem to agree with me, either. I'm allergic to corn. I hate lemon candy because it makes my teeth hurt. Bees scare me because when we lived in Texas, my friend Benetha was stung by what seemed like 10,000 bees because she accidentally bumped into a tree and didn't see the hive. Yellow mustard reminds me of "hotdog girl" who cried at my birthday party.

Harold interrupted my thoughts when he took my calendar from my lap. "This thing is her life." He flipped through it to show the counselor lady. "I appreciate her organization and her budgeting her time, but Nitty doesn't make herself a priority."

That really pissed me off. "What are you talking about, Harold?" I snorted.

Harold kept talking, ignoring my question. "She has color coded notes all over the house reminding us of this thing to do and that place she's going."

"Everything I do is for us." I protested. "I'm building a legacy."

"When is the last time we had a date night, Anita?"

"Remember you took me to…" I was stuttering. "You know we went to…" I searched through my phone's calendar and was embarrassed to see that it had been a year! "Wow, I didn't realize it's been that long. I guess, because I see you every day, I didn't realize we haven't been out."

"Babe, we're in a good place right now," He squeezed my hand. "I want to enjoy you as much as you enjoy helping your clients achieve their dreams. WE have dreams, too."

The counselor chimed in, "What does that mean Anita, building a legacy?"

I pursed my lips before I spoke. I had to bite my tongue so I wouldn't snap on her. It was too soon for her to be getting in my business like this. "How can I explain this to you?" I paused and blinked a few times. "I have things I want to accomplish before turning forty. I have three years, two months and five days. Therefore, I'm stacking money, co-leading my company with my best friend, training our staff and building my legacy."

"I understand," she interrupted. "But what's the goal?"

"What do you mean? I want to make sure I have money for our future children. Plus, we want to be able to help our families if they need it."

"How does taking care of your mothers build your legacy, Anita?"

"She sounds dumb," I thought. "Taking care of our mothers is a Biblical principle." I leaned in and asked, "Am I not communicating effectively?"

"To be honest, you're not. Explain more about the legacy you want to leave. Who's the legacy for?"

Harold looked at me with sympathy and said, "I don't want her to self-destruct, that's why I brought her to you, Dr. Octavia. You came highly recommended from my mother. She doesn't trust everybody." What could I say to that?

"It's fine to want to build a legacy, and we'll unpack that later." Dr. Octavia paused for a few seconds before speaking again. "If I can be frank here, are you building a legacy with Jenga blocks or bricks?"

I wrinkled my face in disbelief, and she continued to fire questions at me. Every inquiry felt like an arrow through my armor, piercing my soul. "What good is it to build a legacy and not be able to enjoy the process?"

That stumped me. "If your memory fades while the legacy you're building stands, was it worth it?" I had to swallow the tears on that one. "Are you rushing through life missing important moments because all you're thinking about is building a legacy?" That led me to ponder moments I've missed with my family. Then she asked, "What happens when the work is complete?" Her final statement hit the bullseye, "I don't know what you think you're doing, but this ain't that, Anita." Harold chuckled.

"Forgive my Ebonics." Dr. Octavia continued, "I need to be blunt. You can keep doing things the way you're doing them, but if Harold's concern becomes a reality and you melt down, or if you burnout, will you be able to stop the work without worrying that no one can help you carry the load?"

"I have a team and. . ."

She put up her hand to stop me. I watched her Kinky Twists fly as she shook her head back and forth. "Those people can't please your husband, nor can they do what you do, like you do it."

"I know, but . . ."

I know she was trying to make her point, but I hated that she kept interrupting me. I felt that she wasn't really hearing me, and it was starting to piss me off. "If you don't teach people how to treat you, or how to respect what you're building, if something happens to you, they won't be able to honor it the way you hope."

That's when Harold piped in, "We tell her she has to teach others how to do the work. She has to let go."

"Mentoring is my passion."

"But are you micromanaging how they learn? Are you giving them grace to make mistakes?"

"I never thought of it that way." I put my head down and sighed.

"You can't bear the weight of everyone else's dreams, goals, and shortcomings all the time. Something will suffer. In this case, something has to give."

"I hear you, but. . ."

Dr. Octavia put her hand up to cut me off for the third time. My insides were seething.

My ears perked up when she said, "Black women need a community to help them lay their capes down. Give me six months; I'll show you how to give yourself grace. I'll equip you to build legacy and teach others to build theirs in a healthy way. Together we process your stressors and triggers." She paused and took a sip of water. "Can you trust me?"

My feet started to burn in my heels and I managed to say, "I'll do my best," before I jumped up, grabbed my bag and jogged out of the office without saying a word.

Behind my back I heard Harold say, "Don't worry, she'll be back."

Chapter 34

A change is coming.

Four months later, I was able to work, only remotely. I participated in our, "Lead Like a Lady" online conference with Sandy and several of our VIP clients.

Sandy was so excited, greeting all of the guests as they joined the call. She blew a kazoo and played inspirational music to keep them engaged. I sat at my desk in front of my laptop with my head in my hand. I couldn't keep myself awake.

"Hello Ladies," Sandy said. "At ElnaHue Consulting, We're here to help you show up with confidence. Let's hear from ElnaHue Co-founder, Anita Pitts."

I felt my head nod and I jerked awake. "Oh shoot! I fell asleep."

"Anita! You're muted."

I turned on my camera not realizing that my lip gloss was smeared, and my hair was unkempt. I turned my camera on, unmuted, and caught a glimpse of myself before I quickly turned off my camera. "Hey Ladies. Thank you first, for being a VIP, and second for investing in yourself and your business." I breathed shakily, "Sandy, what's on the agenda?"

I turned my camera off and stared at Sandy's yellow shirt until my eyes blurred. "Before we do that, tell us in the chat what your expectations are for today." The comment section started to blow up. "I see you, Marilyn. Why don't you unmute yourself and share more."

A young woman spoke up, sounding so chipper and enthusiastic. "You all are mentors in my head. I love everything you do, and I want to learn everything I can!"

"Thank you for that," Sandy said. As she talked, I rubbed my stomach, which out of nowhere started to ache. I turned the volume of my computer to the maximum and ran to the bathroom. My pants and chair were wet when I got up, and I had things coming out of both ends!

I made it to the bathroom just as my stomach erupted. I hurried and sat down so that I wouldn't ruin my dress. I had to wash my face and change my clothes.

"Okay," I looked at myself in the mirror. "Boss mode. I am the head and not the tail. I am in control." I stood up straight and said my affirmations in the mirror, "My spine is straight and nothing can break me." My stomach erupted, and I had to go back to the toilet.

By the time I sat back at my desk, Sandy was putting the women into breakout rooms for an exercise. When we were alone, she asked, "Are you okay?" I shook my head left and right. "You don't look good. Are you cramping? I'm hurting today, too. You know our cycles are in sync."

Ignoring her original question I asked, "Why are you wearing that damn yellow shirt? It's not on brand."

"I just got this shirt." She looked down. "I'm sorry."

Reality hit me. "Oh shoot!"

"What's wrong, Nitty?"

"I missed my cycle. I'll be back." I slammed my computer down and ran back to the bathroom. I went to the drawer where I kept my feminine products. Under a box of tampons was a box of pregnancy tests with one stick left.

"I don't know if I can go through this again, Lord." I took the test, and immediately it appeared positive! I threw the test in the trash and went back to the meeting feeling numb.

After the VIP Zoom call, I changed my clothes and started cleaning. I pulled out my bucket and my homemade cleaning solution of lemon juice, vinegar and tea tree oil in a spray bottle. I sprayed the bathroom down and scrubbed everything. Then, I went into my office to clean. Next, I cleaned Harold's and my bedroom, scrubbing everything, like I was a cleaning fool!

When Harold got home, I was in the kitchen chopping more lemons, deep cleaning the counters. He came in right as I nicked myself with a knife. "Dang," I said, cowering in pain.

"You okay," Harold said, greeting me with a kiss.

"It's been a hell of a day, Babe."

"What happened? How was the Summit?"

I shook my head left and right. "I can't talk about it right now. My head is throbbing." I changed the subject. "How was school? Did you have a good practice?"

"The boys will be ready for their game tomorrow." Harold sat at the table and watched me chop lemons. "Why are you cutting so many lemons?"

"I had to clean everything."

"Oh," Harold said standing. "After I hit the shower, I'll cook."

"No need, salmon is in the oven."

I didn't say anything, but when Harold called my name, I knew he'd found the pregnancy test. The next week we had an appointment with our obstetrician. He told me, "Mrs. Pitts, you need to be on strict bed rest. You have preeclampsia." I dropped my head.

"I need to work, Dr. Song."

"I understand, Mrs. Pitts, but you need to do it from your bed. We want to keep this little baby safe. You're already five months along."

Chapter 35

I see yellow.

On the way home, Harold called Mama first. "I'll be there Saturday," she squealed. "I'm staying until my granddaughter comes. Hold on," she said, clicking over. "I'm back with LJ and Enid. LJ, call Hannah, Nitty has some news."

We shared our news, listened to their delight and made more calls. I had to get my mind right for Mama coming to stay with us for possibly two months. "Mama is going to hover over me so much."

"Let her," Harold said.

On Saturday morning, I woke up to the vacuum cleaner running outside of our bedroom. Mama was humming our song.

"Mama" I screamed, hoping she would hear me over the vacuum and through the closed door. "I have a headache! What are you doing?"

"Sorry baby, I was trying to tidy up for you."

"By vacuuming while I was sleeping?"

I turned on the lamp and saw a vase of yellow gladiolus. I threw a pillow, knocked the vase over and covered my head. Mama banged the door open and ran to my bedside.

"JOYCE? You okay, baby?" Mama lifted the blanket to check on me. "What happened?"

I pointed to the vase on the floor and the water-stained carpet. "I hate those flowers!" I turned over and covered my face again.

Mama picked up the vase, sat on the bed., and patted my leg. "Baby," she said. "They're a reminder of your Daddy because he isn't here."

"Get them out of here!"

"This is a symbol of a peace offering."

"For you, Mama. Not for me." When I was fifteen, I thought I overheard Mama and Daddy having an altercation in the middle of the night. I was clueless to the fact that it was true until the next morning when I was doing my chores before Sandy and I could go to the mall. I had my to-do list on the counter: Wash dishes; Clean counters with lemon; Iron clothes; Do hair; Sweep and mop floor; Mall!

Daddy came into the kitchen with a vase of yellow gladiolus with a card that read: "I'm Sorry." He set the vase on the counter and said, "Give these to your mama."

He poured lemonade into a large yellow cup and plopped in a lemon from the cutting board. "Oops," he said, "I spilled it. Sorry, baby. I didn't mean to do that. You got it?"

He kissed me and exited the kitchen. I slid a kitchen towel, from the oven handle, across his spill and bent to wipe under the counter. While bending, I saw an earring, hair, yellow beads, and broken glass. I stood there, hearing the commotion from the night before. "Joyce, come here!"

Mama's voice was muffled when she said, "Doug, no! I'm not coming over there."

The truth sat on me. "Oh my God! I wasn't dreaming." Mama sat on my bed with her eyes as big as plates. She played with her fingernails as she spoke to me. "I heard everything that night Mama." She dropped her head in shame.

"Nitty, it wasn't your father's fault. I'm sorry, I didn't know you heard that."

"Mama!" I raised my voice. "He bought them dumb yellow flowers for you every month!"

"It's not what you think."

"Mama, I saw your eye patch, your bruises, the broken glass. Your favorite earrings were broken, one lost."

Silence. "Nitty, it was one bad night." She paused, "I was having nightmares, and I was hitting your dad. He was trying to stop me from hurting myself in my sleep."

"Mama! I was wrong. I'm sorry. I always thought about the fact that you stayed with him twenty years and I thought he was hurting you. I vowed never to be weak like that."

Mama cried. "Your dad was a gentle man. He never put his hands on me." She pulled a tissue from the box on my nightstand and wiped her eyes. "All this time you thought I was a weak woman?"

"I did. I'm sorry, Mama. I held this grudge for so long that I forgot I was holding it. I vowed never to be weak."

"I think I became so hard that I couldn't find the soft touch to give you. It's a shame that you almost lost your baby trying not to be me. We both need to unlock that fortress around our hearts."

I rubbed my stomach and patted Mama's hand. "I'm trying to heal, Mama. God gave me a fresh start." I wiped a tear, "Do you think I'll be a good mom?"

"Of course you will! Everyone is excited and baby, we won't let you fail. This baby is already loved."

"I'm scared," I admitted.

Mama rubbed my hand and said, "If we work on our healing, together, we can get through it. When I found out I was pregnant with you, I was terrified. Mother only hit me one time, but she was mean to me for a long time. That didn't change the fact that when I told her I needed her, she was there." Mama rubbed her temples. "She didn't let us celebrate her, nor did she celebrate us. That's why I celebrate you."

"I don't know why I assumed you were weak, Mama. Why did I diminish you to a hero without power? I know you gave up your business and career to be a mother." I put my hand on her shoulder. "I want everything you sacrificed for us to be restored."

Mama blushed. "I'm working on a few things for me." Give me a second. She left my room and came back with a beautiful handmade quilt. "I made this for the baby." She held it up and pointed out pieces of fabric. "It has pieces of fabric from all of our family. And I embroidered everyone's names."

"It's beautiful, Mama!"

"Hopefully, the baby will always feel the love and be able to recognize it." She folded the quilt and said, "I was scared to be a mother, but I had a lot of help to get me through. I know that Mother loved us the best way she could, but her heart was broken. When you came along, she opened her heart. Her love is no longer a weapon; it's her guide."

Mama pulled me into a tight hug. I inhaled the spearmint of her gum and relaxed in her arms. She said, "You and your brother are the best thing that I have ever created."

I held on to Mama for dear life. She didn't let me go until I released my grip on her.

Chapter 36

A second Chance.

When our daughter, Chance, was born, everyone came to the house to celebrate with us. NiNi, was taking over, Aunt Enid was dancing, Aunt Hannah was doting, Uncle LJ was smiling, Elijah was giving fun facts, Sandy was serving, and Mama was proud.

Three months later, I logged on to surprise the VIP "Lead Like a Lady" participants. I was so excited to see them, and they couldn't contain their excitement when they saw me on screen. I cradled a cup of dandelion root tea and said, "It's time I tell you, my truth. I haven't been honoring myself for a long time and that affected me, my family and my business." Some of the ladies nodded in agreement. "I've been holding a grudge against my mother for something she didn't do, and I didn't want to repeat a cycle of anger and rejection, one that Nini and my mother had."

"May I ask a question?" I nodded at Marilyn, a VIP client, through the camera and nodded. "What have you learned about yourself through this process?"

"My mother has a story to tell, and so does my grandmother, NiNi. I saw tension between them growing up, but they didn't talk about it. When NiNi had a stroke, Mama went to her side. Their healing journey started when they began to talk to each other. During that time, Mama and my aunts served NiNi; that love brough her back to health.

I come from a long line of strong women, but I interpreted strength as control. I put so much pressure on myself; I had dangerously high blood pressure. I had to learn how to feel, how to ask powerful, clarifying questions, and how to give people grace."

I looked Chance and smiled at Sandy through the camera. "My nickname has been Nitty since before I was born. My grandma, Nini, said I was going to knit our family together in love." I looked at the baby, "Chance has been a gift from God. I want to be better so I can give her the best of me."

Sandy piped in, "Nitty, tell them why we've incorporated the color yellow into our rebrand."

I cackled, "I have hated the color yellow for a long time. But after I got sick, I began to reflect on the thread of yellow in our lives and how it represents life and new beginnings. My daddy told us to be strong like a dandelion, and we want to honor him by passing that lesson on." I took a deep breath and kissed my baby before looking into the camera and asking the women, "What is the significance of the work you do? If you don't know, figure it out before it knocks you off your feet."

Sandy wiped tears from her eyes and said, "Wow. I hope you ladies tuck that wisdom into your heart." She led the group in applause. "Thank you, Anita. Now log off and go enjoy my niece." Sandy winked at me, and I did as I was told.

Chapter 37

Dear healing.

"Relationships are complicated." I said, putting my leg under my thigh, at Dr. Octavia's office. It was our last counseling session, and I was sad, yet optimistic. I started to tap my foot, but I didn't feel the urge to run, that was a big difference from my first day with her.

"I never understood why NiNi was always at Mama's throat, but so kind to me. She always told me how much she loved Mama, but she didn't tell Mama. You've given me tools to navigate the confusion about all of this."

"What was the breakthrough moment?"

I shrugged. "The last six months we've talked about things I haven't thought to ask. I've experienced healing circles with the women in my life." I exhaled. "I've longed for that space with them for years."

Dr. Octavia smiled. "That's wonderful!"

"I will continue to host healing circles with the women in my family."

"Have you been open and honest with them? What do you think will happen when you let them see you?"

"I think they see me. They just don't see themselves in me or in each other."

Dr. Octavia tapped her chin and said, "Interesting."

"It's not that hard for me to see myself in them, but I've worked incredibly hard to avoid the bad habits that kept them bound. I think they love each other, but forgiveness hasn't come easy for them."

Dr. Octavia asked, "Do you agree that forgiveness is mandatory and reconciliation is optional? "What've you learned from your Mama and NiNi?"

I shrugged. "I come from humble beginnings and a long line of strong people who defied the odds and worked hard to solidify their roots. I've seen Mama fall, but she always lands on her feet. The image of the "strong Black Woman" is a fallacy; I don't have to fight to live the way Mama and NiNi did. I'm strong, but I have safe places to break and be restored. This is what I will teach others."

"Good for you, Nitty!"

I continued, "Mama has given me some of her journals from over the years. Reading them with her has helped me get to know her better. She's always been guarded with me, but I understand why, now. Mama and NiNi have different love languages, but they love each other deeply. I know that love now with Chance. One of my mentors, Ms. Cecelia told me that a long time ago."

"Plant your feet, lift your head, and stand in your truth, Anita. When you feel overwhelmed, inhale courage and exhale fear. You're right where you belong."

"Thank you, Dr. Octavia, for helping me see through God's eyes. Can I read you something from Mama's journal?"

She was excited, "Sure!" I reached into my bag and pulled out a worn, brown leather journal, and began to read my mother's cursive handwriting:

Dear Healing,

Girl, you are everything I never knew that I needed!

I was in the clutches of rejection for a long time. Overlooked, put down, and minimized so much that I didn't recognize my worth. My roots kept me grounded, and for every obstacle, I looked for God all around me.

I didn't feel worthy of love for a long time. My siblings believed in me for me; my husband escorted me back into the arms of God; and my children gave me a reason to stop running from you.

Girl, you took Mother into your arms and cradled her until she was transformed. It was a miracle! We gave each other the best of ourselves until we were the best of ourselves and the sharp edges between us are gone! We promise to cherish our second Chance.

It wasn't always easy to run towards you, but meeting you was worth the journey. Dandelions lean, but they cannot be broken. I can now live up to the meaning of my name, "Joyous."

~Love,

Joyce

I walked out of Dr. Octavia's office, equipped to build legacy. I looked up and stood still under the sun as if I was seeing it for the first time. Taking my shoes off, I stood in a patch of grass and grounded myself next to the dandelions. Out loud, I declared, "I run between dandelions to love, faith, and hope. There is no other way to stop running from me."

FOR DISCUSSION

Use the questions in this section to start and have meaningful discussions. There are several themes in the book including topics about love, forgiveness, relationships, sisterhood, motherhood, and health. You may find other topics that resonate with you as you read.

Feel free to share any other questions that arise with the author at: Scribecoach@inscribedinspiration.com, we would love to hear from you.

Purchase other books at www.pendaljames.com/rbd.

1. Which character in the story do you most relate to? Do you see any similarities between yourself, Annabelle, Joyce, or Nitty?

2. Annabelle, Joyce, and Nitty have similar qualities. Describe some of the commonalities you see between them. What does it mean to give your mother grace? Have you judged your mother without really knowing her story?

3. Share some lessons you have learned from your mother. What do you carry from her that either showed you what to do, or what not to do?

4. Talk about the person who taught you about God. What did you learn from them?

5. Annabelle's faith led her to create strict boundaries for herself and her children. Do you know anyone who acts similarly to her?

6. What qualities did you recognize in Joyce as the oldest daughter? Encourage her to make herself a priority.

7. Talk about a time when you needed to think through your emotions and speak through a healed place. What happened?

8. What do you think about the definition of what it means to run between dandelions?

9. Did you get the chance to meet your mother as a woman? Do you think Annabelle was able to see Joyce as a woman and vice versa?

10. Is it realistic to balance holiness and fun? Do you need to be one or the other? How do you protect your peace?

11. Give a personal example of a woman who spread her wings and explored life without limitations. Do you have a Biblical example?

12. What crown have you chosen to wear that causes you to sacrifice yourself as a priority?

13. When have you been full and hungry for something at the same time?

14. What excuses do you have for not finishing your goals? If someone has said something to you that impacted your belief in yourself and what you can accomplish, how did you overcome it?

15. Women with degrees fight insecurities. What are some ways you push through your insecurities as a professional woman?

16. Are you rushing through life missing important moments because you're thinking about "building a legacy?" Do you have moments when your children said they missed you, yet you thought you were building their legacy? How did it make you feel? How did you respond?

17. What part of *Running Between Dandelions* resonated with you the most?

18. How would you explain this statement in the book, "Complicated relationships require understanding and forgiveness?"